THE GOODMAN CURSE

JOHAN THOMPSON

Tumbleweed Books
Tumble through the pages of our books

THE GOODMAN CURSE
JOHAN THOMPSON

Tumbleweed Books
Tumble through the pages of our books

Https://tumbleweedbooks.ca
Tumbleweed Books is an imprint of DAOwen Publications

The Goodman Curse / Johan Thompson

Edited by MJ Moores and Douglas Owen

Cover art by MMT Productions

ISBN 978-1-928094-76-0
EISBN 978-1-928094-77-7

10 9 8 7 6 5 4 3 2 1

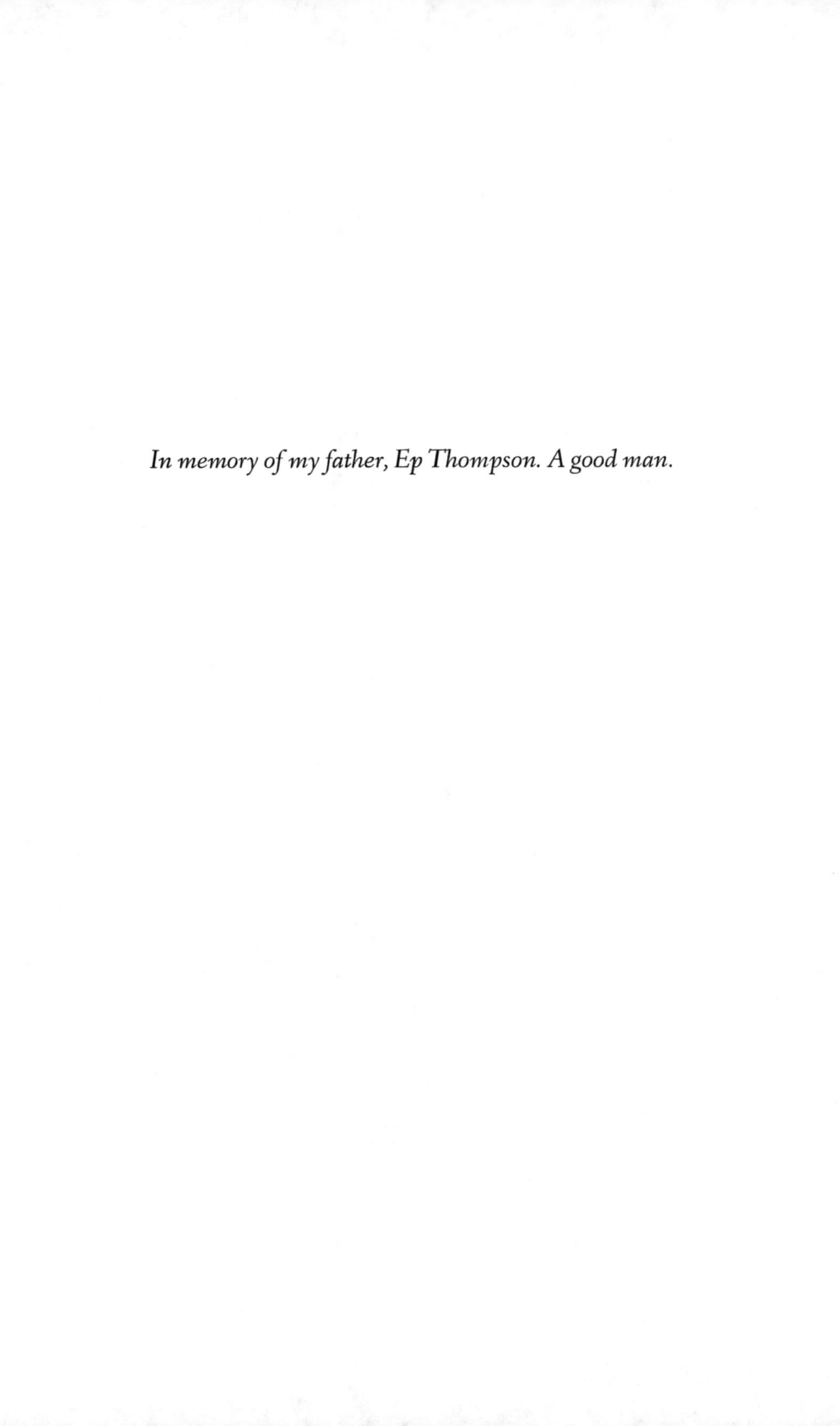

In memory of my father, Ep Thompson. A good man.

1

"No polecat ever smells its own stink."
Zulu proverb

Houghton
August 25, 15:03

What's the meaning of life? For Henry Goodman, the man who raised me, profit, power, and growing the Goodman empire. According to my mom, not being poor no matter the cost and portraying the Goodman name as good. She was like the guys promoting DDT, plastic bags, and pop-up ads. My parents were the perfect couple on social media. Behind closed doors, I'd never seen them kiss, hold hands or shit-talk. Those weaknesses they saved for my sister. So, the meaning of life for me, not be like them, whatever the cost. And the cost was high.

I was on my first assignment after spending three months in an induced coma, cramped into a suffocating minivan with three people who also didn't want to be there.

"Can someone turn on the air-con?" I said, focusing on Tanita's cleavage.

"You'll develop tunnel vision, Sergeant," she said, working on covering the dark lines under my eyes.

"I know Thero won't agree, but a woman's cleavage for a man is like a chalk line for a chicken."

She shook her head with a deadpan expression.

"What's your chalk line?" I asked.

"A man interested in me and not my breasts," she muttered.

"I need to start the engine before I can turn on the air-con," Steward Van Rooyen said where he sat in front of a wall of monitors, paging through a hunting magazine. "I signed this thing out, and I don't want to run up the costs." He swivelled around his chair. "You smell Greg! What time did you arrive at your dump this morning?"

"I don't know Daddy-long-neck." Van Rooyen was a lanky six-four. His head, neck, and body looked out of proportion, as if at birth, when extracted, his big feet got stuck.

Steward's face lit up bright red, even more than his hair. "Call me that one more time, Sergeant! It's Lieutenant!" He turned back to the monitors and muttered, "Respect the rank, bloody tick."

"Heard you killed a defenceless lion the other day." I waited for the reaction.

"What!" Tanita straightened.

Bingo – I'm an artist, creating the perfect snapshot of disgust. I'm usually on the receiving end, so this snapshot directed at somebody else, especially him, I cherished.

"I saved many defenceless animals by killing it," Van Rooyen muttered, paging.

"But that's its nature," she said. "God created it that way."

"I would never kill a defenceless animal." I refrained from sneaking another glance at her cleavage. "Even a criminal."

Van Rooyen glanced over his shoulder. "What about the guy that slit your throat and left you for dead?"

"I think it was a girl." Thero's gaze shifted between Steward and me. "Don't worry, Gee, we'll find the bastard."

"Where were you that night, Lieutenant?" I asked.

Tanita tilted my head back and worked on hiding the eight-inch scar, starting under my right ear.

"You didn't answer my question," Van Rooyen said.

"I'll make sure he's armed."

"Say you don't manage?"

"Then, if not resisting, I will arrest him. That's what differentiates cops from criminals." I winked at Tanita.

Steward snorted. "That's rich coming from you. But I'll remember the next time you beat an unarmed rapist unconscious. We all have a tipping point."

"The seeds of evil buried in the pits of the subconscious mind will sprout given the perfect circumstances." Thero stared with glazed eyes at me. Or Tanita, I couldn't tell. Must be me.

"What the fuck, Thero?" I shook my head. "I said, never kill a defenceless criminal. Nothing wrong with beating the shit out of a thug." I raised a finger. "But you must have the self-control and expertise to know when to stop."

"Please, sit still." Tanita pushed my head back. "You're all over the place."

"Annoying, hey," Steward mumbled, paging, "ADHD, PTSD with a touch of STD."

I rolled my eyes, shaking my head. "I don't have an STD."

She placed her hand on my forehead. "Hold still!"

I closed my eyes and filled my lungs with her arousing perfume. Together, with her warm breath and delicate touch on my sensitive scar, something awakened below.

"Who or how did this happen?" she asked, dabbing.

I swallowed. "Anyway, Lieutenant, I got home, changed into the school uniform, met Tanita at her salon, and went to school. I had no time to take a shower."

"Can I start the engine?" Corporal Thero asked.

"No!" Steward snapped. "Crack open a window."

Thero removed a white hanky from behind his bullet-proof vest and wiped his forehead.

Tanita frowned. "Sorry I asked. Too soon?"

I closed my eyes, trying to remember for the millionth time what had happened that night four months ago. Nothing, like staring at a pitch-black wall. However, her words repeated in my mind. *Hold still!*

"Heard your parents are rich and famous." Tanita reached my Adam's apple with the brush. "They also live in Houghton."

"Moved out on my sixteenth birthday and never looked back." I took another deep breath of her scent – alluring, but something gave me a slight headache.

Tanita frowned. "What's it been, five years?"

Steward sprayed the magazine with his vile spit as he burst out laughing.

"Ten years ago." I scowled. "Why do you think we called you?"

Tanita straightened. "Gee, sorry. I hit another nerve?"

"You think I got all these in school?" I stood up and raised my T-shirt, showing my scars – two bullet holes and six stab wounds.

Tanita looked away, and Thero beamed, but not at my scars. I fell back into the chair and covered up.

"You done?" Steward closed his book and glanced at his TAG Heuer – a gift from my sister. Such a waste.

Tanita blinked, snapping out of her state of disbelief. "Almost." She brushed and dabbed the scar until, finally, reaching my left ear.

"Looking good, Greg." Thero gave a thumbs up. "Can't see the scar."

Tanita picked up a black wig, giving it a few vigorous brushes.

"Forgot about that," I muttered.

"How else are you going to hide your earplug," Van Rooyen said. "And you wore it at school this morning."

Tanita pulled it over my brush cut. "You look cool, like John Wick."

I rolled my eyes and inserted the earpiece. It was safe to stand up.

Van Rooyen crouched, looked me in the eye, and placed his hands on my shoulders. It took all my self-control not to pop his tiny balls with my knee. "You know what to do, and don't screw this up," the asshole said.

"I have your back, Greg!" Thero gave a determined nod, still beaming.

"I know you do, Thero. I know you do." I gave Tanita a gentle kiss on the cheek, tucked a stray blonde lock behind her ear and whispered, "God had you in mind when he created Eve."

Her blue eyes lit up like an armless man winning a lap dance. "Be careful," she whispered back.

I winked. "You saw the scars." And bingo: I had her. I grabbed my backpack, leather jacket, and jumped out of the van. Then, as I closed the door and walked down the street, the A-hole spouted in my earpiece, "Let me save you a lot of heartache, Tanita. To him, it's just a game."

"What do you mean?"

"He wants one thing from you and one thing only. As soon as he gets it, he'll move on to the next... thing. And you saw how childish he is."

"That was the old Greg," Thero said. "After what happened to him..."

"He still needs to go for his psych evaluation," Van Rooyen countered. "If he fails, he's out."

"Should he even be doing this?" Tanita asked. "Why didn't he go for the evaluation yet?" I detected genuine concern.

"Because the little shit is difficult to pin down. You saw how he is," Van Rooyen grumbled. "And he was the perfect candidate for this assignment."

His sarcasm almost dripped from my ear.

"His scores are the highest, Lieutenant," Thero said.

I smiled, taking a breath of Joburg's soot. *He has my back. Take that, Lieutenant Ramrod.* But would he still have my back if I looked like Shrek? And the scores were pre-throat-slid-days. *Am I still any good?*

Steward continued his assault. "So, what do you say, Greg? You still the same childish womanizing shit-seeker?"

My microphone was on speaker in the van so I could respond. *Who am I?* Can an event you can't remember change you? I removed the earpiece. Besides, I was too shocked to reply; he broke the Man-Code by using the Cock-block manoeuvre. He was no friend of mine, but all men knew the Man Code was sacred. Without the Code, man wouldn't survive. Women would realize that our dicks were at the centre of our universe. They would gain the knowledge and power to control us, and we all heard Peter Parker, "With great power comes great responsibility." And women were not responsible.

It took me two hundred meters before realizing I had a job to do. I replaced my earpiece and heard nothing. Thankfully. Again, I shook my head, but not at the Cock-blocker parked up the road, but at the opulence. Five kilometres away, people lived in tin shacks, some up to fifteen in one bedroom. Clive Bolton's house was the biggest on the street with all the trimmings: imposing wall, electric fence, CCTV, infrared beams, and state-of-the-art alarm. Well, with over fifty people killed each day in this sludge-fuck of a country, I guess I couldn't blame them.

I didn't like the style, though. It reminded me of my parents' home – a mansion with pillars that could support a fifty-story building and enough room to house all the prostitutes in Joburg. A Labrador played with the kid on the front lawn as if directed to do so. The perfect picture. Sickening.

The two guards at the gate glared at me, like my dad when I used to walk into his study.

"Sammy," I shouted, waving at the kid as I crossed the street.

One guard, a big guy, glanced over his shoulder at Sammy, waiting for the teen's response.

Sammy recognized me and waved back, excited.

"I'm his friend from school." I smiled up at the guard.

"You seem a bit old for school?" he said and pushed his Ray-Bans back onto his nose.

"I'm eighteen." I shrugged and unzipped my leather jacket.

He frowned. "He's thirteen. Mr. Bolton is very protective. I need to search you for drugs."

"Sammy invited me." I stepped back.

"Come on, Barry," Sammy said, panting, as he reached the gate. "He's a friend." The kid looked at me. "You brought the game?"

"Yep." I slipped the backpack from my shoulder and tapped it.

"Sweet!" His round face lit up like a traffic light.

Sammy was a fat kid: red hair, red face – yes, I know, a cliché. But he was a kid with filthy rich parents who would give him fodder, livestock, or doodah – anything to keep the butterball at arm's length, away from them. Like my parents, but his father wasn't such a dick. I hoped he would lose the fat, as I did – not out of choice, I might add. My weight-loss programme came in the form of another shit, Staff-Sergeant Koonz. The sadistic prick enjoyed seeing us vomit on the red smothering dust of the African Highveld. The crazy glint, the utter satisfaction he had whenever one of his troops cracked. I never gave him that satisfaction – I would've killed him first. If Koonz hadn't joined the Special Forces, he would probably be in jail for torturing little animals or kids. Kids like little Sammy.

"You sure you know this kid?" Ray-Ban man asked Sammy.

"He saved my life," Sammy shouted through the three-metre-high cast-iron gates. "He bitch-slapped a grade twelve, double his size, who tried to split me in half."

Little did Sammy know; I paid the twelfth-grader two hundred rand to wedge the fuzzball and double it if I could slap him. He told me eight hundred, and I could break his nose when defending Sammy's fat ass. Deal!

Ray-Ban man shrugged, waving me in. The massive gates parted, and I walked in – as planned.

We made our way toward the house. "Is your dad here?"

"Nope." Sammy tried to keep the dog from sniffing my crotch – I freaking hated that.

"Isibunu, no!" Sammy pulled the dog away by its collar.

I frowned. "Your dad's going to trend one day." I glanced over my shoulder at the fence and noticed at least seven guards walking the perimeter; another two guarded the front door, all with H&K MP5 submachine guns – the model we use.

"Trending?" Sammy pulled his face as if smelling something dead but wasn't sure if it was human or animal.

"Who named the dog?"

"Precious, our maid," Sammy said, stroking the dog's head. "She said it means warrior in Zulu."

"Of course, it does." I grinned. Precious was precious. Not one of the Zulus protecting their white arses told them it meant vagina or genitals. Even the Boltons took her word.

"You stink, Greg."

Couldn't believe I gave him my actual name. "Is your dad a c–...an asshole like mine?" I kept my head low.

"No, my dad is cool." He pushed out his chest. "He's my Isibunu."

I frowned. "It's because you never see him?"

"I see him every day. We do all kinds of stuff together – we play Xbox every night before I go to bed, he takes me to my dancing lessons–"

"Does he slap your mother around?"

"No!" He laughed. "He loves her, treats her like a princess."

"It's because he cheats on her."

"Why are you so on my dad's case, dude?"

"Sorry, man." I slapped him on his back. "Just messing with you."

"It's okay," he whispered.

I felt sorry for the little guy. His entire world, depending on how this went, might be about to implode.

"You're right. Your dad is a real Isibunu."

The guards at the front door gave each other that knowing look –
the one that would never grow old – these white idiots.

"Wait, you dance?"

"Yes, why?" Sammy pushed open the heavy wooden door.

"Nothing."

I smiled at the two guards as I strolled into the house.

Sammy stopped in the double-volume foyer. "You want
something to drink? My mom makes a killer milkshake."

I couldn't remember when last I'd had a milkshake. The closest
thing I had to a milkshake was three bottles of Amarula. I promised
myself never again; even my vomit tasted sweet the next morning.
Sounds like a good thing, but it's not.

"No, I'm fine," I lied and aimed for the stairs.

"My mom wants to meet you before we go up." He walked
toward a door to the right.

According to the house plans, she must be in the kitchen.

"She's in the kitchen, making us chicken pie for dinner. My dad
loves chicken pie. I also love it."

No shit. "Must I meet her?" I waited at the bottom of the stairs.

"Rules," he said over his shoulder and pushed open the door.

Rules! I almost cracked a tooth. The only rules I had as a kid were
not to disturb the King in his study and to eat all the food on my plate
– because somewhere in the world, there's a starving child. "So, give
my food to him," I told my mom once. "But I'm sure he would die
before eating this shit." It didn't go down well – the broccoli or the
remark.

A guard appeared at the top of the stairs, glaring down at me. He
had a Kriss Vector.45 semi-automatic machinegun over his shoulder –
Made in the USA, nice.

"Okay," I sighed, dropping my shoulders. For a moment, I was
that teenager again.

The smell of pie slapped me in the face as I entered the room. I
filled my lungs with the sweet aroma, and that made the hangover
even worse – as if I had swallowed a tennis ball on fire. Maybe, I was

nervous. I'd done this so many times I couldn't tell the difference anymore. I was hungover or nervous – the former was more likely.

"Mom, this is Greg." Sammy beamed. He held out his arm like a ringmaster introducing his most prized lion. You're introducing a slithering scum-sucking snake. Why, with this assignment, did I feel so shit?

"Is this the boy who saved my Samuel's life?" Mrs. Bolton asked and gave me a playful wink. She placed the milk back in the fridge.

"Ja, tannie." As a kid, all my Afrikaans friends called older women tannie. A sign of respect. Most women took offence. Means aunt. I kept my answer short and remained by the door.

"Tannie? What the fuck, Greg," Van Rooyen said under his breath.

Precious glanced over her shoulder where she stood at the kitchen sink, dressed in a pink and white maids' uniform. I gave her a nod. She was beautiful, with high cheekbones, chestnut skin and eyes that knew all the secrets. Cover model looks. Precious indeed. She smiled and returned to their dishes.

Gloria Bolton looked like a proper mother, not like mine. She was forty-five, a bit taller than me – about five-foot-nine, short brown hair with mommy-perm and warm greenish eyes – loved cooking and food, hence her and Sammy's weight problem.

Gloria walked over, hand stretched out. I hoped she didn't notice the make-up or Stroh rum – women are much more observant, especially with this.

I gave her a firm shake as my grandma taught me. She always said a woman liked it that way; it showed character. Grandma also told me, "When there's a fork in the road, Geegee, always take the most righteous path." I struggled with that one, still taking the road that would upset the most, right or wrong.

Mrs. Bolton's hand was soft and warm. She frowned. Shit! The thought of Sammy standing over his dead mother's body, crying, and eating pie, flashed through my mind, but then she said, "You've got the most beautiful eyes, Gregory. You must be popular with the girls."

"Mo-om," Sammy moaned.

I rejoiced, but only for a moment.

"Why would you want to mingle with a junior? I can see you're not one for rules, with the long hair, tired eyes, and scar you're trying to hide. Sammy is not in your playgroup, if you know what I mean."

Build me up before breaking me down – the oldest trick in the book. I wanted to neutralize her, but she was only looking out for her furry chuzzle. And I would never hit a woman.

I smiled. "I'm trying to change my ways. After saving your boy's ass, I wanted to get out of there as quick as possible, but then he saw my game. So, see this as an extension of my goodwill, nothing more," I said, unflinching.

She flinched, realizing I was only humouring her butterball, the closest thing he'd ever had to a "true" friend.

Gloria looked at Sammy. "Not too loud. Dad's working."

Sammy's face lit up again. "I thought Dad was at work?"

Yes, Mom, I thought Daddy wasn't home. I kept my cool.

"He came in when you were in the bathroom. I thought you heard him?"

"No." He smiled. "Can we go say hi?"

She rubbed his big head. "He asked not to be disturbed, and I don't think he'll like the idea of you playing in your room with Greg." She glanced at me. "You know how Daddy gets."

"Okay." He turned and walked out of the kitchen, his hands almost dragging on the floor.

"Bye, tannie." I had to get that one in.

We left Mrs. Bolton in the kitchen and made our way up the stairs. Pierneef, Monet, and the real Father Claerhout lined the wall to the right. I grew up surrounded by similar names.

The guard at the top of the stairs refused to move.

"Come on, Brian," Sammy said.

He glared at me, chewing on a match.

"Yeah, come on, Rambo," I smirked. "You trying to scare a kid."

"Your friend here is a troublemaker, Sammy," the guard said, glaring, chewing. "Call me if he gives you any shit."

I gasped. "You swear in front of kids? You're the reason we can't ride our bikes to school anymore."

"He's okay, Brian, don't worry."

He glared and chewed a bit longer and then stepped to the side.

We walked down the corridor, passing Clive Bolton's closed study.

"Don't you find it strange, all these guards?" I asked as we entered Sammy's room. "Two at the gate, seven around the perimeter, two at the front door, and one inside – top of stairs."

Sammy frowned. "My dad said he needs to protect us and our money. There are a lot of bad people out there who want to take our stuff. You know, they want to take white people's stuff without compensation."

I restricted my response to an eye roll, closed his bedroom door and threw my backpack on his bed.

"I'm not allowed to close my door when I have friends over." He walked back to the door.

"Sorry, I thought your mother said we must be quiet. I play my games with the volume loud."

He stopped, thought about it, then turned back. "Okay."

Sammy's room was not what I expected. Well, I don't know what I expected, but I remembered my room at thirteen: posters of Britney Spears, Black Sabbath, and Maxim centrefolds covered my walls (my grandma drew the line with Playboy), dirty laundry and stiff socks covered my Van Dijk carpet, and an anxious smell filled the room. Only two things had changed since then: My iPhone replaced Maxim, and no more stiff socks. Sammy's room was clinical, clean and, well, Mom's room. My stiff-neck mom tried her luck with her freaking East Coast Nautical dream theme and Biggy-Best wallpaper. I expressed my discontent by painting over her sea-blue and egg-white, drawing awkwardly posing stick men in blood-red and tyre-black enamel. Sammy had the same problem; the only thing rebellious about his room was the dirty pink bedspread. But I was jealous about the en-suite bathroom; it could've sorted out my stiff-sock problem when I was a kid.

I took out the game and two Cokes. "Here you go." I opened one bottle and handed it to him.

"No thanks – I'm not allowed to drink Coke."

"You're fu-freaking kidding me. Coke is the least of your problems."

"No, it makes me hyper."

"You need exercise then. Take it, live a little."

"Okay." He shrugged and accepted.

"Cheers." I held mine out, waiting for the tap.

"Cheers." He bumped my bottle, and we drank. I finished mine in one gulp, dousing the flaming tennis ball in my stomach. "That bloody Stroh rum," I whispered and gave a satisfied burp.

Sammy took two sips and burped, like stepping on a tiny frog.

"Get the game going." I tossed it to him. He caught it with fumbling hands and studied the cover. "You must work on your gross motor skills."

"Dad gave up," he muttered, reading.

At least he tried. "Put it on, dammit." I waited for the intro to start. "Need to take a piss."

I walked into the bathroom with my backpack and closed the door.

"Why didn't anyone tell me the lion is home?" I asked, tapping my earplug. I waited a few seconds. "Hey, am I the only one working–"

"You mean dad is home. We heard you, Meerkat," Van Rooyen defecated in my ear.

"Do I need to abort? Because to extract the info from his computer without him knowing about–"

"The operation is a go," he said.

"But that will mean–"

"We know what that means."

"Shit," I whispered, turning toward the mirror. The tennis ball reignited as I looked at the teenager facing me. What I would give to be that boy again before my father forced me into the service. I wanted to be a rock star or a kamikaze pilot, or an Irishman, or a hacker: stealing from politicians, fake pastors, crooked Nigerians, and New Zealanders.

"Do you copy, Meerkat?" Van Rooyen snapped.

I hated that call sign. Van Rooyen called me that if I wasn't in the room with him, he knew I'd kill him – Lieutenant, or not. Asshole Koontz gave me that nickname, and it stuck.

"Yes, I copy." I seethed and closed my eyes, thinking about what Captain Modise had said three days ago: "We've got three scenarios." He always had three bloody reasons, holding up three fingers, one half blown off by a stun-grenade. "One, Sergeant Gregory Goodman goes in undercover, retrieves the information and bugs his study without alerting Clive Bolton. Two, we storm the house and get the info we need, risking him destroying all his data and alerting his suppliers and superiors that the police are on to them. And three," two and a bit, "Goodman goes in undercover and neutralizes Bolton before he can destroy the info we need."

"Why me?" I'd asked.

"Three reasons," he said, holding up two and a half. "One, you look like a boy. Two, Sammy would rather invite a white friend to his home than a black friend, and three," two and a bit, "you're the only one who knows computers."

Van Rooyen brought me back. "Remember, Meerkat, you are authorized to use whatever means to get the information."

"Copy, I'm not a retard."

"And another thing, I know it's not procedure, but when the shit hits the fan, you do not let the hostiles know you're a cop."

"So, even if the fact that I'm a cop might stop them from blowing my brains out, I can't tell them."

"Copy that."

"Tell my cat and grandma I love them." Pathetic, but my choice. I needed a woman of a more permanent nature. Lipstick, tampons, curlers, Cosmopolitan, and Vogue filled my drawers, but each item belonged to a different woman. Probably my ADHD. However, I found the one but broke it off. Idiot. I had figured – in my screwed-up mind – I should break up first before she did it to me, before she saw the real me.

My single status was maybe the actual reason Modise had chosen me: to save on catering costs for my funeral – one platter for six. There would be leftovers for the gravediggers.

I pulled out my H&K 9mm from my bag and cracked open the door. Sammy lay on his back, game in hand, snoring. The doctored Coke did the trick. Should have used Dr. Pepper. The bedrooms and study at the rear of the house walked out onto a huge balcony overlooking the pool and tennis courts. I nudged the heavy curtain of the balcony door to the side – no guards. I hoped Clive Bolton didn't lock his balcony door.

"The boy is out cold. I'm stepping out."

"I did not copy that, Meerkat; please follow procedure," Van Rooyen said in his annoying, monotonous tone.

I let go of the curtain and stood back, taking a deep breath. "One, two, three, four–"

"Are you counting hostiles, Meerkat?"

Van Rooyen enjoyed his newfound rank.

"Anger management," I whispered. "I neutralized Chicken Little. Meerkat is leaving his hole, about to sink his teeth into the lion's balls."

Brief silence. "Copy that."

Van Rooyen and Modise had applied for Task Force training the same time I did. Modise was twenty-nine, already ten years' active service in the police and Van Rooyen, twenty-seven, with five years' active service. I was twenty-five, with two years' active service – the minimum requirement. We'd all graduated two years ago. I kicked all their arses, but I had a problem with authority. That's why I stayed behind, and everyone else got promoted. Because of Van Rooyen's fantastic ability to crawl up the arseholes of his superiors, without shame, he made Second Lieutenant. He had a permanent brown ring around his giraffe-like neck. Because Modise showed remarkable skill with a stun-grenade, he made captain.

I nudged the curtain away – still, no hostiles.

"What's going on with Samuel?" Mrs. Bolton spoke behind me. The blood drained from my face, although my heart pumped like crazy. How could I mess up like this, allowing a forty-five-year-old woman to sneak up on me?

I turned around slowly, trying to conceal the weapon in my hand, but it was too late. Gloria ran to Sammy's aid, screaming, "You killed my Sammy."

"He's sleeping, dammit." I ran past her and closed the door.

"Sammy, wake up, my angel." She shook him by his shoulders, but he was out cold.

Gloria looked at me, eyes wild with rage. Unstoppable. No amount of talking would help. She leapt to her feet, kicking off her Christian Louboutin shoes, the ones with the red soles; that's all my mom wears.

She stormed, screaming, her face red and veins bulging. Then, I did something I had never done before: I punched a woman. I had to shut her pie hole. My fist landed on her puffy right cheek. I sidestepped her falling body and grabbed her around the waist, trying to soften her descent. I ended up on top of her. My landing was soft – as if diving on top of a puffball. Gloria Bolton had joined her son in the Land of Nod.

"Goodman, what the hell is going on there?" Van Rooyen said in my ear.

"The Hippo arrived, unexpectedly, but all–" The door handle turned. I sprinted to the side of the door with Van Rooyen still screaming in my ear.

"Goodman, answer me!"

The door slowly opened.

Rambo, I thought, as I noticed the short barrel of the Kriss Vector machinegun. He'd heard the screams. I waited until the safety catch above his hand was in sight.

"Goodman!"

Bingo.

I flipped the safety back on, grabbed the machine gun, and wrenched it from his hands. He stood in the doorway, shocked and raised his hands.

"What do they teach you at that school?" The match dropped from his mouth.

"You must see how I dissect a frog."

"I told you he wasn't ready. He's damaged goods. Goodman, if you don't answer me now–"

"Van Rooyen, please, shut the fuck up," I snapped. "I can't concentrate with you yapping in my ear. Everything is under control," I lied. The irritating voice in my head went away, for now.

"What?" Rambo asked. I could motorboat his frown.

"Get in," I said, flipping the safety off.

"Listen, kid; I can get you drugs. What do you want?"

"I don't want drugs. Do I look like a junkie?"

He raised his left brow.

"Really?" I frowned. "Whatever, we're getting side-tracked here. I'm working for the Triads." Yes, yes, I know, but it was the first group that came to mind.

"The what?"

"The Chinese mafia."

"But you're not Chinese?"

"I'm Siamese cross Minskin. Get inside." I pointed the weapon at his crotch.

Rambo entered and froze as he saw mother and son on the floor. "Are they dead?"

I dropped my shoulders, disgusted. He had his back toward me. "Yes, but don't worry – they went quickly." If he thought I was a cold-blooded murderer, he would listen to me, tell me a few things.

It was his turn to drop his shoulders. "How could you do such a thing?" he whispered.

"It was easy – like swatting a fly." I glanced at mother and son. "Well, with these two, it was more like bumblebees."

Rambo started shaking, sobbing. Shit. Maybe I should tell him the truth. No! Billie Eilish's song 'Bad guy' popped into my head. "Is Clive Bolton in his study?"

The shaking stopped.

I gave a step forward, shoving the barrel into his back. "I asked you a–"

Rambo swung round, hitting the machinegun from my hands. He landed a punch on my right cheek. I staggered back; tiny glitter balls floated in the room.

"Now I'm going to kill you, kid or no kid," Rambo hissed, picking me up by my collar and crotch, throwing me across the room. The fifty-inch LCD television broke my fall.

The screaming started in my ear again. "Meerkat, what the hell is going on?"

Rambo grabbed me by the collar and privates, flinging me into a bookcase. A sharp pain shot through my shoulder as I scurried to my feet, trying to find a footing between all the Harry Potters and Spuds. Rambo went for the machine gun, plucked it from the floor, and aimed. Playtime was over; the kid needed to grow up quickly, and I hated that.

I drew the 9mm, tucked into the back of my jeans, aimed, and fired.

Rambo dropped to his knees, blood trickling from the tiny hole between his eyes. I grabbed my backpack and ran for the door without waiting for him to hit the floor. In one morning, I'd drugged a kid, knocked a woman unconscious, and killed Rambo – forced into something I didn't want to do.

"The shit is going to hit the fan, Leopard. I'm on my way to Lion's den."

"Do you need backup?" Van Rooyen asked, his tone stressed. It was now business; no more grudges, blood, or hatred. Well, he was my brother-in-law.

"Negative. Like you said, we don't want his friends to know the cops are involved."

"Affirmative."

I was halfway down the hall when Clive Bolton's study door opened. He peeked out and slammed the door shut as he saw me. My shoulder hurt like hell, but luckily, it was my right; it wouldn't interfere with my aim. I ran past Clive's room as I heard the drumming footsteps of the guards running up the stairs – the two posted at the front door. I pulled the trigger twice, silencing the footsteps and turned back to Lion's den. Three down, seven to go.

Before running back to Sammy's room, I knocked on Clive's door.

Machine gun fire ripped the door to shreds behind me. That could have been your son knocking, arsehole. I entered Sammy's room.

Gloria Bolton stirred, groaned. I ran to the double glass doors, exited onto the patio and made my way to Bolton's study. His patio doors were wide open. Idiot.

I peeked around the corner. Bolton was crouched behind his desk, facing the door he had turned into Swiss cheese. He fired another volley through the door as he noticed the door handle move.

Somebody screamed on the other side – it must be another guard.

I sneaked up behind him and pressed the barrel of the gun against his polished bald patch. "Drop your weapon, Friar Tuck," I whispered.

He jerked and dropped his MP5 machinegun to the floor. "Please don't kill me."

"That depends on you. Stay dead still." I picked up his machinegun, locked the patio doors, and drew the curtains.

"Who are you?" He kept his head low, not looking my way.

"I can tell you, but then...well, you know the rest."

Somebody dared to knock on the door.

"Tell them to stay away," I said calmly. "If I see movement through those holes, I will kill you."

"Stay away. I'm fine!"

Clive Bolton was in his fifties, heavy-set – like his next of kin – and well dressed. His study was huge, eleven by nine metres according to the plans. Bookshelves covered two walls and an entertainment system the third.

"We can do this with blood or without," I said.

"Who sent you?" he repeated and glanced over his shoulder. "You're just a kid."

"Looks are deceiving." I knelt behind him; one of his men might take a shot through a hole in the door. "I want the list of your suppliers, your superiors, and where the containers are leaving for Dar Es Salaam tonight."

He chuckled, his shoulders shaking. "I don't know what the hell you're talking about; I supply pots and pans to the South African Defence Force."

The annoying voice in my head was back, "He's lying, Greg. Do what you need to do."

"Clive," I whispered in his ear. Because of my size, every oaf thinks he can play with me. The surprise when they realize their mistake... rib-tickling.

"Yes," he said, uncertain.

"I kill men for a living, and I make quite a good living. Job satisfaction is out of this world. Even in my spare time, call it a hobby, I study and practise the art of killing. I once kept a man alive while I painstakingly removed every bone in his body. At the end of the week, he died of a heart attack." I hoped he bought the cockamamie story.

He swallowed. His white silk shirt was soaking wet.

"Where's your laptop? I can see your charger. Tell me, or,"–I pressed the barrel of the 9mm against his lower back–"you will end up in a wheelchair for the rest of your life. No more playing with Sammy, and I don't mean your son or the blonde you've been screwing in Sandton."

He lowered his head with a shake. "They'll kill my family and me if I give you the information."

I gave a drawn-out sigh before I squeezed the trigger. Clive screamed, grabbing his thigh as he fell on his side.

"Why do people always test me like this?" I said for dramatic effect but also meant it. I hoped he'd had enough – I had.

"Because you don't look like a killer," he groaned.

I scanned the room, throwing books from shelves and searching drawers, all the time checking the door. Nothing! No laptop, storage devices, or paperwork worth anything.

"Goodman, stop messing about and get the information." This time it was Captain Modise spitting in my ear. "We can't send in the police, not now. This operation will halt with all the red tape and lawyers. The shipment of weapons and his friends will be in Tanzania by the time we'd struck a deal with him."

I walked over to Clive, aiming the pistol at his healthy thigh. "Where's your laptop?"

"No, no, please, I swear on my son's life. I know nothing else."

Clive was stupid or incredibly stubborn. "Clive, does it look like I'm fooling around?" The second shot was mentally much easier for me because this guy made me angry.

The father of one screamed in pain, crying, "I don't know. Please believe me."

Between screams, I heard a ruckus at the Swiss cheese door. The guards tried to keep Sammy and Gloria away, but together with their mass and determination, they were unstoppable.

I looked at the door, then at Clive.

"Gloria!" Clive screamed as he read my mind. "Take Sammy and get the hell out of the house."

I ran toward the door as I heard Gloria screaming through a hole, "Don't let me get my hands on you...you snot-nosed kid. Leave my husband alone."

"Daddy!" Sammy screamed.

"Greg, time is running out!" Van Rooyen yelled. "They phoned the police. Somebody they know in the force. They will blow our cover."

I wiped the sweat from my forehead "Fuck!" *Breathe.* I pulled back the hammer of my pistol, unlocked, and jerked open the door. Gloria stumbled into the room, followed by Sammy. I surprised the three guards in the corridor. They aimed, but hesitated, afraid of hitting the hippo in front of the meerkat. I fired low, three shots, all splitting kneecaps. I silenced Gloria with a left while Sammy ran to his groaning father. I slammed the door shut and locked it.

"Please, Greg, don't," Sammy cried, lying on top of his father with his arms wrapped around him.

How the hell did it get this far? Not my finest hour. I swallowed the lump in my throat.

"I'm done playing with daddy." In my business, the righteous path does not work. "It's time for you and me to rough and tumble."

"Stay away from my son, you sick bastard!" Clive wrapped his left arm around Sammy, punching the air with his right. His eyes were wild, a mix of fear and rage – Finally, I had his attention.

"You brought this onto yourself, Clive." I stepped on his wound. He slammed his fists into the soft carpet, hollering in pain, allowing me to pluck Sammy from his chest. Clive turned on his stomach and crawled toward me, fingers digging into the expensive rug.

"I'll count to three." I stepped back.

"Greg?" Sammy said as I covered his eyes with my hand.

Clive froze, glaring up at me.

"One." I aimed at Sammy's leg.

"Okay," he whispered. "They might still spare his life." His head dropped to the carpet. "I'm dead in any case."

"Two."

"I threw the laptop from the balcony. It landed in the pool. Everything is on there. Everything."

"Do you have any other backups?" I kept aim. "Do you use a cloud to save your work?"

"No, I didn't want to risk it."

"Was that so freaking difficult?" I holstered my pistol. "Go to your father."

Gloria groaned, eyelids fluttering.

Clive wrapped his arms around little Sammy, tears streaming down his face.

"I knew we could count on you, Goodman," Van Rooyen said.

I nudged open the curtain by the patio door, still no hostiles.

Gloria sat up, stroking her cheek.

"Clive, keep your bitch on a leash," I warned as she struggled upright.

"Take it easy, Gloria. He's leaving."

"Put pressure on the wounds. The ambulance is on the way. They're only flesh wounds. Your pool, is it heated?" Because I hate the cold.

"Of course it is. But why? It's destroyed."

"He's right, Goodman," Van Rooyen said.

"Was the notebook switched off when you tossed it?"

"I closed it before throwing it over the railing. Why?"

I walked away, whispering, "The notebook was in sleep mode when it hit the water, so we can still retrieve the data. A hard drive is a sealed unit, so the physical disks should be okay. I'll take it to our forensics lab for recovery."

"No! There's a leak somewhere in our unit; we can't risk it. Don't you know someone with the right equipment who can do it?" Van Rooyen just wouldn't shut up.

I knew someone, but that someone didn't want to know me. "No."

"What about the girl you brought to the wedding?"

That was the one, the one who left the Cosmo. "No, she will format the drive out of spite."

"I don't have time for shit, Gregory. It's a fucking order. How long will she take?"

"She won't do it!" My eye caught the three confused faces of the Bolton's as I turned.

"If you don't, I'll be very upset when I get home tonight." Van Rooyen confirmed my fears.

"If y-you touch my s-sister I'll f-f-"

Van Rooyen burst out laughing. "This is not the time for one of your p-p-panic attacks."

It's an anger attack! Asshole!

"This is very unprofessional," Modise interrupted. "Sort out your family matters on your own time."

I rushed to Bolton's desk and pulled out the bottom drawer – remembering a bottle of Johnny Walker Blue when I'd searched the place. Blue is my favourite colour. I downed the last half of the bottle.

"And what's that?" Gloria scowled at her husband.

"It was a gift," he groaned, his face distorted in pain as he tried to move.

I slammed the empty bottle on the table and belched in satisfaction. My breathing slowed, and I could feel my face again. "Clive's drinking is the least of your problems, Gloria. You need to worry about Clive's friends."

"I worry more about Sammy's detestable little friend," she sneered and looked me up and down, like a person watching a dog take a dump.

"Stop worrying about Sammy's friend and worry more about Sammy. Look at him. He has no friends. He sits in his room all day and needs to get out, burn some calories. Meet girls. I saw his search history, and it's getting weird."

"Greg!" Sammy made eyes. "I thought you were my friend."

"You see?" I pointed to him with an open palm. "I shot his father...twice, shoved a gun in his face, killed his friend, Rambo, knocked his mother out...twice, and he still thinks I'm his friend?"

Clive stared at me through narrowed eyes. "Don't tell me you're an undercover cop?"

"No." Shit, I flinched.

Clive dropped his head to the carpet, mumbling, "I knew they would turn on me."

"Who do you mean, the cops?" I knelt next to him.

Gloria stiffened as I moved into her personal space. I could see it took everything in her not to grab my scrawny neck with her puffy hands and squeeze the last drop of Stroh Rum from my body.

"You messed up, Greg," Van Rooyen shouted in my ear. "Now he'll tell everyone in his syndicate we're on to them. Everyone will jump ship."

"Why don't we arrest him, take him in, and keep him away from his friends," I said, keeping a wary eye on Gloria.

"No, they'll find out we have him," Modise said. "You need to make this entire thing look like a hit."

I tapped my earphone. "What do you mean, make it look like a hit?" I said, without considering my company.

Clive and Gloria snapped their heads toward me.

"I've already stepped over the line and won't take it further. This is not right." I walked away from the Boltons, whispering, "You're joking, right, Captain?"

Modise continued, "You said it yourself. You've stepped over the line. If his two-thousand-rand-a-minute lawyer finds out about what happened there – police brutality, torture, child abuse – you will go to jail."

My face went numb... again. "You ordered me to get the info by whatever means necessary."

"Within the law, Sergeant," Modise said. "Do what you need to do – no witnesses. Or do you want those Nigerians to finish what they've started? And I promise you, your friend, Sergeant Manana, will not ride in on his black horse to literally save your ass."

"But this o-o-operation, every w-w-word gets recorded." I can't breathe when I get angry; my throat slammed shut. And what made my condition worse was the way people looked at me when it happened; a mixture of pity and confusion because those who gave me that "he is special" look were usually the ones responsible for creating my disability. The people staring at me now, though, were not the ones responsible. They had the going-to-be-killed-by-a-stuttering-mad-man look.

"C-C-Captain, I'm not going t-to do it."

"Then you will go to jail, Sergeant!" Modise almost burst my eardrum. "A pretty white boy like you, especially a cop, will provide hours of fun in jail."

Sammy jumped up as he saw my elevated condition; I couldn't get a word out – not even a stutter.

I tried to catch him as he ran past, but the little butterball was surprisingly quick.

"Don't touch my son!" Gloria screamed, struggling to her feet.

Sammy disappeared behind the desk and emerged moments later with a bottle of Jack Daniels. I broke the neck and gulped down a sizeable portion.

Gloria looked at her husband in the same way she'd looked at me moments before – disgusted and angry.

"That was also a gift," Clive muttered. He was getting weaker and paler by the minute. The surrounding carpet turned into a mush of blood.

My old friend calmed me down, my heart rate slowed, and I could speak again.

"Thanks, Sammy," I whispered, ruffling his red top.

"That's what friends do, Greg." He looked at me like a dog waiting for his owner's next command.

"That's what friends do," I said, but he'd helped me from the cliff into the ravine.

"The police will be there any moment, Sergeant." Modise sounded nervous – well, more than usual.

Gloria had turned Clive on his back and was lying with half her body on top of him, embracing him, sobbing.

"I'm sorry I've got us into this mess," he whispered, straightening one of her locks with his finger.

Sammy returned to his father's side, fighting the tears. "I don't think he' will hurt you anymore, Dad. I helped him get better."

"Three reasons to—" Modise started.

I removed my earpiece, placed it on the table and slammed the bottle of Jack down on it. Then I realized; I would have noticed this jewel on my search expedition. There was a half-opened panel on the other side of the desk. Undetectable if closed. I knelt and slid it open.

"Bingo."

Inside was a big black book – time to go.

Clive stared at me with wide eyes – still uncurling his wife's locks. "Let's talk, Greg."

2

"When you bite indiscriminately, you end up eating your tail."
Zulu proverb

**Police Central
Johannesburg
Thursday, 18:07**

I walked into the police station, backpack over my shoulder, and still
wet from retrieving the laptop. The usual patrons filled the station:
angry drivers without cars, underdressed women with cheap
jewellery, shocked wives without husbands, and crying children
without parents. Quickly and inconspicuously, I glided through the
torrent of intense emotions, weaving my way through antique desks
and minimalist décor – off-white walls, vinyl floors that were never in
fashion, and newly framed portraits of satisfied men and one woman.
I read the classic engravings on the desks for the umpteenth time
while avoiding eye contact: "Fuck PW Botha," "Apartheid bastards,"
and "Free Mandela" – wondering where those "vandals" were today,

maybe on the other side of the desk or in one of the frames. Budget constraints created this time capsule.

There were three reasons why I took the stairs to the seventh floor: to dry, to cool off, and not get stuck in the lifts again.

Sergeant Manana met me on the fifth.

"Modise and Van Rooyen are effen pissed, man. What did you do?" he asked.

Good old Manana; never had I heard a naughty word pass through those lips. At seven feet, two inches, everything about him was big, including his heart. His arms and chest mimicked a gorilla's. He once lifted a Bug (not the insect) with the driver, but that's another story.

Manana grabbed me behind the head with his large hand and gave me a manly hug.

"You're wet," he said with my face buried between his breasts.

"Can't be, I'm having my period," I mumbled.

His bosoms chafed my cheeks as they bounced from laughing.

He pushed me away by the shoulders and glared at me as a father would his son after finding out he'd knocked up the reverend's daughter. "Why wasn't I told about this operation?"

"Orders."

"Since when do you obey orders?" he asked in his Barry White voice.

"I was given two-and-a-half reasons." I shrugged. "And I needed the excitement."

"You look like poop, Meerkat. How're you holding up?" I allowed Manana to call me that, just as I was to call him Banana. He was the brother I'd never had – an adopted, older brother (one of the six at my funeral). He had the characteristics the Task Force was looking for: maturity, leadership skills, and sound judgment. I had none of those. Take one wealthy father with a dash of high-profile friends who wants to set his angry, rebellious, wayward (I can carry on) boy straight. In other words, teach him a lesson.

"You should have seen me before I jumped into the pool. I looked like an eighteen-year-old."

Manana's forehead crumpled. "That was a bad pool."

"You sayin' they're displeased with me?" I changed the subject. This conversation was getting tired.

"Affirmative. They ordered me to come and get you."

"You have my back, brother?"

"Always, like you had mine."

We proceeded up the stairs, with Manana trying his best to keep a conversation going. It was one-sided. My mind raced at warp speed; it made my head hurt, or was it the whiskey? I emptied the bottle of Jack before jumping from the balcony into the pool.

"Is Van Rooyen with him?" I almost strained my neck, looking up at Manana.

"Affirmative." He placed his hand on my shoulder. "I'll be waiting outside."

I turned after a few strides. "They said I'm damaged goods. What do you think?"

He scowled. "Who?"

"Modise, Van Rooyen."

Manana smiled. "They thought you damaged since the day you joined the force. Forget about it and move on. You still the old Greg."

Modise sat behind his desk with Van Rooyen standing behind him. Both watched the news. Van Rooyen whipped his head toward me. Modise kept his eyes on the flat-screen television.

I pulled the laptop from my bag and threw it on the desk. Water still seeped from it, soiling some paperwork.

Van Rooyen returned to the news.

"The upmarket suburb of Houghton was rocked this evening when a security guard of business tycoon, Clive Bolton, went on a rampage. He wounded five of his colleagues, including Mr. Bolton, before he was shot and killed. The motive of the attack is still unknown. Mr. Bolton was taken to the hospital and is in stable condition. Our news correspondent on the..."

Modise turned the volume down and threw the remote on his desk. "You disobeyed–"

"What order?" I interrupted and fell into a chair. "To kill an unarmed father, mother, and thirteen-year-old boy? Please, bring me up on charges. My orders were to retrieve all data regarding Clive Bolton's business dealings and to find out more about the arms shipment to Dar Es Salaam. This was all that I could find." I pointed at the laptop and black ledger. I had to give them something to keep them busy with; accounting was never my strong suit.

"But he knows now that we are on to him," Van Rooyen spat. "The container has probably left the harbour by now, including all his friends. This will be an international disaster."

"Just another day in Africa."

"Everything is a fucking joke to you." Van Rooyen slammed the desk with closed fists.

I leapt to my feet, almost a reflex, and said with a locked jaw, "You wanted to throw me to the wolves. I don't think my father would be too pleased." I surprised myself, keeping my cool.

Van Rooyen straightened, chuckling, "Now he's your father. And I'm damn sure he'll take my word over yours."

"How did you get Clive Bolton to play along?" Modise interrupted the stare-down.

"I don't know." I shrugged. "I wasn't there. You saw the news." I turned and aimed for the door.

"Innocent people will be killed with those weapons, and all because of you." The satisfaction dripped from Van Rooyen's thin, snake-like lips.

"There's something more to this story." I searched for some reaction or emotion. Modise glanced at Van Rooyen. "But now we'll never know." I gestured at the laptop.

"I thought you said they could retrieve the data." Modise sat up, his stomach already bulging under his shirt because of his new position.

"The notebook was on when it hit the water. The hard drive is fried. But send it to forensics, see what they can do. I'm not going to send it to Nicole – I won't involve her in this shit."

"You're dismissed, Sergeant. Get out of this office," Van Rooyen pointed at the door. "I will convince your father to allow you to leave the force without him kicking you out of his will. Your dream might just come true."

"And don't disobey me again, Sergeant. You messed up your career." Modise tapped his shoulder. "I worked hard for these stars."

I snorted and glanced at his belly. "I carried you in training. Doubt if I still could."

He fell back into his chair and smirked. "So who was the smart one? Brains get you into this chair, not balls."

That was a good comeback, I had to admit. I could have continued our little scuffle, responding with: Was that why you were so easy to carry – you had no balls? But I was tired, my shoulder ached, and I needed a smoke. It was so out of character, leaving without chirping something over my shoulder.

My father demanded I join the force by threatening me with my inheritance. I could have stood up for myself, showed some guts, walked out of the house, and did the thing that gave me that warm fuzzy feeling inside. But, as any normal person would do, I betrayed myself for money.

I did it for four reasons, not three.

One: I didn't want to work all my life. I figured if I did this thing, I would only do it until my father croaked. Then, I would show character, grow a set of balls because nothing else can make your nuts grow as quickly as money – lots of it. Nothing.

Not that I don't have a set now.

Two: I did it for my grandma. She said if I honoured my father's wishes, for once, maybe it could mend our relationship. The old lady told me that deep down, my father – her son – was a good man, that he would come around someday, and nothing would give her greater joy than seeing our family united again. Although, he did put her in a nursing home since then. He can afford a hundred full-time nurses to look after her in his mansion, but no, he screwed her. So, I would do this, pretend to try until she dances through the Pearly Gates. I think she convinced me to join the force to get me out of her house. I moved in with her on my sixteenth birthday. My mom reluctantly agreed with me. My father and I needed a "time out" – things were getting way out of line between us.

Three: I didn't know what would give me that warm and fuzzy feeling inside. Had no freaking idea! The only thing that gave me a warm fuzzy feeling was a bottle of Jack. So, I joined because I needed some time, and this had some excitement – shooting bad guys. I figured if I hadn't joined the police, they would have killed me by now.

And four, the most important: Beatrice. Still a raw open wound. I had to get out of the house, away from my parents. What they did, what I did, was unforgivable.

I exited the office, leaving Modise and his pile simmering. Manana was still waiting in the corridor, reading Men's Health.

"That's a magazine for whites," I said, slapping the glossy to the floor.

He bent down, picked it up, and searched for his place. "That's why I'm reading it." He flipped through the pages. "Know thine enemy. Besides, I like reading about white-man problems – Premature ejaculations, small penises, and impotence."

"Well, I've got a little black in me then," I said, proceeding down the corridor.

"You almost had," Manana followed.

"You will never let up. The one time you had my back."

"We going out tonight – the guys want to beat your record," Manana said.

I laughed, throwing my head back and almost walked into the wall. "I'm already there. I don't need another drink."

"So, pick you up at nine." Manana grabbed me behind the neck and steered me into the open-plan office. A chaotic room with about twenty "antique" desks covered with papers, coffee mugs, Simba wraps, and bulletproof vests.

The thirteen men glanced at us and started with their usual wisecracks.

"Manana!" Thero yelled. "I see you brought your dildo."

"Hi, Bilbo Baggins," Craig smirked.

"Look who's here, Manana and his albino Mini-me." I did not see who yelled that, but it was a new one.

"Fuck off, girls." I placed my backpack on my desk.

"Hey!" Manana hollered. "He's not in the mood tonight."

The remarks ceased.

"What's wrong, Geegee," Dudu said with a deep frown.

"I'm tired. Rough day."

"Don't worry; there's nothing that a stripper and alcohol can't fix." Thero walked over and pinned me under his arm.

I snapped.

The next thing I remembered was Manana's arm around my neck, Thero groaning on the floor, holding his head, and everyone else staring at me with wide eyes.

"Take it easy, man," Manana whispered in my ear. "There you go." He almost sang in my ear. Not that I could do much with a tree trunk wrapped around my neck.

"I'm okay; let me go," I wheezed, red-faced, like a chain-smoking, eighty-year-old woman.

The arm relaxed.

I rushed to Thero's side. "Shit, I'm sorry. I don't know what's going on with me today."

"No," he groaned and sat up, shaking his head. "It's my fault. I got too close."

"What's going on in here?" Van Rooyen stood in the doorway.

"Nothing, Lieutenant," fifteen voices said as one – including the injured.

"Thero tried his backflip from a desk again," Manana said.

Van Rooyen shook his head, glaring at me, knowing I had

something to do with it. "I'm leaving. See you guys tomorrow." He turned and walked down the corridor.

Thero raised his hands as I tried to help him to his feet. "Don't worry, I'm fine."

I stood up, staring at my white sneakers, and muttered, "I'm sorry." I turned and walked for the door. "Enjoy your piss-up tonight," I said over my shoulder. There was no reply, making me feel even worse. The path that upsets me the most – I never disappoint. I was irritated with how this whole operation went down, the way Van Rooyen and Modise pushed me into a corner. That they were prepared to throw me under the bus. I was still angry, fired up. *Something smells about this.* I raised my arm and took a whiff, almost walking into a wall again. Before I could go to Nicole, I needed a shower. She was heavy on that. What also pissed me off was the way everyone looked at me lately. The glances they gave each other when I entered a room. I was away for too long; I'm not part of the team. It must be that.

* * *

My place
Thursday
20:02

I lived in a two-bedroom flat in Melville. A bit rundown, but it was mine and a springboard to the library and the retirement village. Sometimes, when I wasn't shooting bad guys, I picked up grandma at the retirement village and dropped her off at the library. My sister did the rest. Mom was always too busy – shopping, manicures, pedicures, and bikini waxes. I shuddered.

The elevator worked, but I took the stairs to the third floor because the building had the same maintenance plan as a government building. Why fuck with something not broken?

As usual, Peter, my neighbour from flat 306, was hanging over the railing, wearing his washed-out green robe and blue slippers. Peter, or Peebiscuit, as I called him (he always reeked of piss and was hung like a horse), was about forty-five and had wavy blonde hair gelled back. He tied his robe's belt in a neat bow to support his sagging bay window. Sometimes the curtain slipped open and revealed his turtlehead sleeping on two duffel bags. I'm sure he did it on purpose.

His eyes lit up as he saw me. "Gregory!" He stretched his arms wide, pushing out his belly. The curtain parted, revealing his awakening old man. Another shudder ran down my spine. It was difficult not to look at it, like watching a horrible train crash – this one was derailing to the left. If it weren't for Mercy, my cat, I would've tossed him over the railing and watched him, robe flapping, to his merciful death. Why, oh why, did he not wear anything under that thing?

"Peebiscuit, please!" I snapped. "I have not asked for an encore. Close the curtain."

"Oh, sorry, Gee." He acted flustered and retied his robe by opening it before closing it.

"Is Mercy all right?" I asked as I inserted the key. "Because if something happened to my cat, I will castrate you. It's easy enough to get to." I walked into my flat, glaring at him, noticing the twinkle in his eye, the sheer excitement. It might have caused my cat's imminent death. "I took care of her for three months when you were undercover."

"Thanks, Pee," I sighed. "I'll drop off some cat food before I go."

"No problem, Gee."

"Who told you I worked undercover?"

"Manana." He winked. "Don't worry, your secret is safe with me."

The door slammed shut on his smiling pasty face. Undercover? I was in a fucking coma.

I liked my cat and nobody else's. She left me alone, and I left her alone. Sometimes, when I got teary-eyed, like when the Springboks lost a game or when my satellite dish had gone, or when I thought of Beatrice, or lately the nightmares, she would come and purr on my lap. The rest of the time, we stayed out of each other's way. I wished everyone was like that.

Before jumping into the shower, I locked the front door. With Pee next door, one can never be too safe. Nicole liked a clean man – shaven and everything.

* * *

Nicole's place
Northcliff
21:05

The last time I saw Nicole was at my sister's wedding. I dropped her off at her apartment, kissed her goodnight, and that was that. We'd been dating for four months before our break-up – the longest I'd been with a girl, ever. She was beautiful: golden brown hair, big amber eyes, a cute button nose, and perfect lips. Nicole was a little overweight, not too much, and about my height. I hated it when girls looked down at me.

She lived in the same townhouse complex in the northern suburb of Joburg. Nice place – clean, modern, and expensive. She worked for an international IT company as a data recovery specialist. I'd met her a year ago when our forensics team, including me, couldn't retrieve sensitive data from a hard drive. We approached the company, and they assigned Nicole to us. It took her two hours to work her magic and about the same time to work my magic on her.

I stopped by the security gate and removed my helmet.

"You again," the twenty-rand-an-hour security guard asked. I was sure he wouldn't take a bullet for any of these inhabitants, even though they thought he would. Hilarious. He looked at me as if I'd just impregnated a three-legged dog. "What makes you think she'll let you in this time?"

"Nicole, 69." I'll never forget that number. "Please."

"What's your name again?" He snapped his fingers, frowning. "What did she call you? O, yes, Dickhead."

"Greg Goodman."

He unclipped his cordless phone from his belt and dialled the number. The phone was on speaker. It rang a few times before she answered.

"Greg Goodman to see you, Ms Roberts."

I was glad it was still Roberts.

Silence.

"Ms. Roberts?"

Silence.

Then, "Tell him, tell him to fuck off."

He looked at me with a satisfied smirk.

"Tell her I'm here on business."

"He says it's business."

"Tell him then to really fuck off." Her voice cracked through the receiver.

"Tell her I want to apologize."

"He said he wants to apologize."

"No, Greg. Please go away. Please." She whispered the last word, but it was the loudest.

The guard shrugged. "You heard the lady." He turned and walked back to his cage.

I leaned on the helmet between my legs, staring at the gate. For two weeks I avoided her calls. That's all. If I were such an arsehole with women – why would any girl be angry with me if I left? I would be ecstatic if I left me. Now what? Where to find another IT specialist at this hour? I shrugged, put my helmet back on and started my other addiction – my Triumph, the American Cruiser. It growled to a start and then purred like a satisfied lion between my legs.

The white gate rolled open.

"He said you could go in and apologize." The guard waved me in. If it were up to him, I would never get in.

Two weeks after I had fled from our relationship, I wanted her back; left messages, texts, emails, visited the guard. All had the same reply: Fuck off, Dickhead!

I rolled in, past the communal piss-infested swimming pool, down a paved road lined with palm trees, and up to her townhouse, a square grey block with huge windows.

The door burst open as I lowered the side stand. He stormed out, wielding a baseball bat, dressed in shorts and a vest.

So, the guard didn't have a slip of the tongue; her boyfriend let me in.

"What the hell you want with my fiancée," Byron Wolf screamed, bat raised above his head. "Can't believe you're back here again! Didn't you get the fucking message to stay away!"

"What's going on here?" Nicole came running.

We made eye contact. That was the moment I knew; something in her gaze told me.

"I told you not to let him in!" she screamed, hands in hair. "Byron, don't! He'll kill you."

The steroids baby was huge but slow. He left himself wide open. I still had my helmet in my hand. The bat scraped my back as I ducked, throwing him off balance. I swung the helmet up, hitting him under the chin. Byron staggered back, eyes glazed. Blood gushed from his mouth and nose.

"Greg, no! Don't hurt him, please," Nicole screamed, pulling Byron by his arm.

Shit. If I beat the crap out of her boyfriend, she'd never speak to me again. It would destroy any chance of us getting back together. She would also not help me with recovering the data. If I turned the tables, she would send him packing and take pity on me – all I needed; a bit of sympathy mixed in with my charm.

"Come on, wet fart," I stepped back. "You done already?" I

removed my backpack and dropped it into the flowerbed lining her footpath. "Let's even the playing field." I tossed my helmet.

He yanked free from Nicole and stormed, bat in hand. The bastard. I was hoping he would toss the bat before beating me up.

"Byron, he's playing with you." Nicole tried to grab his arm, but he was too quick out of the blocks. "He's dangerous!"

As he ran toward me, I had about seven ways of neutralizing him, but I chose none. I stepped back, stumbled over her flowerbed, and fell on my back. This is going to hurt. I raised my arms, protecting my head and face, waiting.

His first blow struck me in the ribs, the second, my arms, and the third, my legs. He then started kicking me in the nuts. I caught a glimpse of him through my arms and turned cold. This guy had lost it: red face, wild eyes, and clenched jaw.

Nicole stood by the front door, under the light, with a surprised expression – almost amused. Did I hurt her that badly? *Don't worry, Greg, she's going to run to your aid at any moment.*

He swung the bat like pro-golfer, striking me on my injured shoulder. I let out a yelp, surprising even myself. This smart plan of mine was going south quickly.

Nicole now would be a good time! She stood, arms crossed, emotionless –well, it was better than the amused expression a moment ago.

The arsehole clubbed me in the ribs again.

Nicole! I screamed in my head. It had to come from her.

A sharp pain shot through my body. I gasped for air, crossing my arms, trying to protect myself, but left my head wide open.

A loud thump, darkness, then finally Nicole screamed. *Finally!* Fuck! I blacked out.

3

"Cunning men do not deal with each other."
Zulu proverb

Nicole's Place – I hoped.
23:25

Hold still! The darkness engulfed me. I couldn't breathe. Couldn't move. Someone whispered, "This is for..."

Something pressed against my throat. I gasped. *Help!* I couldn't get the word out. *No!* My mouth opened but again, nothing. Warm water or something soaked the front of my shirt.

I regained consciousness as if hoisted from a water-well, wrapped in barbed wire, and pummelled in the head and nuts by a nail-bat.

"Fuck." The word slipped as I tried to move. I wasn't in the garden.

"Don't move," Nicole said. But it wasn't a gentle, sorry-my-boyfriend-almost-killed-you tone. "Must I call an ambulance?"

"You haven't already?" It took a moment to open my eyes. I was on her couch in the living room.

"You're cold-blooded, like a lizard. I wanted to wait and see if you couldn't get out of here yourself."

I glanced around. "How thoughtful." I groaned.

"I asked Byron to carry you in, against my moral judgment, but I was worried about the neighbours. I became friends with them again. If they see that you're back in my life, they'll never speak to me."

"Where is Byron?" I asked in a hoarse whisper.

"I asked him to leave for the night. He needs to cool off, and I need to ask you a favour." She spoke in a heartless, monotonous tone.

"What?" I pulled my face excessively as I tried to move.

"Please don't report him to the cops or to your friends. It's my fault he hates you so much. He was the one there for me when you ran away. He listened to my cries and bitching about you."

"What did you tell him about me, that I burnt you with cigarettes?"

She didn't even crack a smile. "Only the truth."

I raised my head and tried to assess the damage. My new white shirt's buttons were torn off. I hadn't even washed it yet. My Diesel jeans seemed intact. *No, wait, shit, knees torn.* I would hang on to them until back in fashion. I'd google how to get the bloodstains out.

She knelt beside the couch, wiping blood and sweat from my chest – mostly blood from my nose and sweat from the nightmare. I hardened my stomach muscles, emphasizing my six-pack. That usually worked. She drove the cotton ball over my ripples but said or showed no emotion. Her hair brushed over my chest. It felt amazing. I filled my lungs with her scent, letting it out slowly – like a craved cigarette. Perfect, no after effect. A strange feeling flared up in my stomach. Was it the butterfly feeling? I raised my hand and touched the back of her neck.

Nicole jolted, leaping back as if I'd just hit her with a stun gun. She stood over me, teeth clenched, trembling.

"What are you doing?" she seethed. "I'm getting married! Can't you see how upset I am that you're in my house?" She threw me with the blood-soaked cotton ball. "I'm only doing this for Byron. I hate you." Her eyes welled up. "Your looks are the only thing you've got going for you. Inside, you're empty, just an empty shell. Women are nothing but a hole you can stick your dick into." She pointed at the door. "Get out. Go!"

I worked myself into an upright position. Byron did a bloody good job. Asshole. I remained seated, not knowing how to respond, staring at my torn jeans. There was no comeback. For a moment, but only for a moment, I wanted to jump up and scream, Bitch! But that would only prove her point, and I liked her too much for that. And I would pee my jocks. I tried to look shocked, but couldn't fake that emotion, not now. She would know.

I stood up, clutching my aching shoulder. She was wrong; I wasn't an empty shell. Fuck, was I? No, an empty shell would feel nothing. I didn't want to acknowledge what she said. Agree or disagree.

My backpack stood next to her white dining-room table. The dirty green bag stood out like a dog-turd on a putting green. I made my way to the table. She was silent – thank God. I couldn't get myself to look at her. From the corner of my eye, I noticed her glistening tears in the dimly lit room. I picked up the bag and removed the notebook.

"I will not press charges if you help me retrieve the data." I gathered enough strength to look at her. "Someone threw it into a pool." The throbbing headache and my shame forced me to turn for the door.

"Leave it on the table."

"It's sensitive information, so nobody must see it."

"I'll call you when it's done. And this time, you better answer because I will phone only once." Her voice cut through my back.

"I'm sorry." I closed the door behind me and picked up my helmet from the flowerbed. "Fuck." My motorcycle lay on its side, dented and bruised – like me.

Byron vented his anger when he left.

It was the longest ten minutes of my life, struggling with one arm to get my bike upright, wiping my tears, and arguing the empty shell statement. I would forgive him for my wounds, but not for this.

* * *

Melville
    Friday, 8:22

I lay in bed, drenched in sweat, staring at a daddy-long-leg in the corner. The bastard grew by the day. I became afraid of it. A symbol of how useless my one-day-a-week house cleaner was. I must get her for two days. But not now. The laptop I bought and destroyed besmirched my fucking budget. How long would it take forensics to figure out there was no data on it from the start?

My cell phone rang for the fourth time this morning.

Probably the office. I had to be there at six-thirty. I tried getting up at five-thirty but couldn't move. My body was fifty shades of purple and one ball of pain. I gently touched my swollen right eye, where Byron had struck me with the bat. Mercy was draped over my left leg, weighing a ton. I moved, almost pissing my briefs.

She raised her head, staring at me with those green condescending eyes.

"I know," I whispered. "Don't say it." I reached for the bedside table, popped three pain pills, and downed them with the last bit of whiskey left in the bottle.

My cell phone rang again. I waited until it stopped before reaching for it.

Ten missed calls.

Asshole Van Rooyen, three missed calls.

Mom, two missed calls.

Dominique, three missed calls. Can't she catch a hint? I went out with her after Nicole – before I had my throat slit.

Two missed calls from an unknown number – been getting them since leaving the hospital. Tele-fucking-marketers.

No missed calls from Nicole.

The front door opened.

I leapt from the bed to the utter dismay of Mercy and grabbed my pistol from under the pillow. The pain for now forgotten.

I dropped my weapon on the bed as my mom called, "Geegee, where are you, my sunshine!"

"I'm coming!" I frantically searched for a shirt and pants. "Just a sec!"

My mom stormed into the room, followed by Tito, followed by another woman, and to my utter shock and horror, followed by Peter – you guessed it, dressed in his green robe and blue slippers.

All froze as they barged into my room.

"Geegee, my darling, what happened?" Mom called out, placing her hand, with red manicured nails, in front of her mouth.

Tito, her bodyguard-cum-personal-assistant-cum-driver – I called him her third nipple (the only natural one) – placed his hand on her shoulder for support. The other woman tried to leave, but Pee blocked her escape. He stood, wide-eyed, taking in every inch – his curtain parting.

I grabbed my weapon and pointed it at him. "Peter, if you don't leave now, I will shoot you."

He flew around and left, his robe flapping in his wake.

"That goes for all of you!" I snapped. "Wait in the living room."

The room emptied, and I threw on a t-shirt and denim. The painkillers didn't work.

* * *

My mom approached with outstretched arms as I entered the living room. If it were somebody else, I would've said "no hugging" because of my bruised body, but I knew her too well. She was always afraid something of me might rub off on her designer outfit. Mom cupped my cheeks and gave me a peck with her blood-red lips.

"What happened, Gee?" she asked with pouted lips, reaching for my swollen eye.

I pulled back. "Just work."

She turned without missing a beat, pointing with an open hand to her latest asset. "I want you to meet Drew – my new Ray of Light foundation manager. I'm doing so much good I can't keep up."

I gave Drew a nod and a weak smile. She was a beauty: long wavy brown hair, big brown eyes, and full lips that would keep you occupied for a weekend – Easter weekend.

"Morning, Greg." She smiled, her puppy brown eyes not so innocent anymore. "You better keep her away from Dad."

My mother rolled her eyes. "Oh, please, I wish. He can have her if it will help to get him out of the canyon he finds himself in." She waved Tito closer. "I bought you new clothes. You're still wearing your boy size?"

"Fuck," I whispered, glancing at Drew.

"Nothing to be ashamed of, darling." She slapped me on my butt.

I wanted to kill her, but she was my mom.

"You okay, Mr. Goodman?" Tito asked in his hoarse voice as he placed the bags by my feet. He rested his hand on my bad shoulder.

I didn't flinch as the pain shot through my body, not to offend. Tito had been with the family for as long as I could remember. Always neat as a pin, dressed in his black suit and tie, crisp white shirt, and shiny black shoes.

"I don't look as bad as I feel inside," I said and winked at him with my good eye. *Shit, he's getting old.* His hair was as white as the shirt he wore and skin as leathery and wrinkly as Pee's scrotum.

He stared at me until he heard the words he wanted to hear that everyone else wanted to hear because nobody had the time to listen to anyone's freaking problems anymore.

"I'm fine, Tito."

"Good." He smiled and shuffled back to his corner.

"How's your grandma?" Mother took a seat on the edge of my couch, clutching her lime-green crocodile-skin handbag with one hand and stroking her long blond hair draped over her right shoulder. She looked damn good for her age. Okay, she had some work done. Still, at sixty, she could pass as a forty-year-old.

"Your mother-in-law is fine," I lied, because what's the use.

"I'll visit again soon." She glanced around the room as if something was about to jump on her. I found it amusing; my mom grew up in an orphanage.

"Maybe with Drew around, you'll have more time on your hands to visit," I said, glancing at the new Ray of Light foundation member. "Because we all know charity starts at home."

Drew suppressed a smile, admiring my entertainment system, which took up one wall of the living room. I liked her.

"The reason I'm here–"

"I didn't know you needed a reason to visit your son."

"You also don't need a reason to visit your mother," she fired back.

Ouch. I made wide eyes at Drew.

She smiled, pulling up her shoulders.

I couldn't get Nicole out of my mind. Even with this gorgeous woman. I took a slow seat at the kitchen nook. "Sorry, Mom, you were saying."

"Your father wants to speak to you."

"He always needed a reason. What did I do wrong?"

"It's not that kind of talk. He's in a slump lately, and he asked if you could come over."

"Just for a talk." I frowned. "You expect me to believe that."

"I think it will be something good, Geegee." She smiled, but I detected sadness in her eyes. "It's time you sort out your differences. You know he visited you almost every day in the hospital."

"Yeah, right," I whispered.

"Please, ubaba," Tito whispered.

"No, call me indoda. I'm not a father."

He grinned. "That's the problem."

Mother stood and placed a tentative step toward me. "We'll be leaving for the farm this weekend and will be there for the holidays. Can you see him at his office today?"

"Not Monte Carlo or Greece or France, but the Limpopo River. What happened, someone pissed in the tank of the jet?"

"So, can I tell him you'll see him?"

I removed a packet of cigarettes from a fruit bowl on the kitchen nook and lit one up.

Mom frowned. "I didn't know you smoked."

I filled my lungs and exhaled slowly for dramatic effect. All eyes were on me.

I stared at Drew. Hell, she had beautiful eyes. A flash of darkness. *Hold still!* I thought of Nicole.

"I've been smoking for fifteen years, Mom. There's a lot you don't know about me."

"Then I think it's time I get to know you better."

I took another slow puff, toying with the audience. "Okay." I gave a slow nod. "He can pencil me in."

"What time? You know how he is."

"I don't know; you know how I am."

Someone shuffled behind me in the kitchen.

"Your milk is off," Peter said.

* * *

Johannesburg
    Task Force Operations Room
    Friday, 10:05

Captain Modise stood behind his altar, scanning faces. Twelve pairs of eyes stared back at him, three rows of four – all men – standing at ease, dressed in camouflage-green uniforms.

"Does anyone know where Sergeant Goodman finds himself this morning?" Modise asked, scribbling something in his notepad.

Manana raised his hand.

"Yes, Sergeant." Modise glared at him over the rim of his frameless glasses.

"He phoned me just before the meeting, Captain, told me he was not feeling well."

Modise held his glare for a moment and then scribbled something.

"So, he was not at weapons training this morning?"

"No, Captain, but he sent me a photo of his misfortune." Manana held up his phone.

Modise narrowed his eyes and waved Manana closer.

"What's his excuse?" Modise took the phone from Manana.

"He walked into a revolving door; it struck him again and again and again."

Subdued laughter rustled through the room.

Modise stared at the picture with a raised brow before a slow smile formed. He removed his wallet from his back pocket and plucked a fifty-rand note from it. "Buy the revolving door a fruit basket." He glanced around for a response but received none.

"Fine, I'll buy it myself," he muttered, stuffing the note back into his wallet and noted the absent member.

The door opened, and Lieutenant Van Rooyen peeked inside.

"Good." Modise smiled, relieved. "The lieutenant is back. He will proceed with the briefing."

Van Rooyen waved Modise closer and stepped back into the corridor.

"They couldn't retrieve any data from the laptop," Van Rooyen whispered as Modise joined him.

"So, the data was destroyed," Modise said, scratching the side of his nose.

"No, I mean, it never had data on it."

"So, Bolton still has the info?"

"There's more." Steward glanced up and down the corridor. "That notebook was purchased yesterday." He leaned forward. "After they took Bolton to the hospital."

Modise's eyes shifted, processing the info. "That fucking, worthless Goodman. I want him arrested. I want that little shit behind bars. That means he and Bolton made a deal."

"We can't arrest him," Van Rooyen said.

"Why not?" Modise placed his hands on his hips. "Because of his father?"

"Because yesterday's operation was such an absolute disaster that we will lose our jobs if any of it gets out. I've already destroyed the audio recordings. Besides, CCTV footage of the shop shows a bm making the purchase and not a white male. It was a cash transaction."

"So, we are just going to carry on as if nothing happened? Goodman will get away with it again. His insubordination–"

"Greg didn't get away with anything," Van Rooyen interrupted. "Someone stabbed him in the gut and slit his throat." He smiled. "Karma's a bitch."

Modise stared at his Lieutenant with a concerned frown. "I know he's an annoying piece of shit, but he's still part of our team."

Van Rooyen swallowed his smile and nodded, averting his gaze.

"The most important thing for us to do now is to find Bolton's laptop. I'll leave it to you." He walked away. "Do what needs to be done, Lieutenant."

4

"The nice fig is often full of worms."
Zulu proverb

Goodman HQ
Johannesburg CBD
Friday, 14:42

I parked my banged-up Triumph under a No-Parking sign in front of the seventy-story skyscraper and hung my "disabled" sign over the handle. Joburg did not disappoint on my way here, as overloaded taxis disregarded every middle finger, horn, and profanity known to man. Illegal street vendors lined the sidewalks, selling everything from fruit to chicken feet to Eveready batteries. The smell of piss burnt my nose as I made my way to the polished brass revolving door. I was here about five years ago when my father made me the deal I couldn't refuse – join the service or else...

So, I joined, but for my reasons and never took a cent from him since. He did offer via mother. *Why am I here now?* Curiosity – to find out why the sudden interest in my life? He visited me in the hospital almost every day – so they told me.

The metal detector's alarm sounded as I walked through, attracting the female guard. I presented my green SA Taskforce identity card and raised my T-shirt, showing her the holstered USP 9mm pistol.

She squinted at the card and then at me. Her doubt was clear. "Goodman?" she replied.

"My father."

She shook her head and waved me in.

The "important" people, dressed in their suits, wearing work faces, scurried past me in the foyer, taking their next step in the hamster wheel. Some noticed the odd one out with his battered face and enlarged their personal space. The trained receptionist didn't even bat a false eyelash as she looked up from her switchboard. She could land the Space Shuttle Endeavour with it.

I scanned the wall behind her as she organized my security card.

Goodman Mergers & Acquisitions
Goodman Transport & Freight
Goodman Financial Services
Goodman Global
Goodman Arms & Ammunition
Goodman Pharmaceuticals

Goodman this, Goodman that – the list was longer since the last time I was here.

"Top floor." She handed me the access card.

"Of course."

A group of suits waited by the bank of elevators, thumbs furiously working their smartphones – without them, the world would stop turning. They only noticed me when we herded into the elevator. Those who entered behind me made an about-turn and scurried away as if forgotten to turn off their stoves. None wanted to occupy the same space as me, or they didn't want their tailor-made bubbles invaded by someone not from their planet. It suited me fine. The elevator caught two of them. I stared at my reflection in the polished chrome doors – I couldn't blame them. *Is this me?* I grew up turning into the man my mother warned me about.

"Floor?" the one closest to the control panel asked as he pressed number nine.

"Twelve," the other suit replied.

"Seventy," I said as he looked at me with an expression expecting the basement.

He frowned, his finger creeping up the panel as if his hand weighed a ton. "You sure?"

"Why?" I played along.

"It's Mr. Goodman's floor."

"So?"

He glanced at his colleague before pressing the number.

"See, you're still breathing."

The elevator started its ascend.

I scratched my side, revealing my weapon on the reflective surface. They glanced at each other while shifting away.

Both ran out as the doors slid open on the sixth, almost knocking over a woman.

"Hey!" she scowled and entered the lift without giving me a second glance.

"Floor?"

"Sixty-nine, thank you." She looked like a typical tight-ass corporate with her polished ponytail, black-rimmed pointy glasses, high heels, and power suit.

"My favourite position." I pressed the button.

She looked me over with a gaping mouth, repulsed. "Please don't tell me it's one of your pickup lines?"

"No." I shrugged. "I was trying to make small talk. It's still a long way to go."

Her eyes shifted to the control panel. "You're underdressed for that floor. You family?"

I stuck my hands into my pockets, sighing, "Father."

"You're short for a Goodman. Must be such a disappointment to him."

Ouch! Am I that transparent? It came from a stranger who only knew me for fifty floors. "Try to be," I muttered, keeping my cool.

The doors slid open. "Talk about cutting off one's nose." She exited the elevator like a racehorse from its cage and turned back after a few strides. "Be careful what you say to a respectable woman. Here it's called sexual harassment."

I had a million comeback lines but decided against it. The doors closed, leaving me with my reflection. The thoroughbred only echoed what Grandma said every time she saw me. I'm like a drug addict who knew he had a problem but still had a few good veins left before hitting rock bottom.

The receptionist frowned as the elevator doors opened. I heard my father in his office. Mother designed this office space; the pastel-green carpet, white walls and impractical furniture told me so.

"Can I help you, sir?" the receptionist asked, still with a cute frown. She had long black hair, the bluest eyes, and the brightest smile. I thought of Nicole – she had the same smile, although I didn't see it last night.

"I'm here to see him." My stomach cramped.

"I don't have anyone scheduled to see him." She stared at her monitor, tapping the mouse.

"Good." I smiled. "Then I don't have to wait."

"I'm sorry, but if you don't–"

"Tell his highness that his son is here to see him."

"Oh, Mr. Goodman." She leapt to her feet. "Sorry, you don't look like him at all." She stuck out her hand. "I'm Tracey."

I thought her blue eyes could not get any bluer.

"Hi, Tracey." I smiled and shook her hand – deciding against kissing it; I didn't want another elevator scenario.

"Mr. Goodman told me I could send you in as soon as you arrive."

I gave Tracey a final peek over the shoulder before opening the doors to hell.

My father sat behind his desk, back toward me, and talking on the phone.

"Harry, this strike is killing us." He shook his head. "These fucking unions." Chuckled. "Yes, send them all to Robben Island or Ireland – the Irish would know what to do with them." He scratched his thinning-grey hair. "You're crazy!" He burst out laughing. "Not my island... Yes... We're still busy with the paperwork. Can't wait... I'm going to retire there... No, I'm not afraid. They'll never take my farm. It's just hoo-hah to calm the masses. Populism. They won't slap the hand that feeds them."

I panned the horizon: a suffocating, sinus-inducing grey cloud covered mine dumps and buildings in the distance. To the left, a towering skyscraper with burnt-out windows and laundry blowing in the mucky gale – another highjacked building.

"You heard about the oil they struck in Nigeria... not even enough to run my Bentley." My father swivelled around and froze as his gaze landed on me. He played with one of his awards, Rolex on the wrist. The three-piece Armani flashed even when no one was watching.

He stared at me in silence, those piercing, judgmental eyes scrutinizing every flaw, every imperfection – it felt like an eternity. *Five years, what must I do? What must I say?* I felt awkward and exposed.

My father blinked and cleared his throat. "Harry, I've got to go. Something came up."

Why did I come today, bringing along my bruises and scars? I'd just proved his point – I was a failure, a loser, a disappointment.

He stood, also unsure, unsmiling. His lean, six-foot-four posture towered above mine.

"Greg, you came." It was hard to read that gaunt face, but I detected a whisper of a smile. "It's been, what, five years since you saw me." He moved from behind his desk and replaced the golden tower in his trophy cupboard. "I visited you in the hospital."

"I-I-I know." *No! Fuck! Not now, you're pathetic, Gregory. Pull yourself together*. I took a deep breath and gave my legs the oxygen they needed. They felt like another man's legs, the legs of a coward. I took an awkward step and seized his reaching hand. "Father," I got it out without a stutter. Since stepping out of the hospital, the problem had worsened.

We shook hands like two strangers – which we were – one firm shake, looking him in the eye. His hand was clammy, not the cold, firm shake I once knew. Was he also nervous? I used that weakness to pull myself together.

He pointed to a private lounge in the corner of his office. Four leatherback chairs surrounded a big, solid wood coffee table. My mother had no hand in decorating his office; thick dark-grey carpet, grey walls, and larger-than-life dark wooden furniture – it had to scream money, balls, and intimidation. Even the chairs on the other side of his desk were smaller than usual, so he could look down on his prey. I took a seat on one of the big leather couches, feeling like a hobbit visiting Gandalf the Grey. He was more like the All-Seeing Eye in the tower.

"You want something to drink?" the Eye asked and took a seat opposite me. "Maybe some coffee to sober you up?"

And there it was, one minute in his company, and already he took a swipe. After five years, and that was the second thing he'd said.

I stood up. "This was a m-mistake."

My father stood. "I'm sorry, it was uncalled for." He pointed to the chair. "Please."

I glared up at him. *Why must I be so bloody short?*

A clock chimed three times as I took a slow seat, breathing. "It's Friday afternoon – I had a drink with my friends," I lied.

He forced a smile. "So, how are you keeping?" He sat clutching the armrests, upright, legs crossed, watching my fiddling hands.

"I'm fine," I said, the words they all needed to hear. "And you?" I asked before he could drill deeper.

"I'm also fine." He raised his hands, touching fingers as if praying. Those judgemental eyes shifted to the right. He wasn't fine.

I was more in control, my inferiority dissipating like the grey blanket behind him on a rainy day.

"Any pain?" He swallowed.

I frowned. "What do you mean?"

"I mean, are you a hundred percent." He took hold of the armrests as if preparing for a rollercoaster ride.

"Look at me."

He smiled. "I mean from that night."

"What do you know of that night?"

My father shrugged and looked away. "Only what they reported. That they attacked and robbed you." He cleared his throat. "Left you for dead." He looked at me and waved a finger at his jugular. "The loss of blood and oxygen caused memory loss. Can you remember anything?"

"Nothing at first."

"What do you mean?" he said, shocked.

"Not much, only a voice."

"A voice?"

"Whispering, hold still, and this is for."

"This is for?"

I nodded. "Can't remember the rest."

"Maybe it's better you can't remember."

"Maybe."

He stopped white-knuckling the armrest, the colour returning to his cheeks.

"Mom said you're not yourself." I struggled to force some emotion into my tone.

His eyes narrowed. He seemed angry by the fact I knew. "It's December – the working class gets very demanding this time of the year." His Adam's apple bobbed.

He wanted to continue, but again, he reined himself in. He wanted to elaborate on his "working class" remark.

Strike two.

"You wanted to see me?" I sat back.

He took a moment to answer, choosing his words. "For five years, my wallet was open, and you never took a cent. I don't know why because you obeyed my wishes to join the armed forces."

I let him finish. This I wanted to hear.

"According to the deal we've made, you had to stay for a minimum of two years. Still, you stayed, and not just stay. You joined the Task Force." He picked at something on his armrest before looking at me. "Why?"

I glared at him, mind racing. "Waiting for something... better." I shrugged. Shit answer.

He raised a brow.

"I wanted to prove to myself I could do it. I wanted to be away from you. I wanted to–" Shit, I choked. *Don't cry, not now.* "I wanted to prove to you I'm not the worthless piece of shit you think I am." I took a deep breath and folded my arms, trying to hide my shaking hands. "But you know what? I don't care what the hell you think anymore because I'll never be good enough for you. I'll always fall short." I dabbed the sweat from my face with the hem of my T-shirt.

"Why did you bring your gun with you?" My father searched for something behind me: the nearest exit or security, I don't know.

I frowned, taken aback. "Relax, I'm a cop, remember." He was afraid. I should be ecstatic, but it angered me. My father didn't know me at all. "You think I brought it with me just in case."

"I don't know, did you?"

I shook my head, amazed. "Why did you wanna see me?"

He glanced at his fidgeting right hand. "I know you hate me. I messed up so many times with you. When I saw you in that hospital bed..." He shook his head. "I want to make things right between us."

"Because I was beaten up?" I scowled. "I'm still the same Greg; that same worthless piece of shit you hated. That same k-kid you belittled and yelled a-at f-for just being m-me. I-I know I'm n-not a Goodman, but f-fuck, you made it hell for me. Y-your hatred switched o-on like a light when I w-walked into y-y-your office. I-I could feel it." I grabbed the hem of my shirt and pretended to wipe the sweat from my brow. *Fuck! Don't cry!* I hid behind my shirt. "Why?" I whispered.

The beat of the clock was ear-splitting. Tick-Tock, Tick-Tock, Tick-Tock. "Okay, I owe you this," my father said. "You were created by the people I hated the most at that time. Your mother slept with my attorney before our marriage to prevent him from registering our antenuptial contract. He told me this."

I could finally lower my shirt. "So, you stayed in the marriage because you refused to give Mom some of your millions."

"Some," he scoffed. "I'll be damned if I hand over three generations of wealth."

"It doesn't make sense," I said. "Why didn't you take her to court. With the lawyer's testimony and proof of her screwing around, you could have annulled the marriage."

"My ex-lawyer only came clean four years into our marriage. Your sister was three months old." He shook his head. "Your dear Mom vowed I would never see Tracey again if I took her on." My father shrugged and looked me in the eye. "The lawyer also hanged himself in his garage, between his Mustang and SL. The little shit took the easy way out."

"Because of your shit?"

"You know me." My father scratched his head. "I make it difficult for those who cross me." It seemed as if he regretted the fact.

"Because you couldn't vent your anger on my father anymore, you took it out on his son." Take that, you son of a bitch.

He flushed, fingers digging into the armrest. "I want to make it up to you. In fact, I already did – that's why I called you here." His words did not mirror his facial expression.

"What have you done?"

"They have released you of your duties. You're a free man."

"What are you talking about?" My world crumbled around me.

"Clearly, you're not happy. Your drinking is proof of that. Your brother-in-law, Lieutenant Van–"

"I know who my f-fucking brother-in-law is!" I jumped up.

He swallowed. "He told me you were unhappy, that you wanted out. So, I phoned my friend, the Minister of–"

"No!" I shouted. "What did you d-do?"

"I thought you would be relieved. You just need to hand in your gear, your weapon and walk away. You can do whatever you want to now. I'll pay for everything." He reached into his inside pocket and removed a piece of paper. "Here is a cheque for a million rand. See it as a down payment." He held it between his two fingers. "There will be a lot more."

I fell into the chair and buried my head in my hands. The ever-present anger festered like a stomach ulcer. Trust my father to tear it open. I raised my head, taking gulps of air.

"I don't know what to say." He acted flustered. "According to Van Rooyen, you made it hell for them. You were miserable and–"

"I know!" I leapt off the chair once more and stormed around the room. "I know, I...know, I know, b-but it was my choice." I cried and didn't care. "You know how f-fucking hard it was to join the T-Task Force." I stood over him, fists clenched. "Do you have any fucking idea? It was my only fucking accomplishment." That sentence echoed through the room and in my mind. How pathetic does that sound?

I noticed an emotion I'd never seen before, dismay, sadness, and fatigue. The mask had fallen off. He sniffed and blinked. I kept my stance, my anger.

"Phone your friend and tell him you made a mistake," I said through clenched teeth.

He shook his head. "I can't. Believe me, I can't. It's over, Gregory."

My father covered his eyes with a shaking hand.

Strike three. He'd done it again; he'd broken me. Every little grain, every little stone I'd balanced on top of the other, he crushed into a fine powder. This job was all I had. It kept me sane. I wanted to kill him, grab him around his neck and squeeze every grain of life out of him. Instead, I walked over to his trophy cupboard and pulled it from the wall. The glass doors and every fragile accomplishment shattered into a thousand pieces. He remained seated, one hand still covering his eyes, the other clutching the cheque.

"You almost died, son," he whispered. "I don't want to see you like that again."

I walked out and made a point of not closing the door behind me – he hated that.

I was a dog chasing a car, catching it, and then realizing he lived for the chase. *How could he do such a thing!* Was this necessary to understand what I had, what I'd accomplished? The old story – you only realized something's value once you'd lost it. I was angry at the world, at my father, and I took it out on my job, my friends – a spoiled kid, refusing to grow up, refusing to commit. One option remained; go back to Modise and do the unthinkable. Beg for my job, my life. To get something back, your love was worth the embarrassment.

A suit bumped into me as I stopped, exciting the revolving door – my bike was gone. Not a surprise. This was the next logical obstacle before falling face down in an open sewer. *What is the world coming to, somebody impounded or stole a disabled person's mode of transport?* I glanced at my Casio – 15:12. Modise ran away at two – that's after taking lunch from midday. I needed time to think; figure out my life.

I wanted to phone one of my six funeral buddies to pick me up but decided to hail a taxi. Another first. I didn't want to wait for an Uber. After a crash course by a professional hailer on the side of the road, I gave the hand signal to Melville – moving a limp hand from side to side with fingers pointing down; like a limp dick flapping in the wind, more or less like what I was feeling at that moment. Within one minute, I was on my way, travelling west, sitting in a fifteen-seater, surrounded by eighteen jovial commuters – not one gave the banged-up white a second glance. I thought of phoning Manana but decided against it. Not now. I chose not to call anyone because it was impossible to hear anything with all the screaming and laughter. It was Friday.

* * *

Johannesburg
    Task Force Central
    Friday, 15:14

Lieutenant Van Rooyen slammed the phone down on his desk, picked it up, and slammed it down again. He did so three times before falling back into his chair, rocking back and forth, staring with glazed eyes at the fire-drill procedures behind his closed door. A knock on the door jolted him out of his reverie.

"What!" he barked.

Thero stepped inside. "Excuse me for disturbing, Lieutenant, but Craig heard from Captain Modise, just before he left, that Goodman was no longer with us."

"You heard correctly." He raised his eyebrows. "Anything else."

Thero gave a step toward him. "But this was his life. This will...push him over the edge."

"Then he should've taken better care of his life. Besides, it came from the top – I had nothing to do with it."

"I doubt that Lieutenant," Thero said, glaring.

"Careful, Sergeant." Van Rooyen rose to his feet. "He pissed in his own pond, don't make the mistake of drinking from it."

"This is a big setback for our team. He was one of our best. If it didn't come from you, sir, then find out where it came from and sort it out."

"Is that all, Corporal?" Van Rooyen took a seat, pushing papers around on his desk.

"This is not right." Thero shook his head and turned for the door.

"Since when is anything right in this place?" Van Rooyen muttered as Thero turned the corner. "Suck it up, princess."

* * *

Melville

15:23

I was exhausted, sticky, and sore but took the stairs. It was a slow ascent, smoking two cigarettes before I reached the third floor. As usual, I didn't take Dominique's call. *Maybe a quick text to tell her she's wasting her time.* No, then she'll know I knew about all her calls – that I was still alive. I met her at Pixies. *Was it at Pixies? Was it the night?* I couldn't remember if it was the night before my attack or that night. But I knew she wasn't the one for me – too skittish and shy – couldn't look me in the eye. Dominique had bumped into me on the dancefloor, spilt most of her Blue Hawaiian cocktail over my white shirt. I had to break a beefcake's nose for calling me a Smurf. They always try their luck – so tiring.

Luckily, the old man sleeping on two duffel bags wasn't waiting for me. I tiptoed past Peebiscuit's flat but halted midstride. My door was open.

Perhaps crazy Pee was inside, feeding Mercy because I locked this morning. The door was undamaged. I nudged it open and peeked inside – Pee's blue slipper lay in the corridor.

That weirdo is going through my underwear again! "Peter!" I stormed inside and froze – Pete lay sprawled on his back, in the middle of my lounge, arms and legs stretched out. No blood. I drew my pistol, tiptoed down the corridor, and searched the rest of the flat. All was clear; only the main bedroom remained. I turned the knob and pushed open the door.

Mercy hung by a rope from the light, sliced open, blood still dripping from her carcass. Above the bed, written in blood across the wall: *Where is it?*

The man who did this to her will die. I wanted to cut her down, but the policeman within held me back. My eyes stung, remembering that weight on my legs, her judgemental stare, her sudden want for affection. The fucker who did this knew what she meant to me.

I left the room and returned to Peter, searching for signs of life. No such luck. His body was colder than my father's heart – neck broken. Pee probably thought it was me returning from work and caught the intruder by surprise.

Where was what? I fell back, shocked, staring at the lifeless body. I glanced at his privates – so used to checking if he covered up. Poor Pete soaked the carpet in his dying moments. I'd seen many dead bodies in my life, but none so close to me. Not that Pee was close, but he was a friend – a good guy. Forget that; he was okay. A lonely guy.

I left him exposed – guess he would want it like that and not to disturb evidence. I tried to make sense of it all while I waited for the cavalry.

"Where is it?" The only thing I could think of was the notebook. Had Van Rooyen and Modise discovered the laptop I gave them wasn't the one? Or was it one of Bolton's men, or his enemies, or his friends? I didn't think it was Bolton; we made a deal. I would let him go, but he had to forget I was ever there. It didn't take much because they would've thrown both our asses in jail. I had to give Van Rooyen and Modise something, so I convinced Bolton that his notebook was fucked. Maybe he figured I lied.

* * *

Wolf Recovery Inc.
    Sandton
    Friday, 15:27

Nicole stared pensively at the computer screen, biting her lower lip. She removed her librarian glasses and took a deep breath, exhaling slowly. "You're not going to like this, Greg."

She jolted as her office door burst open.

"Byron." she scowled as her glasses flew from her hands and landed on the keyboard. "You should learn to knock!"

"Oh, please, I thought we were long past knocking." He strolled around the desk and stood behind her. "Why are you so jumpy?"

She switched off the computer screen. "Sensitive data."

He placed his big hands on her bony shoulders and started messaging. "Have you ever heard of data that isn't?"

She closed her eyes, tilted her neck, and sighed. "I mean, it's private."

"So, the other data is public domain." He crouched down and kissed her on the neck.

"You know what I mean, and stop it. Somebody might walk in on us." She stroked his cheek.

"I don't think anybody would storm into the Technical Director's office," he whispered in her ear. "And is there somebody else who isn't knocking?"

"Technically, yes, the Managing Director." She leaned back and kissed him on the lips. "But he's also in the office."

Byron turned her monitor back on while lip-locked.

"Hey, smooth move."

"Are you doing private jobs on company time, Mrs. Roberts?"

"Technically, yes, but this is to keep your ass out of jail."

He straightened. "What do you mean?"

"I agreed to help Greg with this, and in return, he won't press charges against you."

"I can look after myself." He glared at the screen.

"You beat up a cop, Byron." She swivelled around. "And I would be more appreciative if I were you."

He frowned at the monitor.

"What?"

"Nothing." He smiled. "I'm sorry I placed you in a difficult situation." He went down on his knees in front of her and pushed her legs apart.

"I hoped he enjoyed his walk home." Byron grinned.

"What do you mean?"

"After I carried the asshole inside, I vented my anger on his bike."

"What!" Nicole jumped up, shoving him back. "That was his baby. Why did you do such a stupid thing?"

He leapt to his feet. "Why are you so upset?" His eyes narrowed. "Don't tell me you're falling for him. After everything we went through."

"Don't be ridiculous. I know how much that bike means to Greg." She walked around her desk and opened her office door. "You're kicking at a sleeping snake. God help you when he realizes he doesn't stand a chance with me"– she smiled –"or if I fall for him. Now, if you'll excuse me."

Byron stormed around the desk and grabbed her around the arm. "Don't fuck with me," he said through gritted teeth, cheeks flushed. "If I find out you're screwing with me, you'll regret the day you crawled into my office." He walked out and barked over his shoulder. "I want that NSI job on my desk before six... tonight."

"Oh, is that how it's going to be. I'll come up later and burp you," she yelled and slammed the door shut.

Nicole took a few breaths, chewing her lower lip. She walked over to her desk, picked up her cell phone, and searched for Greg's name.

* * *

Melville

15:35

Everybody and his little sister were there: police, ambulance, coroner, forensics and three of my team – well, ex-team. Two of Brixton's murder-and-robbery unit and Manana waited outside with me. They pretended to chat, but I knew the drill; they fished. One of Brixton's finest, sixty-year-old Inspector Coetzee – a relic of the past with his beer belly, bushy grey hair, and penetrating blue eyes, had already offered me a smoke, which I accepted, of course. Inspector Nichols, his sidekick, made notes, scribbling in her little notepad, now and then wiggling her hand to readjust her bulky black diver's watch. Although, I'm sure she'd never seen the inside of a wetsuit. Her mullet haircut also convinced me she disliked MacGyver.

They went through the usual list of questions until they asked me the one they wanted to ask first.

"Where is what?" Inspector Coetzee said, eyes narrowing.

I shrugged, keeping eye contact. "I've got no idea."

He stared at me for a few seconds, then smiled. "I can see you're having a bad day, but if you want things to get worse–"

"Inspector Coetzee!" Van Rooyen yelled as he stormed around the corner. "Thank you for securing the crime scene, but we will take it from here."

Coetzee closed his eyes as he took a deep breath.

"You're lucky," I said. "He's family."

Coetzee turned to face him. "Did your car break down?"

"No," Steward heaved. "The elevators."

"Someone killed a civilian in my jurisdiction. How is this your crime scene?"

"As you know, Sergeant Goodman is one of ours, they found the victim in his flat, and this letter from the top makes it so." He shoved the paper in Coetzee's face. "So, thank you, and goodbye."

"This was quick," Coetzee said.

"This is bullshit." Inspector Nichols gave a step toward Van Rooyen, pushing out her breasts.

Manana stepped in and eased his big arm in between Van Rooyen and Nichols.

As I watched the scene unfold, three things I found ironic popped into my mind; now I'm suddenly one of them, Manana standing up for Van Rooyen, and Nichols using her breasts.

"Well, it's less paperwork for us." Coetzee shrugged, turned, and strolled down the corridor. "You coming, Nichols?"

"This is bullshit," she muttered again and flipped her notepad closed.

We watched in silence until the two inspectors descended the stairs.

"I don't know if you've heard, but I'm not one of you anymore," I said.

"What?" Manana frowned.

"It didn't come from me," Van Rooyen defended.

"From who then?" Manana asked.

"His father spoke to the Police Commissioner." He shrugged. "I just follow orders."

"Then why, if I'm not with you anymore, are you here?"

"Because what happened here, I think, is part of our Bolton operation."

"Why do you say that?"

Van Rooyen looked at Manana. "Give us a minute."

Manana glanced at us before walking into my apartment.

Steward leaned in and whispered in my ear, "We know that the notebook you gave us was not Bolton's, and I'm sure that the people who broke in here know as well."

His cologne burnt my nose. I couldn't believe my sister had fallen for him; he was such a dick.

"What are you talking about?" I frowned. "That's the notebook I took from Bolton."

"Stop fucking with me!" Van Rooyen's permanent blush morphed with the rest of his face. "You've forgotten something; you are now a civilian – unprotected."

"Is that a threat?"

He smiled. "Hand the notebook over, and I'll talk to your father and the commissioner. If not" – he glanced into my apartment – "I'm sure that if we dig deep enough, the evidence will show you had something to do with that man's death."

I clenched my fists, trying my damnedest not to break his crooked nose. If I were to open my mouth, I would stutter, so I just glared at him. It was him, cluster-fuck. He killed Mercy and Pee, or he ordered it. Somebody on the team was working for him.

"Bring the notebook to my house tomorrow at seven." He scratched his chin, thinking. "No, make it eight. I like to screw your sister in the morning."

I shuddered.

"If you're not there at eight, I'll get angry and might just rough her up."

"I-I." I grabbed for his collar, but he was expecting it. He lifted his knee, hitting me in the groin. I stumbled back and grabbed the railing, not giving him the satisfaction of going down. It took some doing to stay on my feet. I'd been kicked so many times in the nuts these last few days, my mouth tasted like scrambled eggs.

"Tomorrow, at eight, don't forget." He strolled down the corridor.

Manana emerged from my flat. "What's wrong?"

"Nothing," I groaned. "Thanks for having my back."

He shook his head. "I think before I act. You should do the same."

"In other words, be a coward." I immediately regretted it. "I'm sorry," I mumbled.

"You see what I mean." He gave me a supportive pat on the back before he made his way down the corridor.

My cell phone rang. Nicole. I still had her number saved. I swiped to accept the call.

"You answered this time."

"You warned me."

"What's wrong?"

"I'm having a kak day."

She went silent for a moment. "I'm sorry about your bike. Byron told me what he did. I'll pay for the repairs."

It was so good to hear her voice. Even my balls felt better. "That's the least of my problems."

"What happened?"

I wanted to spare her, but I had to tell someone my sad story. "Someone butchered my cat in my bedroom. I've got a dead guy in my flat, I got fired, and someone stole my bike. Oh, and an arsehole destroyed any hopes of me ever having children. Not that any kid deserves a loser like me."

How pathetic! I expected the line to go dead and to never hear from her again.

"Who would do such a thing to Mercy?" She was upset.

And she remembered her name! I choked, closing my eyes. "Any news on the... thing?" It came out squeaky.

Again, she was silent.

I sniffed.

"Yes, I've got it."

Nicole waited for me to say something, but I couldn't get a word out.

"Listen, uh, I can hear you're upset. I told Byron to stay away tonight. Why don't you come over to my place, so we can discuss the thing? I'll make you dinner, and you can sleep on the couch. You can't stay in your flat tonight."

"Thank you." I sounded like a four-year-old girl.

"And remember, this will not go further than tonight. It's just to help you, nothing more. I'll be home at seven."

"Okay." I wiped away the tears before anyone noticed. The line went dead. I turned around, still teary-eyed, and looked into Thero's pity-filled eyes. He grabbed and hugged me.

"It's okay, Greg, let it out."

I wanted to lift my knee but remembered our scuffle the day before and how bad I'd felt. Instead, I stood motionless, arms dangling.

"I'm sorry about your cat and... your partner."

I felt the blood rush to my head. *Shit!* I realized how this had to look: a dead guy in my flat, wearing only a bathrobe. Peebiscuit did it again – even in death, but this time the old man would never lift his head from the duffel bags.

5

"Fire and gunpowder do not sleep together."
Zulu proverb

Millpark Private Hospital
Friday, 18:21

The nurse admired herself in the elevator mirror, stroking her black curly extensions. She made sure everything was in place. The stockings were surprisingly comfortable, as were the hospital shoes – like slippers. The bra was a bit tight, though. The doors slid open on level two. She exited, and made her way to the nurse's station. The corridors were empty. Visiting hours were between seven and eight. The two nurses at the station sat in deep conversation. She unhooked a clipboard next to the whiteboard and searched for a name.

Bolton, Room B8 – Surprised they used his actual name. She proceeded farther down the corridor.

Two nurses came round a corner, speaking Xhosa.

"He doesn't like the food," the one to the left said.

"He said his wife would bring him food later," the other replied.

"It won't be chicken legs."

They passed without giving her a second glance. A guard sat by the door, focused on his smartphone. He looked up and smiled; she was probably the most attractive and slender nurse he'd seen all day. She smiled and dipped into her clipboard. He returned to his phone as she entered the room.

Clive Bolton lay in bed, watching television with his earphones on. The nurse drew the curtains and removed his file.

"What now?" He removed his earphones. "The other nurses just left."

She cleared her throat. "Doctor's orders." She removed a capped syringe from her pocket.

"What's this for?" Clive asked as she injected the contents into his drip.

"It will help you relax."

Clive placed his earphones back on his head as she tucked in his sheets. He watched television, but only for a moment before removing his earphones again.

"Why did you draw the curtains?" he asked.

She stopped her faffing and stared at him in silence.

"Why did you–" He opened his mouth, but nothing came out. His arms fell limp to his sides. His eyes filled with fear. The nurse bent down beside him.

"You've been a naughty boy, Clive," the man whispered in his ear. "You know you can't come clean. Fortunately for us, you spoke to someone involved in our business. You know the rules. By tomorrow, your fat wife and kid will join you. We have to make an example of you, prevent someone else from getting similar ideas."

The nurse remained by Clive's side until his heart failed. He left the curtain drawn, tucked the syringe back in his pocket, and walked out of the room.

* * *

En route to Northcliff
    Friday, 18:48

My flat was still sealed and out of bounds. They considered me a suspect – standard procedure – so Thero and Manana packed me a bag. I couldn't shower in Pete's apartment because it was part of the investigation.

The only place left and within walking distance for a good scrubbing was Grandma's place. Like old times again, but with one difference, I decided not to confide in her. I wasn't in the mood for any wise words or speeches. She would only confirm what I already knew; my life was a series of unfortunate fuckups – mostly caused by yours truly. I told her I had a plumbing problem and a date. An hour later, I was ready, showered, shaved, and shampooed, waiting for Tito to pick me up with my mom's Porsche Cheyenne.

"I'm glad you and Nicole are getting back together," Tito said as he turned the corner onto Beyers Naude Drive – the name had changed from DF Malan Drive, but still the same houses, shops, and people. Beyers Naude had to have done something right for the government to name a street after him. Usually, street names changed from ivory to ebony and not from ivory to ivory. I guess it took some balls for him to go against his kind – no matter the cost to himself – to have fought for something he believed was right. In my mind, it was harder to become a hero like that than running into a burning building because the latter was cut and dry and instant.

"We're not getting back together. It's just business." I turned on the radio.

He smiled.

"She's engaged."

His smile widened. "You've never given up on anything you wanted. Good or bad...or stupid. So why stop now with the best. You have to fight for the things you want. Ask Mandela."

"You can't compare my relationship to your people's struggle."

"Your people?" He frowned. "I thought he did it for all of us?" He shrugged. "I guess that's why we are where we are."

"You know what I mean," I mumbled.

A few blocks went by. "I heard the meeting with your dad didn't go as planned."

"You heard right."

Another block. "Your father is not the person you think he is."

"You mean he's not egotistic, sadistic, and arrogant."

"He's not a sadist," Tito snapped. "A rebellious little boy who made it hell for his father might think so. He put all four of my children through university and went to their graduation."

"Why did he not come to any of my stuff?" I reined myself in out of respect for the old man.

"He was. I saw him there when I brought your mother and gogo." He shrugged. "There weren't many occasions, but he was there when you made Sergeant and when you made the Task Force. Not even your mother knew he was there. He was always in the back and left before the end."

"Why?"

"He didn't want to spoil your night."

"Even if he was there" – I shrugged – "he wasn't there when I grew up."

"Because he worked his fingers to the bone to build a company for you and Stacey."

I snorted. "I'll never work for him. Why did he then force me to join the police?"

The old man shook his head as if dealing with an idiot. "Because you needed direction, to grow a set of balls, and get some life experience. He told you that many times."

"Well, if by life experience you mean getting shot at, throat slit, pulling a dead child from a boiling bathtub, and walking into a farmhouse where the family was hacked to pieces, then, yes, he accomplished that. I don't know if I have balls left after yesterday."

"You are a stubborn boy, Greg."

Boy! "Anyway, I'll never forgive him for Beatrice. You weren't there that night."

The GPS was the only thing that spoke the rest of the way. I climbed out and mumbled, "Thank you."

"Everyone does something in their life they regret."

I turned and held the door open for him to finish.

"You need to forgive. Otherwise, it will eat you up inside. He needs you now, Greg. They're leaving for the farm tonight – why don't you visit them for Christmas."

"You don't need to pick me up tomorrow." Every corner, an Oracle awaits.

"Umfana," Tito said before I could slam the door shut.

"Yes."

"Can you remember what happened that night?" He pointed at his throat.

I held still and shook my head.

"Maybe it's better that way."

"Not knowing what happened is far worse because your mind exaggerates the missing parts."

"So true." Tito nodded. "Just like you're doing now with your father's absences."

Respect your elders. Respect your elders. "His presence fucked him, not his absence." I winked. "Peaceful dreams, ntate. I slammed the door shut. I can also talk proverb.

The gate opened as I approached. Easier than the last time. The guard even waved at me. Only then did I hear Tito drive off. Kids playing in the piss-infested pool pulled me away from the dark hole in the back of my mind. But only for a moment. The hole got bigger the harder I tried to remember. *Fuck!*

"Greg!"

I turned around, startled.

Nicole stood in the street, three driveways back.

"Shit, sorry!" I hurried back.

"I saw you walking by. A penny for your thoughts."

I raised my pinkie finger and said in a British accent, "Just a cuppa and a squeeze of your booby will do milady."

She shook her head and thankfully cracked a smile. "From a penny to my boobs, trust you to find a way."

I shrugged. "No, I was trying to remember that night."

"What night?"

I looked at her, annoyed. "The night this happened." Pointing at my throat.

"Oh, yes," she said, inspecting my scar. "Figured you got it in a bar fight."

"Really." I placed my hands on my hips. "Got my throat slit in a bar fight? Is that what you think. I was three months in a coma. Almost died."

She frowned, shocked. "Why didn't anyone tell me?"

"Well," – I shrugged – "why would anyone?"

She touched my arm. "You okay now?"

"Nothing a massage can't fix."

"Dream on." She turned and walked toward her front door. "What happened?"

"That's just it, I can't remember." I fell in beside her.

"So, it could have happened in a bar fight." She flicked me a playful glint and opened the door to her townhouse. "What's the last thing you remember?" She stepped to one side and waved me in.

I walked in, filling my lungs with her soft mind-numbing scent. It drove me crazy. For the first time in Pete's existence, he did something worthwhile – he brought me to Nicole's door.

"I was walking to my bike."

"Where?"

"Pixies parking lot."

"The bar Pixies?" she said with a raised brow, hand on hip.

I placed my gym bag on the floor next to her leather lounge suit. "That's all I can remember."

"Did they catch them?"

"Them?"

"It took more than one guy to do that to you." She smiled. "With a snake, one must hold the head and the other the tail."

I narrowed my eyes. "Where were you that night?"

She pensively scratched her cheek. "Selling knives in the parking lot of Pixies. Who was the dead guy in your flat?"

"My neighbour–"

"Peter," she gasped, placing her hand in front of her mouth.

I noticed the ring, a big shiny thing – even for my untrained eye. It was like staring into the headlight of a Metro train. She did it on purpose because she couldn't stand Peter. He flashed her once, or was it twice, behind my back. She only told me later. I did nothing to him because I thought he only made me look good; it gave her a proper comparison like Beauty and the Beast, or New Zealand and Australia, or Simon and Garfunkel. Size didn't matter.

"He probably thought it was me arriving home and caught the bastards in my flat." I hoped she would leave it there.

"So, they killed Mercy after they'd killed Peter?"

"Yes."

"So, it wasn't a random break-in. What were they looking for?" Nicole asked.

"I don't know, but it was someone I'd pissed off."

"And there must be many of those," she muttered, turning to the dining-room table. "I know you're not telling me everything because you don't want to upset me, but the people who broke into your flat were looking for the laptop, weren't they?" She turned and glared at me; her eyes were more yellow than green tonight.

"We did it again, didn't we?" I asked, avoiding the question.

She gave a stiff smile. "Dressed the same, yes, I've noticed."

"We're connected, in a way." I meant it.

"It's a popular outfit," she shrugged. "There are probably a thousand other guys who dressed in jeans and white shirt tonight." She sighed. "We were connected. I realized it when we were still together, but you didn't. You broke that connection." Her eyes narrowed. "Forever."

"I knew it then, but I was a coward, scared. An asshole. I'm–"

"You didn't answer my question. Were they looking for the laptop?"

"Yes." Our eyes locked. "And I'm sorry for bringing you into this. Nobody, and I mean nobody, knows you have it."

"While we're in an apologetic mood, I'm sorry for what Byron did to your bike. I didn't know."

"I know."

"However, I will not apologize for him beating you up because you allowed him to."

I gave a sheepish smile.

"You figured that if he broke your scrawny neck, I would feel sorry for you and maybe take you back."

"Did it almost work?"

"No." She pulled the laptop closer. "I struggled in the beginning, but I've copied about ninety-five percent of the data onto this memory stick." She removed the device from the laptop carry bag and placed her notebook on the table.

"You can throw this notebook in the bin." She pushed it toward me.

"Good." I placed it beside me. "I've got someone who wants it, and I don't want him to know what was on it."

She inserted the memory stick into her laptop and turned it sideways for me to see. The wallpaper was of her and Dick Head kissing in front of the Eiffel Tower. "When was this?" I asked, biting my inner lip. The metallic taste of blood filled my mouth.

"He asked me to join him on a business trip, about a month after you'd left me." She clicked on an icon to cover up the wallpaper. "It was to pull me out of the hole I found myself in."

"The same time, I had my throat slit. If I could get my hands on a DeLorean, I'd go back in time."

"In life, most of the time, you only get one chance," she said, hitting each key harder and harder. "I haven't gone through all the data, but what I've seen is not good."

"What do you mean?"

A spreadsheet opened, but before I could make out anything, she slammed her notebook shut. "Just tell me the truth. Why did you run away? I thought everything was going okay. We argued sometimes but afterwards had great make-up sex." She closed her eyes, biting her lower lip. "I mean, we had normal sex." She leapt from her chair. "It drove me crazy trying to figure out what went wrong." Her eyes welled up. "I liked you."

I avoided her piercing eyes for a moment, building up the strength. "Please sit," I whispered, staring at my lap. She slowly obeyed. I gathered strength and looked into her tear-filled eyes.

"That night, at my sister's wedding, I got scared. The marriage thing scares the shit out of me. The commitment. Kids. I knew that you loved the entire marriage thing and that if we had continued, you would've wanted me to take the next step. I didn't want to waste your time and...love. Every marriage I know is a fuck-up. And I see every day what happens to kids and babies in this country." I shook my head. "Why awaken a new life and bring it into this world? Punish something so innocent. Give it a life sentence just because we want something to love, to give our life purpose. It's selfish."

"So, you can't blame me for trying to stay away from you. All you've been telling me is why you've left, and nothing has changed." Her tears had dried.

She was right: What had changed?

"Because I've changed." Shit, not even I believed it.

She tried to hide a smile but then burst out laughing. "You haven't changed a bit, Gregory Goodman."

I smiled. "What I meant was–"

"Yes," she interrupted, giggling.

"For you, I will change." I stared deep into her eyes. "I can't get you out of my mind. The only thing I know for certain is that I want to be with you. I realized it two weeks after our breakup. That's why I tried so hard to get in touch with you. Explain to you why I had left that night."

"What do you mean?" she said, shocked.

"So, you can't remember all the fuck-off dickhead replies you send me every time I texted and e-mailed you? Your guard at the gate had the same message for me."

Nicole stared at the laptop, thinking, mulling something over in her head. Her frown faded. "Well, I was mad at you. I take a relationship serious, and you don't. You'll drop me like before as soon as the commitment thing dawns on you. As you've mentioned, I love the whole marriage thing; commitment, kids, until death do us part. I want to hear that promise."

I nodded but said nothing because nothing I could say would change her mind. With certain things in life, you only get one chance, and I guess betraying someone's trust was one of them.

She changed the subject to one of the failed marriages I'd mentioned. "What's wrong with your sister's marriage?"

"I don't know what my sister sees in Van Rooyen. I know the marriage won't last. I warned her, but she wouldn't listen. She's such a kind person, and he's such a..." I hesitated.

"The C-word, I know, you told me many times."

I smiled; she was a real Manana. The four months we'd been together, she'd always tried to make me walk the path of the righteous. She had improved my grammar by replacing my cursing adjectives with more acceptable descriptions like bloody or freaking. It had reached a point where I looked over my shoulder, searching for her, before cursing. So, I kept with Nicole's adjectives. For those four months, even my liver thanked her; she knew when I'd had enough to drink, dragging me away from a shot or two before I was about to make a fool of myself.

"I know he slaps her around. But she's too proud or afraid, or I don't know, to admit her mistake. She's like a butterfly caught in a spider's web. So many times, when I still did patrols, they sent me out to homes where the same thing was happening."

"If a man did that to me, he should never go to sleep," Nicole said, with such an expression she scared me.

"I'm sorry for what I did to you."

She smiled. "I'm sorry too, but I'm getting married, and you had your chance. You won't hurt me again."

I was angry at first for laying myself bare before her, but she had all the reasons to be pissed. For tonight, I'd pushed her far enough. Any further, and I'd have no couch.

"I've said what I had to say," I whispered and opened the laptop. "I wanted to make you understand that it wasn't you."

She sat for a moment, staring at her ring. Was it sadness I detected?

But then she returned from wherever she was and dropped the bomb. "Your father is involved in weapons smuggling."

My broken heart jolted alive. "What do you mean?"

"There's a letter Bolton wrote to the President and Minister of Defence asking for immunity for him and your father. In return, he would provide a list of names within the government and private sector of who was involved. The package they had prepared includes conversations, videos, pictures, and amounts paid."

"Was the file also on the laptop?"

"Yes, but they encrypted it. I found a spreadsheet with dates and amounts paid to certain people. Unfortunately, he only used what I think are initials."

She opened the spreadsheet. "You see, here they paid DG one hundred thousand rand on the fourteenth of April. MM was paid twenty thousand. BW, fifty thousand, SVR a hundred thousand, TT, twenty thousand. There're about thirty names on here."

At the top of the list was only a reference number: C542278.

"The encrypted file, can you–"

"Yes, but I need more time."

I raised a brow, glancing at her and then at the notebook.

"Not tonight, I'm tired, and I'm going to bed now." She stood up. "I've made some ravioli. It's in the oven. I'm not hungry."

"My favourite."

"I thought you needed something uplifting after today. Read

nothing into it. It's just ravioli, nothing more." With that, she retreated to her room.

"Thank you," I said before she closed her bedroom door.

What the hell can I do now? Who could I trust with this? Not Van Rooyen. That's why he wanted this laptop. He was probably the SVR on the list. But why did my father not include him in the letter? I thought they were close; Van Rooyen married his precious daughter.

They encrypted most of the other files, so I called it a night. I removed the USB stick and tucked it into my pocket, right next to the condom. Might as well fill it with water and toss it out of my flat window at the prostitutes below, as Manana and I did a few weeks ago. I turned on the television and changed the channel from E-Entertainment to the news. Why did she have satellite? It was always on the same channel. I strolled over to the stove but turned back as I heard the breaking news.

"Prominent businessman Clive Bolton and his family were murdered in two separate attacks. Mr. Bolton, who was still in hospital after his first attack, was found dead in his hospital bed early this evening. He was believed to be poisoned... Also, this evening Gloria Bolton and her thirteen-year-old son were murdered in their house..."

The news presenter's voice faded as my mind processed the information, but I was brought back to reality as I heard the words: "execution-style."

Fuck, Sammy, I'm sorry.

I wanted to break something but couldn't. Someone wanted to send a message. I fell onto the couch, staring at the images of the family and their home. Little Sammy played with his dog on that same lawn now covered with police cars, ambulances, and yellow tape. I'm the one that had killed and wounded their guards. I left them vulnerable.

Nicole's bedroom door opened. "I saw the news." She walked out, dressed in white pyjamas. "Is that the same Bolton that..."

I cleared my throat. "Yes. The boy's name is Sammy. Good boy."

"I'm sorry," she whispered.

I sensed her turmoil. She wanted to comfort me but was afraid; comfort, with me, leads to more. "You're right. I'm a snake." I fell back and covered my eyes.

"I didn't mean it, Greg." She stepped toward me, folding her arms.

"I should've been there for them, just like I should have been there for you. I'm such a fucking loser."

She took a seat next to me.

Bingo.

Sammy didn't die in vain. *Fuck!* This is wrong; using his death to get closer to Nicole. I was back in Sammy's room, raising our Coke bottles. Then it came to me. I sat up.

"What?" Nicole asked.

"That means my family will be next." The other person named in that letter was my father.

She nodded with a concerned frown.

Her pyjamas' top button was undone – exposing half her right breast. I caught her gaze just in time as she turned to me. I clenched my fist, resisting the urge to reach out. Our most memorable time together was movie night; me sitting in front of the couch, Nicole wedged between my legs. Halfway into a film, I would slip my hands in under her t-shirt, resting her breasts in my palms, kissing her neck, circling and thumbing her nipples until they were rock hard. They rested perfectly in the palms of my hands. I licked my lips, swallowing. I could taste it. We'd never finished a movie.

"What were you thinking just now?" Nicole asked, eyeing me.

Really Greg! After hearing the devastating news, you thought about movie night. I cleared my throat. "Sammy and... and the farm and things like that."

"Don't lie to me!" She jumped up. "I know that look. You weren't thinking about Sammy." She looked down and noticed her exhibit. "Stand up!"

"What! Why?"

"Stand up!" She repeated, buttoning up. "You were thinking about movie night, weren't you?"

I remained seated. "Listen to me! Sit down. We need to talk about my dad and things like that."

She shook her head. "You're the reason there're so many lesbians in the world."

"Wait a second." I grinned. "So, you were also thinking about movie night?"

"What?" She shook her. "I just–"

I placed a finger over my lips.

Nicole stared at the window; her face edged with fear. "What?" she whispered.

The familiar click of a gun's safety switch.

I leapt off the couch and lifted Nicole off her feet. The curtain to the left juddered as if someone poked it with a stick from the other side. But it wasn't a stick; someone fired at us through the open window with an automatic machine gun, fitted with a suppressor.

The bullets ripped apart Nicole's pride and joy: her leather three-seater chesterfield couch. The trail of destruction followed us as we fled toward the bedroom, destroying Nicole's high-end décor, African art, and flat-screen television. I threw her over my good shoulder and ran into her bedroom. She stayed surprisingly quiet. I slammed the door shut, slapped the light off and dived over the bed. Nicole landed headfirst on the other side of the bed.

The gunfire ceased.

"Stay down and shut up," I whispered. The light from the television still illuminated the room. I jumped up. "Before you shut up, do you have any weapons?"

She took shallow breaths. "No, wait, no, yes, no," she whispered. "You're the cop. Where are your weapons?"

"My gym bag. Stay under the window and behind the bed." I went down on my stomach.

"Greg," she whispered.

"What?" I glanced over my shoulder. Her eyes and ring shimmered in the flickering light of the television. She was petrified.

I gave a nod. "Don't worry; we'll be okay."

"Be careful," she whispered as I leopard-crawled to the door. I jiggled the handle and stood back, standing flat against the wall. Bullets ripped through the door, casting light beams into the room. I waited until the salvo stopped and yanked open the door. The masked intruder had another full magazine in his hand, inserting it with skill into the MP5 submachine gun. I darted toward him. He needed to charge the weapon and load a round into the chamber. A lengthy two metres spread between us as he completed the task. *Now or never.* I went in low and hard.

The MP5 spewed its first volley as I made contact. *Am I hit?* We landed on the chesterfield couch. I pushed the searing-hot suppresser away from my body and pummelled him with my right. The fucker also punched but could only reach my ribs, my fractured ribs. I felt no pain as my heart pumped pure adrenalin.

"How does that feel, you fuck?" With every word, I connected with his head. He was a tough bastard, staring at me from behind the balaclava with cold eyes, showing no sign of dizziness. His eyes shifted to his left, but only for a fraction of a second. I was so into him I'd forgotten to scan the room for anyone else.

Someone slipped way in through the shattered window. I had to finish cold-eyes first. I pulled back and slammed my head into his face. That had the desired effect; his rib punching stopped, and he shook his head, blinking. I head-butted him again. Blood streamed down my face, stinging my eyes. I wasn't sure if he was unconscious, but I could pull the MP5 from his hand.

The second visitor appeared from behind the curtain, aiming his weapon. He hesitated, afraid he might hit his partner. I had no such problems and pulled the trigger.

"Greg, no," the man screamed as the first few rounds slammed into his body. I released the trigger, shocked. Too late. The man stumbled back, pulled the curtain from the rail, and fell back through the window.

I had no time to think. Cold-eyes leapt on top of me and grabbed the weapon. We stumbled around the room – a dance – weapon pointing at the ceiling. He was taller than I and lead. We burst through Nicole's bedroom door and fell onto the bed – him on top of me. He returned the favour and head-butted me in the face. The weapon slipped from my fingers. I searched for Nicole but couldn't find her in the television's dim light.

"The police is coming," I seethed.

"Police are coming," he corrected, hardly audible.

"You're not my fucking father!" I let go of one hand, punching and clawing at his face. His balaclava came off, but it was too dark to discern his face. He kept both hands on the weapon and wrenched it from my grip. I sunk my teeth into his neck, tearing and tugging at the flesh. His blood filled my mouth. He didn't make a sound, even when I ripped flesh from his neck. Hold still. The whisper in the shadows was back. *Not now!*

This song and dance had to end. I spat out the vile pulp and pushed my thumb into the open wound. It gave him the strength to pull the weapon from my hands. He sat up, straddling me. In the flickering light, the gun pointed at my face.

"I'm sorry, Meerkat," the man whispered, again too soft to recognize.

Was this it? No flashing memories? Not that there were any I wanted to relive. I settled on movie night. *Nicole! Where the fuck is she!*

A dark figure jumped up behind him and jabbed something into the back of his neck.

Cold-eyes groaned, arched his back and reached for the object. I grabbed the weapon with both hands, twisting it from his hand and fired one round aimed at his shoulder; I wanted a heart-to-heart with him. He fell backwards and landed on the floor, his boots still on the bed.

The room lit up as Nicole switched on the light. She stood wide-eyed and shaken.

"Are you all right?" she whispered.

"Stay there." I jumped off the bed. "Fuck! No! Fuck!" I froze over the sprawled body. "Thero?" I scratched my head. "Oh, I'm so fucked." I took deep breaths, placing a hand over my pounding heart. "Oh, fuck."

He stared at me with fading eyes, unable to move. The pool of blood grew around his body.

Was this a sanctioned operation? I kneeled next to him and looked at Nicole. "What did you stab him with?" I snapped.

"Scissors," she cried. "He... he was going to kill you."

"I know, dammit!"

She looked at her shaking hands, eyes welling up.

Fuck! "It's okay," I said as calmly as possible. Every ache and bruise awakened as my adrenalin level tumbled. I glanced at myself in the mirror. "Bloody hell."

"I know." Nicole reached for my head but pulled back as if realizing I was a prickly pear. "You covered in blood." I detected a tone of sympathy.

"Thero!" I patted his cheek. "Come on, buddy." He opened his eyes. "I take it this tango wasn't official."

"Sorry, Gee," he whispered. "I had no choice." His face distorted. "I'm in too deep."

"I thought you were gay," I said.

He gave a laughing cough. "What the fuck does that have to do with anything."

"I thought you guys were sensitive and honest."

"How'd you know?" he whispered, but his smile faded. "I'm sorry, Greg, I didn't know you'd be here."

"You knew Nicole was here. Who sent you?"

"You're not getting it that easy," he whispered.

"Did Van Rooyen send you? Please, give me that."

He stared at me for a moment, then shook his head.

"Who then?"

"It would have been so easy. In and out. Nicole sleeping. No one was supposed to get hurt." Thero shook his head. "You always have a way of fucking things up." His eyes flickered and closed.

"You packed heavy for a quick in and out." I used the bed to push myself upright. Nicole was not in the room. I shuffled to the door, clutching my ribs. She sat on her Chesterfield De Fucked, face buried in her hands. I couldn't believe the carnage; plaster and glass covered the floor, bullet holes riddled kitchen cupboards and walls. She glanced up as she heard the glass crunching under my boots.

"You would think somebody would've called the police by now." She reached for her cell phone on the dining-room table.

"This was the police," I said, making my way to the window of entry.

"So, what are you saying? I shouldn't call them?"

"What I'm saying is, until you decipher the file, we do not know who to trust."

I glanced out the window. "Shit."

"What now?" she sighed.

"He's gone. Probably wearing a vest." I glanced at the dining-room table. "I hope you made a backup of your data."

"What!" She jumped up. "He took both laptops."

I removed the USB stick with a smile and dropped the condom on the floor.

She shook her head. "After I told you on the phone that there's nothing between us anymore."

I shrugged. "It's a habit." The police might still find two bodies when they get here. I won't admit the thought had crossed my mind of us getting back together again, maybe tonight.

She looked away, glancing around at the destruction instead. "What do I do now? I need a case number for my insurance."

"You serious?" I scowled. "Your life, as you know it, is over. You need to get somewhere safe until I can figure this out. You also need to break this code." I waved the memory stick at her.

Shit! She's biting her lip. Prepare for the wrath of Khan, Goodman.

She clenched her fists. "You're the reason my place looks like this. You" – she pointed a finger at me – "are the reason I'm in this mess. I was happy, had a nice job, fiancé, and townhouse." She pointed at her couch. "Look at my fucking Chesterfield, twenty-five-fucking-thousand-rand." She stomped her slipper with every syllable.

Two f-bombs in one sentence. "If it's about the money—"

"No! It's not about the fucking money. It's about you. Everything is always about you. The more people try to help you, the more you push them away. I wish I had parents like yours. Get over yourself!" She turned away and muttered, "Self-righteous prick."

"Okay!" I snapped. "I'm freaking sorry. Sorry for saving your life. Why don't you pick up the gun and shoot me while you're at it?"

"If I can remember correctly, I saved your life."

"Whatever," I muttered and picked up my bag.

"What now?" she asked, bewildered. "You leaving?"

"Yes, we've got about five minutes before Thero's friends are going to come back for him. They're parked outside somewhere waiting for him. They can't leave him here for an honest cop to find."

"Where are we going?"

"I'm going to the farm; my parents are there for the holidays. If I were the bad guys, I would hit them there. It's secluded, and the security's not that tight."

"And me?" she asked, staring at the open window.

"I'll take you to Manana. You'll be safe with him."

"No! It seems like most of your friends are involved."

"Not Manana. I know him."

"I don't care."

"What about Byron?" I gave the obvious solution.

"No, I don't want to involve him in this. I want to go with you."

"Why?"

"Because, because you're trained for this." She searched for the right words. "And I know you're not involved."

"But they might hit the farm. You'll be in the middle of it all."

"You don't know that, and besides, it'll give me time to work on the file. By the time we get there, we'll know who to trust and who to call for help."

I shook my head. "No, it's too dangerous."

"I feel safe with you, okay?" Nicole cried. "I killed a man. I can't believe I killed a man." She looked at her bloodstained hands.

I walked up to her and held her trembling body in my arms. *What have I done?*

"No," I whispered. "I killed him. I shot him, remember. You can't kill someone with scissors. You're good, but not that good," I lied.

She looked at me, eyes filled with expectation. "Really?"

"Like you said, I know these things." I wanted to kiss her. "Pack a few things. You've got a minute."

She ran into her room and filled a bag. I washed my face and changed clothes. Five minutes passed.

"I thought so," I muttered as we entered the garage.

"What? It's a great car," she protested.

"Nothing," I shrugged. "You drive. My ribs are killing me."

"You need to drive. I need to work on the file." She tapped the notebook.

"I thought they stole your notebook." I groaned as I fell into the driver's seat of the Mini Cooper.

"This is my old one, but it'll do."

I stared at the piece of hardware for a moment. "Don't you have another one?"

"Makeup with your dad, and you can buy yourself one, and then buy me one as well, because I'm not getting that case number."

I closed the garage and drove to an empty, out-of-sight parking spot close to the gate.

"Aren't we wasting time?" Nicole asked, peeking over the dashboard.

"They know what car you're driving and will be waiting somewhere down the road."

We stared at the gate for about a minute before Nicole started fiddling in her handbag. She removed two breath mints, one for her, and the other she pushed into my mouth.

"Is it that bad, or do you want to kiss me?" I said, monitoring the gate.

"Stop analyzing everything. It's just a mint," she whispered, also staring at the gate.

Another moment of deafening silence followed, interrupted only by an occasional leather rub.

I raised a brow as Nicole's stomach growled. "You should've had some of your ravioli."

She cradled her flat abdomen with her arm, gave a sheepish smile, and tucked some of her sandy locks in behind her ear.

The butterflies were back. "You lost a lot of weight."

She scowled at me.

"I mean, not a lot," I corrected. "You weren't fat like Gilbert Grape's mom."

She frowned.

"Not that I'd cared how fat you were." That sounded all wrong. "What I mean is you look amazing."

She burst out laughing, throwing her head back.

I blushed, feeling like a blabbering idiot.

Nicole nodded, smiling. "I know what you mean. I was messing with you." Then she looked at me, eyes gleaming as she did when I first asked her to go out with me. "Thank you."

I gave an inconspicuous sigh of relief.

"That's one perk of going out with a gym fanatic." She returned her gaze to the gate.

"I also go to the gym," I muttered.

"But you never asked me to go with."

"I didn't know you were the gymming type."

"Because I looked like Gilbert Grape's mom." She smirked. "There's a lot you don't know about me."

One thing I knew about her was she loved movies. So did I. "Leonardo DiCaprio should have won the Oscar for that."

She gave a determined nod. "Yep."

"I think he lost because he went full retard." I referred to another one of our favourites – *Tropic Thunder*.

Nicole burst out laughing. "We didn't watch it to the end, though."

Shit, how I missed that laugh, our time together. How could I have been so stupid? Well, that's me, always screwing up a good thing. For that moment, we had forgotten about the shit we found ourselves in. Maybe that's what true love does to you: It freezes time, like a drug; subdued the bad memories.

"There were a lot of movies we didn't watch to the end."

She flushed.

Bingo.

My battered body brought me back to the present as I shifted, groaning.

"You okay?" she asked with genuine sincerity but returned her gaze to the gate.

"I'm fine."

"That's a woman's line."

"Look at me. I guess I deserved it, the wheel turning, I mean." I looked at her. "For the way I treated women."

I detected a crease in the corner of her mouth.

"Are you enjoying this?" I asked.

The crease turned into a full-blown smile. "A little."

"I missed your smile."

She kept her heart-stopping smile, staring over the dashboard, but not at the gate.

"Now that I've been punished severely and repented my sins, how about forgiveness?"

Her smile faded. She shook her head. "I can't. Then you'll think you have a chance again."

"I won't, I promise."

"I saw you had your fingers crossed."

"They were not," I protested. "I crave a cigarette. Don't worry, I won't dare smoke in your car."

We stared another minute at the gate before she said, "Give me one."

"What?" I frowned.

"A cigarette."

"What!"

"Oh, come on! It's your fault. I started after you fled."

"It's not good for you, you know." I reached for my bag on the back seat. "It causes breast cancer and–" The glint in her eyes caught me by surprise. Was it love? "What?" I asked.

"Nothing. Do you want to die healthy?" She held out her hand.

"No, but I want you to die old." I opened the pack and offered her one – like handing a condom to a twelve-year-old girl.

"I need it after tonight." She plucked one from the pack.

I lowered both windows, letting in the summer breeze. "I take it Byron does not approve?" I lit her up, and then me.

"You crazy?" Nicole said and filled her lungs. She held it for a while and then blew a cloud of smoke out the window. "He's such a health fanatic; he doesn't even drink. Who doesn't like a glass of wine now and then?"

"Is that the same guy you're going to marry?" I started chipping at the wall.

"Marriage is a balance between give and take. And a healthy lifestyle is not a bad thing."

"What did he sacrifice for you?" Another chip.

She took a long drag, exhaling, playing for time. "He helped me to get over you, and that took a lot from him."

"You love him like you loved me?" I slammed the wall with everything I had, and then a little crack formed.

She looked at me surprised, with a little hesitation, and then she answered, "Yes, yes, of course."

"Remember, I was in the hospital for three months. Before that, I really tried to get back to you. I'm still here if you ever change your mind. I still love you." Before she could reply, I said, "And now, I'll leave you alone."

I flicked the cigarette and made myself comfortable, keeping sight of the gate. From the corner of my eye, I saw her stare at me. Strange, not once did she try and call Byron to tell him what had happened.

"What the hell?" I whispered as my cell phone vibrated in my pocket.

"Who is it?" Nicole asked as I removed it.

Shit! Dominique! I looked at Nicole. She will know if I lie – no more secrets. I showed Nicole the screen. "Can't believe this woman. I went out with her for about a week, and that was just before my... incident. I never saw her since, but she keeps calling. What do you think? Should I answer and tell her I'm not interested?" Even in the dimly lit car, I noticed her shocked expression – the colour draining from her cheeks. Is this her jealous look? "What's wrong?"

"Don't answer," she scowled. "She's crazy if she's still phoning after all this time. Remember *Fatal Attraction*." She grabbed my phone and unlocked it. "Soon, you'll discover Mercy in a pot, boiling–" She covered her mouth. "I'm sorry, I... I forgot about Mercy."

"It's okay."

"There." She threw the phone on my lap. "I blocked her."

I stared at my phone, frowning. Then I arrived at the only logical conclusion – she must be jealous.

"I'm not jealous." She folded her arms and wedged her knees up against the dashboard. "I can't handle a desperate woman."

"Get down," I said as the main gate opened.

"I'm not jealous," Nicole muttered, shifting down, peeking through her knees.

A black Mercedes Vito with tinted windows drove into the complex.

"It's them."

"How do you know?" she whispered. "I can't see who's driving."

"We used that van a few times on stake-outs. They probably flashed their police identification to gain entry."

We waited until the van pulled out of sight before driving out the gate.

"Are you going to call your dad to organize us one of his helicopters?"

"No, I want nothing from him," I said it harsher than intended. "And I don't want anyone to know we're on our way. By now, Van Rooyen knows I'm involved; he'll have a tap on all our phones, including my dad's. It'll force their hand and speed up the hit on my family."

* * *

Northbound on the N1 Highway
    Friday, 23:01

It was a great car, but the hard suspension didn't help my damaged body. With every bump in the road, I stiffened with a clenched jaw. I had to remain within the speed limit for obvious reasons. All the way, Nicole worked on the file, saying very little. After two hours, we stopped at a filling station for a Coke and a pee, keeping our heads down.

"How much farther?" Nicole asked as she walked out of the bathroom. My penis caught the beat my heart skipped. She had squeezed into white gym shorts and a pink T-shirt; they fitted her perfectly – about two sizes too small. Shit, she looked unbelievable. The only good thing that came out of her relationship with the gym bigot. What was she trying to do, drive me crazy, or did she want me to drive to the farm without using my hands? *She wants to show me what I threw away.* I leaned against the car, devouring a piece of biltong. Through her eyes, I probably resembled Pluto, the dog, when he discovered a bone, jaw-dropping to the floor, eyes popping and tongue rolling. I was ecstatic learning my nether region still functioned.

She glanced at her tight body, chuffed. "I had no time to pack. I grabbed whatever was on top."

"I wish I could grab whatever's on top." That sounded stupid, but I thought the more I brought up the subject, the more chance I'd have of success. When we were still an item, she enjoyed my dirty talk.

She shook her head. "I want to be comfortable, maybe take a nap on the way. And again, it's just clothes, nothing more."

I offered her a piece of my biltong.

"Thank you." She smiled with that same sparkle. "How much farther?"

"Another three or four hours before we get there." I slammed the door shut. "How far are you with the file?"

"Another hour or so." She opened her laptop. "Just a question, your father must have this list of names. Why not get it from him?"

"Because I don't trust him, and he'll deny everything until I can shove the list in his face."

"I don't think—"

"And I think that Bolton was the front, he did the admin, paid the bribes, my father wouldn't know most of the people on the list. If there's one thing I've learned in my volatile career, it's that you must keep your contacts to yourself – it gives you the edge. Because a contact is only loyal to the one carrying the thickest wallet. Bolton knew that, and that's why he encrypted the file. He only would have supplied the list after he received a pardon from the president."

I started the Cooper, adjusted myself, and drove off into the night.

* * *

Northbound N1

23:30

. . .

All eyes focused on the two LCD televisions suspended from the ceiling of the twenty-five-seater bus. Bafana played an away game against the Lions of Teranga, Senegal's national football team. The game was well into the second half, with South Africa leading by two goals to one. Chatter, roars, and moans filled the bus as fourteen passengers vocalized their professional, unbiased opinions. All wore their corporate wear: grey pants, white shirt, black jacket, red tie, and 9mm pistols. The driver glanced at his watch and stepped on the accelerator, oblivious to the rump-clenching game behind him.

"How long till the final whistle?" Simon yelled over his shoulder, hands clutching the steering wheel.

He heard no reply, just profound encouragement.

"Hey, wena! How much time is left?" he repeated.

"Only twenty minutes," Banele yelled, holding his head with both hands.

The driver looked at his watch again and gave a nervous smile as he noticed the approaching off-ramp.

"I need to make a quick stop," Simon said over his shoulder.

Most didn't hear, and those who did didn't care. All fourteen pairs of eyes were transfixed on the game.

They'd left civilization over an hour ago; the only life visible was a porchlight of a derelict farmhouse nestled in the bush's blackness about two kilometres from the highway. The driver eased off the main road and took the off-ramp, again glancing at his watch. He drove two kilometres on a tar road before turning right onto a dirt road. Simon glanced up at the full moon and shimmering stars; he'd forgotten how bright and awesome the sky was out here. For the millionth time, he doubted himself.

The bus exploded in a chorus of screams and laughter as Bafana kicked another goal. Two men jumped up and slapped the driver on his back, shouting, "Goal!"

He jolted, almost veering off the road. "Hamba!" he yelled, wiping sweat from his face.

Shit, no extra time, he thought. He glanced up at the brilliant sky and wanted to say a prayer but knew he could not. Again, he thought of turning the bus around. It felt as if something, maybe God, was squeezing the blood and air from his heart and throat.

"Only one minute," someone said from the back. Another pulled out a Vuvuzela and emptied his lungs into the effective instrument.

He accelerated, driving mercilessly over protruding rocks and eroded soil.

"Take it easy, Simon!" the young man behind him moaned as he bounced off his seat.

"Sorry, we're almost there," he said with a raised hand. The passengers were now much less jovial, frowning and shaking their heads at each other.

"Where?" the young one asked.

"Mr. G asked me to pick something up on the way to the farm."

"What? A bag of gold," Moses, the oldest of the group, said. The laughter turned into screams as the final whistle blew. The bus rocked from side to side as the group jumped up and danced. The celebration only died down after five minutes. The time Simon needed to reach his destination. The time Simon needed to avoid too many questions. The time Simon needed to fulfil his contract.

He sweated like a marathon runner, wiping his face with a handkerchief. He brought the bus to a standstill in front of the old farmhouse. The moon peeked over the high-pitched roof.

Moses took his place next to Simon and opened the glove compartment. He removed a thick envelope and held it out to Simon. The passengers in the back were silent, staring at the two men in the front.

"We all chipped in to help you get through this difficult time. Raising five kids on your own is not easy. Since your wife's death, we noticed you were not yourself, understandably so. We wanted to give it to you at the Goodman farm, but we've decided to do it now because you seemed very worried and anxious."

Simon fell back into his chair, staring at the envelope.

"Take it, my friend," Moses said in his raspy voice, extending his arm.

Simon closed his eyes, shaking his head. "I'm sorry," he sobbed.

"No, don't be." The words echoed through the bus.

"Hey, Simon, isn't that one of your kids?" Simpson, the young one, said behind him.

A white man emerged from the farmhouse, his hands resting on the young boy's shoulders. The boy showed no emotion, just stared at his father. The man smiled, waving Simon closer.

"Simon?" Kagiso glanced at the boy and then at the father. "I remember him from the other day when you brought him to work."

"I'm sorry," he repeated in a whisper. "Stay here." He opened the door, removed the keys from the ignition, and fiddled with something under his seat.

"That's a surprise," Moses said, waving at the boy with the envelope, but the boy did not wave back.

Simon slammed the door shut and walked toward his son. He pressed the remote and heard the locks engage behind him.

"Close your eyes, Tshepo," he ordered his son as he knelt in front of him.

Simon heard the muffled pop and then the screams. Please, God, take them quickly. He embraced his son, covered the boy's ears, and cried. Simon glanced up at the white man who stared at the macabre scene, excited as if waiting for the bouncing ball on a roulette wheel to hit his mark.

"You see, I told you the gas would kill them quickly." The man glanced at his watch. "Fifteen seconds. So effective they weren't even thinking about using their weapons." He glanced down at Simon. "You did good, Samson."

The boy looked up and said in a trembling voice, "His name is Simon."

He glanced at the boy. "It doesn't matter, boy."

The weather-worn wooden door behind him creaked open, and fourteen men strolled out wearing Goodman security uniforms.

6

"Life is like a shadow and a mist; it passes by quickly and is no more."
Zulu proverb

Northern Limpopo Province
Goodman farm
Friday, 23:46

Henry Goodman stood on his balcony staring at the full moon's reflection in the Limpopo River. On the other side, Zimbabwe, another African failure run by a power-hungry dictator, who lived like a king while his people starved, resorting to the dwindling wildlife to relieve their hunger. Where once he could hear the roar of the lion and the laugh of the hyena, he now only listened to the annoying tick of the high-powered electric fence.

"Are you still out here in the dark?" Jessica Goodman said, stepping out of her room onto the balcony. "Why are the floodlights not on?" She wore a white silk robe, her blonde hair glistened in the moonlight like a golden waterfall.

"What do you care?" he said, returning to the ominous tick.

She stood next to him and leaned on the railing. "You're out here in the open; you want to make it easy for them, like Bolton?" Her grip tightened around the railing. "Serves him right; I heard he wanted to cut us out of the immunity deal."

Henry glanced at her, frowning. "How did you know that?"

She blinked from her spell of rage. "You're not the only one with informants."

"I can't believe they killed Gloria and her son." Henry closed his eyes, shaking his head. "What the fuck are we going to do?"

"Just do what they ask." Jessica placed her hand on his. "You told them that Geegee is no longer involved in the investigation? That he's not a policeman anymore? That Van Rooyen was the one that placed him back on the Bolton case when he came out of hospital." Her hand tightened around his. "Please, Henry, they can't go after him again. Did you tell them that we're back in?"

"Of course, I did!" He pulled his hand away. "It fucking drives me crazy knowing that we're responsible for what happened to our son! What they did to him!" He grabbed a wrought iron patio chair and threw it over the railing, screaming, "And I can't do anything about it!" Henry stormed back into his room. "Fuck!" He marched back, pointing at Jessica. "And you're the reason why our family is now in danger! You introduced me to that snake!"

"I didn't know he was such a dangerous man," she muttered. "He tricked me too."

"He didn't trick you." Henry threw his head back, reaching for the heavens. "He screwed you, and now he's about to screw us all."

"You could have pulled out at any time, but you carried on dealing with him." She turned back to the full moon.

Henry froze, staring toward the barking dogs somewhere near the river. Two guards ran toward the noise, their flashlights slicing into the night. A minute passed before they returned, strolling back to the house.

Jessica shook her head. "How did we end up here?"

"I can tell you where it all started." He wrapped his arm around her slender waist, seething in her ear. "It all started the day you convinced my attorney not to register our antenuptial contract."

"It kept you by my side, didn't it?"

"Divorce is not the only way." He broke free, walked back into his room, and switched on the balcony light.

She rushed in behind him. "I know we've got our problems, but why the sudden animosity?" She closed the balcony door.

"Animosity." He laughed. "I'd call it something else." He glared at her while loosening his tie. "You are the reason why your son hates me so much."

"You just said it, your son. You've never accepted him. That's why he despises you so much. Stop blaming the world for your fuck-ups."

"I never accepted him because I thought he wasn't my son!" Henry threw his tie on the bed. "Your infidelity gave me that doubt."

"He *is* your son." Jessica stamped her slipper.

"I know!"

She gasped, shocked. "What? When? How did you find out? Are you sure?"

"See," he pointed at her, "all these years, you also thought he wasn't my son."

"Well, I, um." She turned away.

"I did a paternity test when he was in the hospital."

"Does he know?"

Henry took a seat on the edge of the single bed, burying his head in his hands. "I thought that if I had proof that it wasn't my son lying in hospital." He sighed. "It would ease the pain and guilt I felt."

Jessica took a seat next to him. "Did you tell him?"

He shook his head. "I, uh, I'm too embarrassed. And it would only make things worse between us. Because, why now the sudden love?"

Jessica chuckled, covering her mouth with her hand.

Henry scowled at her. "What's so funny?"

"I never wanted to do the test because I didn't want to confirm your suspicion. And you didn't want to do the test because you were afraid he was your son. A Goodman couldn't create such a devil."

Henry waved his bony finger at her. "And swear you won't tell him. I'll tell him when the time is right."

She nodded, smiling. "What makes you think Stacey is your daughter?"

"She has my characteristics, my strong will and," he shrugged, "she's taller than him."

Jessica stood, walked to the door, and turned. "Her strong will is keeping her in a marriage she does not want to be in."

"Ditto." Henry unbuttoned his shirt. "Tell me, were you ever in love with me?"

"I first fell in love with the way you made me feel." Jessica beamed at the memory. "Like a princess. And yes, I fell in love with you. Still am." Her expression hardened. "However, the hatred for where I came from overshadows everything else. I will do whatever it takes. Never will I go to bed hungry again. Or cold. Or worthless. Hopeless. Or reeking of the vile sweat of another." Her eyes glistened with anger. "I wasn't born with a Krugerrand under my pillow; I was born in a storm drain and left for dead." Jessica blinked her past away and smiled. "You must have a good night, darling." She blew him a kiss and closed the door.

Henry fell back onto his bed, trying to ease the sudden wave of nausea.

* * *

Limpopo
    Five Kilometres South of Musina,
    Twenty Kilometres from the Zimbabwean border
    Saturday, 02:08

. . .

I glanced at my sleeping passenger. Nicole lay with her head against the headrest, mouth open, snoring, hands resting on the keyboard. She moaned as I closed her laptop and placed it on the back seat.

I kept to the speed limit as I drove through the small town of Musina; the traffic cops' motto this time of year was – catch-cash-release. They wouldn't bribe a cop, but Nicole's licence plate might alert the bad guys. I took the R572 west toward Mapungubwe, taking it slow; a Mini Cooper colliding with a Kudu or ox would be like crashing into a Land Cruiser – another favourite in these parts.

The snoring to my left grew louder the deeper I drove into the Bushveld. I thought of reaching into my gym bag to remove my companion – Mr. Daniels. *It's been twelve hours!* My body involuntarily reacted; my head throbbed, and my mouth dried up. I felt like a ragdoll with a baseball as a head. The Sandman was paid overtime or bribed as everyone else in these parts. I reached for my gym bag on the back seat but stopped as I came within an inch of Nicole's cheek. It would be so easy, just a soft kiss.

I left the bag and divided my attention between the road and Nicole, admiring her beauty – her firm, full breasts lightly bouncing when I hit a bump in the road, her toned legs, her–

"Keep your eyes on the road," she said through a yawn. She turned her back and pulled up her legs. A minute later, she was back in the Land of Nod, hopefully dreaming about me.

I glanced at my watch as I took the Goodman farm's turnoff: 2:45 a.m. My last visit was five years ago. Mom had begged me to come for Easter weekend. I stayed a day and left after my father, and I had another argument. That was the time he forced me to join the police.

Almost there. I reached into my backpack and removed the unopened bottle of stutter-stopper. My insides fizzed as the cap cracked open.

"Not now, Greg," Nicole whispered, her back still toward me.

"I need it," I said, studying the label.

She sat up, staring at me with pity-filled eyes. "If you want him to respect you, then don't." She turned her back on me again and whispered, "And if you love me, you won't."

What was that? I didn't know where the hell I stood with her.

"If you admit that you still love me, I won't."

"Not now, please. I'm tired."

I studied the bottle again, thinking, glancing at Nicole. *Dammit! Shit!* My hand worked the neck. Just a quick sip ... *Fuck!* I tightened the cap and threw the bottle on the back seat.

Another board: *Private property, trespassers will be shot!*

Why had my father not fixed the sign yet? Bad spelling and grammar drove him crazy.

I remembered the time I brought home my fifth-grade English test. As my first B for the semester, I was ecstatic. That was the time I still wanted to impress him. I ran into his study and plonked the test on the table in front of him, covering the work he was scrutinizing.

"You know you're not allowed in here," he'd snapped, without even looking at me. Strange how you remembered every tiny detail when reliving a bad event; the way his hollow cheeks had changed colour from a pink to a flaming red. The way the test shook as he held it in his bony fingers. The disgust in his eyes as he looked up at me and said, "Beautifuller, beautifullest?"

How the blood had drained from my face. "I know... more–"

"A Goodman will never make a stupid mistake like this!" He shouted and threw the test at me. It landed at my bare feet, the red B, screaming back at me, "Failure!" It might as well have been an F.

He jumped up. "What does your teacher think of me now! They know a man by his failures."

I was ten and knew what he had meant. "I-I'm sorry," I whispered.

He leaned forward, fists pressed on the table, his judgemental blue eyes drilling into me. "That just confirms that you'll never be able to take over my business one day. Now go to your room and write the degrees of comparison of beautiful and stupid, a hundred times."

"But I have rugby practice!"

He frowned. "Rugby? You're too small to play rugby. I guess the only reason you made the team is your surname is Goodman."

"I'm scrum-half. I don't need to be tall. And if you take the time to watch me play, you'll see that I'm... good." I struggled to utter that word.

He straightened, pushing out his chest. "How much do you think does it costs to keep you and your mother going? Your private school alone, which clearly is a waste of my money, is over two hundred thousand a year." He shook his head. "No more rugby. You need to concentrate on your studies."

"Please, s-sir." I had to call him sir back then.

"Get out!"

I backtracked away from his desk, fighting back the tears.

The Sir pointed his finger at me. "Remember, beautiful and stupid. A hundred times. Before dinner."

My eyes settled on the test lying on the red carpet in front of his imposing mahogany desk. I wanted to leap forward, pick it up, and tear it to pieces, but I had to escape, get away from him.

His eyes narrowed. "What's the degrees of comparison for stupid?"

I swallowed, my mind a complete blank, and then it started. "M-m-more stupid and m-m-most stupid."

At first, he was shocked, like me, then he smiled, "You even said it correctly. like a retard."

* * *

The eight-kilometre tar road leading to the Goodman farm was the best in the Limpopo province – no potholes and as smooth as Nicole's legs.

My stomach churned as I made the turn and the Victorian

double-storey house stood illuminated in the moonlight. All lights inside the house, and the balcony, were switched off, but the fence and lawn were lit up like Times Square. Two uniformed guards approached the gate. I didn't recognize them.

"You lost?" a guard asked, one hand resting on his weapon, the other wiping his eyes.

"I'm Greg Goodman, King Henry's prodigal son." I handed him my driver's licence. He stared at it, frowning. "I didn't know Mr. Goodman had a son."

"Mr. Goodman also doesn't know if he has a son."

"Gr-e-g," Nicole sighed and sat up.

"We were only expecting one person and not you."

"When?"

"For security reasons, I'm not allowed to say." He walked back to the guardhouse with my licence. Two minutes later, he appeared with his two-way radio. He seemed more humble. "Mrs. Goodman answered, and she wants to make sure it's you, Mr. Goodman."

I took the radio from him. "Hey, Mom."

"Greg! I can't believe it's you. It's Grandma," she said in a shrill voice. "Bongani!" I handed the radio over to the guard. "Open the gate, my sweetie."

"Yes, Gogo." He smiled and held out his hand. "I apologize, Mr. Goodman, but everyone is on edge lately. We are expecting your sister later this morning."

Bongani was a scrawny man, short – like me – with dreadlocks pointing all directions.

"It seems as if we're making it easy for them, all packed into one place," I muttered.

"Them?" Bongani frowned.

"The ones that make you feel on edge."

"Mr. Goodman felt that it would be easier to protect everyone here. We're expecting another fifteen guards later today."

"How many are you now?"

"Four."

"Please, can we get to bed now," Nicole muttered.

Bongani signalled the other guard a thumbs-up, and the massive steel gate slid open. Gogo was waiting by the front door dressed in her robe and slippers, her silver hair tied in a pony. Grandma was a real bore-tannie: warm, bubbly, and loved food – milk tart, koeksisters, and anything with a sugar content of more than eighty percent. I drove around a smashed patio chair and parked by the stairs leading up to the front door. Grandma held her arms out, the robe belt stretched to its limits, her hands opening and closing as if I was still four. Grandma would be the one making the savoury trays at my funeral. Scratch that – she'd be making the dessert.

"My little devil." She squeezed the shit out of me. "I haven't seen you in over a week."

"Been busy." I groaned.

She pushed me away and tried to touch my bruised eye. "Who did you piss off this time?"

"What's with the patio chair?" I asked the rhetorical question.

Nicole emerged from the car, clutching her bag under her arm.

Grandma tapped my shoulder, leaning over. "You back together again?"

"No, Mrs. Goodman." Nicole smiled. "I'm here on business." She glanced at me. "Nothing more."

"Oh, dear," Grandma said and winked at me. "There's only one room left."

I was confused; Grandma would never allow an unmarried couple to sleep together under the same roof – another bore-tannie thing.

"Oh, dear," Nicole smirked, knowing Grandma's conviction. "Then you need to sleep on the couch."

Grandma gave Nicole the same hug, almost crushing her spine, I was sure.

"And to answer your question, Mrs. Goodman, my fiancé did it to him."

Grandma chuckled. "Knowing my little devil, he allowed it to win your sympathy."

"*Grandma*." I made eyes.

"Oh, grumpy." She jiggled my cheek. "Nicole, you sleep in the room next to me, and Greg can sleep in the cottage." She walked into the house. "Come, Nicole, I'll show you the way."

They left me by the front door without so much as a nighty night. I walked to the back of the house on a lit footpath. The four-bedroom cottage wasn't visible from the house. My mother usually housed annoying guests there. The key was at its usual spot, under the welcome mat – genius. I dropped my gym bag on the floor and heard the clinking call of my friend, Jack.

* * *

Henry Goodman woke at four fifty-five, as he did every morning. A cock broke in the new day with a drawn-out crow, coaching the blackness into a bruised purple. He threw his feet off the bed and built up strength for his morning ritual – fifteen push-ups, ten sit-ups, and a brisk walk alongside the perimeter of his estate.

At five-fifteen, he was done with his first two rituals and dressed for his walk-in La Sportiva Boots, khaki cargo pants, and shirt. Henry stopped in the doorway, spotting the black Mini Cooper in the driveway. *Maybe Stacey bought herself a new car? But they're early? And why a Mini? She should have consulted me first; it's not built for Africa.* He stepped off the porch and made his way around the house, taking the paved footpath that zigzagged its way through and around the property.

"Sawubona, Mr. Goodman," a guard greeted.

"Sawubona, Ishmael." Henry smiled. "Thanks for working double shifts. Your replacements will be here soon, then you can get some sleep."

"No problem, Mr. Goodman, I would work another one for you."

Henry walked a few steps, then turned. "Whose car is that?"

"Your son and his girlfriend's. They arrived early this morning, sir."

"You mean my daughter and her husband."

"No, sir, I haven't met him before, but he showed Bongani his licence." Ishmael scratched his head. "His name was Brett... Ned, no, Greg."

"Where's he now?"

"The cottage, sir. Why?"

"Come with me!" Henry turned on his heel. "It can't be my son."

Ishmael unclipped his radio with fumbling hands. "To the cottage, now!"

The two men ran down the paved path but slowed their approach to a tiptoe twenty yards from the cottage.

"Hand me your weapon," Henry whispered as they reached the front door. Ishmael shoved the weapon into his hands.

"Let's wait for the others," the guard whispered.

Henry approached the front door and pressed his ear against the door. Nothing. He eased the door open and entered, finger on the trigger. Ishmael slipped in behind him. The lights were off, and the curtains drawn. Henry waited a few seconds for his eyes to adjust before walking to the nearest room. He paused before entering the room, listening; the only noise he heard was the drumming footsteps of the three guards sprinting toward the cottage. *I must act now; they will alert him. Or them.*

"It might be a monkey, sir," Ismael whispered.

Henry stepped inside the room, one sweaty hand clutching the weapon, the other on the light switch.

He took a deep breath. One, two...

Before reaching three, his head slammed back as something collided with his face. A sharp pain shot through his wrist as the intruder wrenched the weapon from his hand. He staggered back when another blow to his face knocked him off balance. Ishmael grabbed him from behind before he fell.

"Run, he's got the weapon," Henry yelled, pushing Ishmael

toward the front door, all the time keeping his eyes on the room. The bedroom light turned on, and Greg stood in the doorway.

"It's me, dammit!"

The front door burst open, and three guards stormed in, weapons raised.

"Greg?"

A shot rang out.

"Stop, it's my son!"

* * *

Zimbabwe

Seven Kilometres North of the Limpopo River

Saturday, 05:55

Byron leaned with his back against the bus, arms crossed, dressed in khaki pants, a white T-shirt, and hiking boots. He glanced at the gliding arrow of his Rolex and then at the rising sun.

"Come on," he muttered and fetched a Stetson hat from the passenger seat. He needed it for his sensitive skin.

Muffled shots rang out in the distance, followed by shouts. *It's about time.*

He waited another half an hour before a group of men approached from the east, making their way through the knob-thorn and baobab trees. The fifteen men were dressed in Goodman security uniforms, wearing bulletproof vests, and armed with automatic assault rifles. Their five hostages were dressed in rags, hands tied behind their backs.

"Any witnesses?" Byron asked.

"No," Manana replied. "We took care of them."

"Good."

He grabbed Byron by his designer white T-shirt. "It's not good."

"Okay." He raised his hands.

"How many people have to die for our greed," Manana seethed and let go.

"Many still have to," Byron muttered, glaring at the bloodstain on his T-shirt.

"I should never have gotten involved with you." He loosened his bulletproof vest and threw it into the bus.

"You didn't complain every time you received your cut." Byron plucked a bottle of water from the cup-holder in the passenger door and dribbled water on a white handkerchief. "And for the sake of your men and family, you better lose your conscience." He rubbed at the bloodstain, chin pressed against his chest, muttering, "Otherwise, all of us will be someone's bitch."

"You will never get it out like that," Corporal Lebo said, shaking his head. "Fill a spray bottle with one tablespoon of ammonia and one cup of water. Spray it on the stain and wait for at least half an hour. Rinse and wash."

"My wife soaks our whites overnight in a solution of cold water and bleach," one advised from the back of the group.

Over half the group nodded, murmuring their agreement.

"And never, ever, use warm water," another added.

Byron gave up with a sigh. "Why not?"

"It sets the stain," Manana said, annoyed, wiping his bloodstained hands on his pants.

Byron stared at the group. "I find it amazing that you could involve so many men."

"It was our decision," one of the fourteen said. "We knew the risks. And fuck them, with the crumbs we get as a salary, how can they expect us to live?" The man spat at the dust. "They drive their Range Rovers pleading poverty. All corrupt. We don't know who the good guys are anymore." He shrugged. "So, like they say, if you can't beat them, join them."

"And there's still a lot more after today." Byron smiled. "So, are we all on the same page?"

The fourteen gave a solemn nod.

He glanced at the fifteenth man to the right of him, waiting.

Manana glared at his men. "Remember, it has to look like a farm murder. Sloppy, bloody, and barbaric."

The bullet ricocheted from the doorframe, whisked past my head, and shattered the bedroom window behind me.

My father yelled again, "Don't shoot!"

Bongani holstered the 9mm with shaking hands. "What the hell is going on here?"

"I thought he was somebody else." My father tried to stop the blood from gushing from his nose.

"Who? One of your partners in crime?" I asked.

He turned to the four guards. "Leave us."

Ishmael walked over to me, holding out his hand.

I handed him his weapon, smiling. "You shouldn't hand your weapon over to old, inexperienced men."

He grabbed it and exited the cottage with the other guards.

My father disappeared into the bathroom and emerged a minute later with toilet paper stuck up his nose.

"You got lucky," he muttered.

"You were lucky. I could have killed you." I smirked. "I heard you when you took your morning pee."

He walked over to the windows and opened the curtains, one by one. Dust motes played in the morning light. "So, you knew it was me."

"If I hadn't known, you would've been dead."

He fell onto a couch. "How do you feel?"

"For the millionth fucking time, I'm fine."

My father crossed his arms, staring at the zebra-skin rug sprawled on the polished concrete floor. "I uh." Swallowing. "I'm sorry about your job."

"You know me, I'll get it back."

His eyes darted from the zebra's tail to me. "No! I don't want to see you like that ever again."

I frowned. "Why the sudden affection?"

"I won't apologize for being too hard on you. You needed a firm hand."

"You never saw me as your son."

"I blame your mother's unfaithfulness for that."

"Leave Mom out of this," I snapped.

"It's hard to," he muttered, plucking at an invisible thread on the armrest.

"I want to check on Nicole," I said and climbed into my jeans. I wasn't in the mood. And I wanted to check on Nicole's progress; the more evidence I had against him, the easier he would admit to it – that he was flawed like me.

"Running away again." He shook his head.

"What's done is done."

"Well, I'm willing to start over, forget the past."

"So, if I handed you a syringe with my blood, would you take it?" I asked, buttoning a fresh shirt.

"No, because it doesn't matter anymore if you're my biological son or not. You are my son." He stood up and adjusted his nose plug. "I want to make things right between us." He stuck out his hand. "Please."

Just like that? I glared at the hand.

"Please."

I turned away and walked to the kitchen sink. My tears were too close, and a moment longer, I would've taken his hand. I waited my whole life for this moment. But why now? What did I do to deserve it? Because, fuck, I tried as a kid. *Can he get away from being a shitty father that easily? No. Maybe.* I made it difficult for him. But he started it. He seemed sincere. *No.* I steeled myself, praying my legs would carry me, and walked over to my gym bag, extracting my friend, untouched. *Unbelievable.*

"Okay." He stuck his hand into his pocket. "Is that always going to be your first port of call when the going gets tough?"

"You can't help yourself." I forced a smile. "Belittling me is your first port of call."

He closed his eyes, mouthing, *Fuck*.

"I wasn't planning on ravishing this beauty this morning, but I expect things to get heated." I removed a couple of glasses from the cupboard and poured two doubles with my back toward him - I didn't want him to see my shaking hands. "Yesterday somebody broke into my flat." I took a deep breath before turning around. "They killed my cat and neighbour." I slid my father his drink as I took a seat at the nook.

He shook his head, took a seat across from me and pushed the glass away.

I kept my hands on my lap – out of sight. "They were looking for Clive Bolton's laptop, which contained the evidence you wanted to use as a bargaining tool to ask the president for a pardon."

He paled and swallowed.

"They couldn't find it in my flat, so they went to Nicole's place. And that was after they had Clive Bolton killed and executed his little boy. Luckily, I was there to screw things up for them. You know me. I killed one and wounded another, but I'm sure there won't be anything on the news this morning.

"As we're sitting here, having our father-and-son chat, Nicole is unlocking the evidence, trying to find out who's involved." I shrugged. "Because the next person they'll kill, including his family, will be you. So, my question to you, Dad, is how the" – I looked over my shoulder – "fuck did you get your family involved in this." I stood. "These men always get their man. Do you have any fucking idea how many lives your greediness endangered? You, the righteous, the faultless, the saintly Henry Goodman."

Twice in two days, I had a go at my father. It felt good. I took my seat.

My father picked up his glass and emptied the contents with one gulp.

"I thought you might get thirsty." I pushed my glass toward him. "Nicole will not approve."

Henry kept his eyes on the granite nook and asked, almost in a whisper, "What do you know about Nicole?"

"Why?" I frowned.

"Is she still working for Wolf?"

"Yes, why?" It was my turn to whisper.

"Is she involved with him?"

"What the hell has this got to do with your shit?"

My father picked up my glass and took a sip, eyes still pinned on the nook. "Everything." He looked up from the granite. "Where is she now?"

"In the house."

"Why don't you call her over?"

"I want her to sleep late. She went through a lot yesterday."

My father pushed himself away from the nook and stood up. "I'm going for my walk."

"You serious?"

"Why don't you join me?"

What the fuck, dude? Wait. He wanted to spill his guts en route while not looking at me. And hell, why not? It'll be a first. Maybe our first steps toward something of a relationship. Perhaps he'll tell me why a father could be so cruel to a son.

* * *

Johannesburg
   Winchester Hills
   Saturday, 08:06

.   .   .

Stewart Van Rooyen dropped the suitcase into the boot of his black BMW 530d and slammed it shut. Stacey sat in the passenger seat, reading *Mother & Baby*. She'd realized from early in their marriage her husband did not like to wait. He also didn't like cats, children, chocolates, and Chinese food, well, any takeaway food. After work, he wanted his dinner prepared, waiting, and hot. It wasn't like that when they'd dated. Saturday nights, they'd cuddled in bed, watch rom-coms and eat Chinese. Then, after their marriage, everything changed. All he cared about now: cycling, guns, and surfing the internet.

She had fallen in love with his assertiveness, the way he treated her – like a princess – and he reminded her of her father. Now, she would've loved falling for a guy like her brother: funny, disorganized, passionate, and a cat...and takeaway lover. And always late.

Stacey glanced in her rear-view mirror, searching for Stewart. He stood on the edge of their driveway, dressed in his white rugby shorts and sneakers, glancing up and down the busy street. She hated those shorts, more for the way he wore them – pulled up high with T-shirt tucked in. *Probably wants to show off his shaved legs.* She shook her head and opened the door.

"What are you waiting for?" she dared.

He glared over his shoulder and mumbled, "Your little brother."

She frowned. "But he's already at the farm."

He turned around, fists on hips. "What do you mean?"

"My mom phoned me about an hour ago and told me Greg was there. He arrived about three this morning."

"Why did you not tell me this sooner?" He marched back to the car. "We could have been past Pretoria already."

"You didn't tell me you're waiting for him."

He opened the door and grabbed her by the arm. "Don't talk back to me."

"You're hurting my arm." She looked away. "You want my parents and brother to see your handiwork?"

His fingers bore into her fleshy arm. "I'm not afraid of your little brother," he seethed. "And as for your stingy father, fuck him." Stewart let go and slammed the door shut. Stacey clenched her jaw, crumpling the glossy. *I will not cry. I cannot cry; he hates crying.*

* * *

Manana and Byron stood side by side, staring through binoculars at the farm below. Manana's squad stood a few meters back, hiding in the tree line.

"How many do you see?" Byron asked.

"Two at the gate and two patrolling the grounds." Manana turned to his men. "Remember, no names or rank. We'll handle this like any other operation. My call sign will be Mamba and his"–he pointed to the man next to him and smirked–"the Hog."

"What!" He dropped the binoculars to his side. "Why the Hog? I want to be Cobra."

Mamba's men glanced at each other, amused.

"It means pig, referring to the colour of your skin." Mamba turned back to the cliff and peered through the binoculars. "Craig, our sniper, is called Cobra."

The Hog also returned his gaze to the farm. "Then I think Black Mamba will be more fitting for you."

"I'm in charge of the operation, so I decide on the call signs."

"Whatever." The Hog rolled his eyes. "I'm not into this shit. Just call me Wolf."

"Okay, Hog." Mamba chuckled, peering through the shaking binoculars.

"How are you going to do this?" Byron asked, removing his Stetson hat and wiping his face with a handkerchief.

"We first need to take out all communication; satellite and two telephone lines."

"What about mobile phones?"

Mamba snorted. "Out here?"

Byron removed his phone and stared at the display: No network. "And the satellite?"

"Craig," Mamba called. "Time to take out the satellite."

The sniper turned his Sharks rugby cap front to back, smiling.

"You mean Cobra," Byron muttered. "And how the hell is he going to do that?"

"You see that little box on the arm in front of the dish," Mamba pointed at the chimney of the house far below.

"The LNB. I'm not a fucking idiot. What I mean is, it's the size of a cigarette box almost a kilometre away, and won't they hear the shot?"

"I can circumcise a fly from a kilometre away." Cobra went down on his stomach. "We're too far away. My rifle has a suppressor, so the only thing they might hear is the exploding LNB." He sprinkled dry grass.

"I could've told you there's no wind." Byron wiped his face again. "It's not even eight, and I'm already choking."

"You better brace yourself, whitey; it gets forty-five in the shade here," one of the group said with a grin. "You're already the colour of a pig."

"Don't get familiar with me." Byron snapped, pointing a finger. "I'm not your fucking buddy." The laughter died down. "You're here because of me. Do you like your shiny BMW and two-thousand-rand-a-night hooker? Fuck with me again, and you'll be back to eating pap and chicken legs. Fucking dog."

"Thabiso!" Mamba hollered as the comedian reached for his sidearm.

"Please try," Byron grinned, hands on his hips.

"Fuck you, pig." Thabiso drew his sidearm.

Two shots echoed through the valley below, scattering birds. Everyone went down except for the comedian. Thabiso went down slower, falling to his knees, his flickering eyes pinned on the shooter. He swayed, fell backwards and gargled his last breath.

Mamba and Hog peeked over the edge of the cliff at the

farmhouse below, searching for suspicious movement. The patrolling guards on the stretched-out lawn below paused for a minute, explored the surrounding hills, and continued in their direction.

"Hopefully, they'll think it's hunters," Byron whispered.

"Look what you made me do," Mamba scowled. "We've alerted them. We need to wait."

"I'm glad to see you know where your priorities lie," Byron smirked, eyes fixed on the farmhouse.

"God help you if your little fountain dries up because I will kill you myself."

7

"A leopard eats by means of its spots."
Zulu proverb

I kept my mouth shut and eyes on the dusty path, now and then sidestepping a mountain of shit. We left the fenced area about half an hour ago, under protest from me. *Stubborn old man! Like me.* As if I was his son. He said very little, in fact, nothing, as we speed-walked through the tall grass, knob-thorn, and insects. I walked a full circle around anything resembling a spider web – I hated the eight-legged creatures like Monday mornings.

Why did he ask me along? I felt like Julia Roberts in Pretty Woman walking Beverly Hills before spending Richard Gere's money, dressed in denim, sneakers and a T-shirt. Every creature knew I didn't belong, punishing me for it, sinking their little teeth into my sweaty flesh, sucking me dry. It reminded me of basic training, and I hated basic training. I hated every step, every scorching wheeze, every spider. I hated it so much that I avoided many hiking weekends with the guys. Don't get me wrong – give me a campfire, alcohol, profanity, and the stars, and I'm in, but to roam the bush for days just to get back to the spot where you started from is crazy. My father ran in front as if chased by something. Perhaps he ran from himself or me, afraid of more questions about Beatrice. Then, as if walking into a spider's web, he stopped.

"I knew it," he whispered, staring into the distant tall grass. The shrill, irritating scream of the summer cicada distracted me, elevating my need to take a piss.

"What's wrong?" I asked, unzipping.

"Another rhino." He shook his head.

Then only did I notice the grey heap in the tall grass about thirty metres in front of us. I pee-shivered.

"I heard shots yesterday but thought it was a trap. A way to lure me away from the farm." He walked closer and then hesitated.

I shook and zipped up. "Shit!"

"What!" He went down on one knee, searching the surrounding bushes.

I carefully unzipped. "Something caught."

My father shook his head, annoyed, and rose to his feet.

I walked past him and inspected the majestic beast. The animal had no chance. Over a dozen bullet holes riddled the carcass. The fucking poachers hacked off the horn with half the head as if blown off; cruel and barbaric.

My father walked up to the beast. Was he angry, sad, or disappointed? Never could tell growing up. Only after the outburst I realised he was angry. He would come to my room after he and my mother fought – most of the time about her infidelity – and stand in the doorway looking at me. I didn't know what to expect, and then he would start screaming, crapping on me for something I did days before. He never raised a hand. It was unnecessary because he was an intelligent man. My father knew exactly which words in the English language would inflict the most pain: disappointment, dwarf, inadequate, worthless, bastard, and the most painful of all, whoreson. For a moment, I revelled in his pain, but then the pointless killing of this beautiful animal enraged me. This mountain of flesh and soul killed for a horn that bears no medicinal value, killed because a rich Asian somewhere couldn't get a boner.

"I lost thirty-four this year," my father said, still in his trancelike state.

"I heard it's over six hundred this year." I leaned against the carcass with my hands.

"Shit." My father kicked at a rock. "Africa is like the child of this world; every country grabbing at her beauty with hungry hands which will never be satisfied, beating her with a stick, raping her of all her resources." He walked away, then turned back. "And the worst of it all is African governments and politicians allow it. Fuck! And I joined the feeding frenzy."

I turned around, leaned with my back against the rhino. "Have you heard about the incorruptible politician who became a movie star?"

My father looked at me, shaking his head, frowning.

"He played the *Invisible Man*."

He sighed, shaking his head. I detected a glimmer of a smile. "It's all that fucking Wolf's fault."

"What wolf?" I asked.

"Nicole's boss."

"What?" I pushed myself away from the carcass.

"He approached one of my directors with the info he retrieved from the National Intelligence database. His company manages the data storage for the NIA. He had at his fingertips a list of names of people under investigation for corruption. Approachable people. He also had a list of rebel leaders within Africa. It contained everything he needed to do the deal."

"What deal?"

"He approached Bolton, who worked for me at the time, and who was also under investigation–"

"For weapons smuggling, I know."

"I didn't know. He had his own side-line business within my company."

I didn't believe him for a second. My father knew everything that went on in his company. Down to who was taking a dump when. "Okay, so Wolf approached Bolton?"

"To supply weapons to the rebel leaders."

"So, Goodman Enterprises supplied rebel leaders with weapons to overthrow their governments?"

"I didn't know." He kicked another stone. "It passed my desk as legitimate sales to governments within Africa, but the weapons went to the rebels."

"And how did these rebels pay for the arms?" I already knew the answer; I just wanted to hear it from him.

"Blood diamonds." He mumbled the two words, staring at his expensive boots. "Goodman Consolidated received it, then paid Goodman Arms, thereby balancing the books."

"So, you pulled in Van Rooyen to clean up your mess." I would go along with his story for now; I couldn't force the truth out of the man, but if he told me enough lies, maybe I'd be able to catch him out.

My father shook his head. "I can't stand the–"

Two gunshots in the distance silenced him and the summer cicadas.

"The farm!" he yelled.

* * *

Nicole opened her eyes, unsure of what woke her. She glanced at her wristwatch – 8:15 a.m. The unforgiving morning sun already warmed the room to an uncomfortable temperature. She threw off the suffocating duvet, stumbled into the en-suite bathroom and stopped by the mirror.

"What do you expect with four hours' sleep," she muttered, ruffling her tangled hair. *I look like a thirty-year-old.*

She stepped into the shower, gradually closing the hot water. She gasped as the icy spray worked its magic. The events of last night flashed through her mind – the sound of the scissors disappearing into Thero's flesh, his shaking body, his dying eyes. She turned and gasped, letting the cold water wash away the image – her guilt.

A warmness within the pit of her stomach grew with intensity as she thought of Greg. His image shielded her from the cold and chased away her troubled thoughts. *Bastard.* She extinguished the rising flame, recalling his disappearing act. He broke her heart.

Unbelievable that she had therapy because of a man. *Not Nicole Roberts!* Sitting in that chair, sobbing like a little girl. He had almost derailed her plans. She knew before she went to the doctor why Greg's disappearing act had hurt her so. Her parents also said, just like Greg, that they'd see them later. She was fifteen and her brother thirteen. Later never came because of a broken-down transport truck. Nicole's mother drove because her father had too much to drink at his company's Christmas function. The fucking truck broke down in the fast lane, without hazards or a cone. Mom crashed into the back at a hundred and ten. Her father died in his sleep, face ripped off.

There were many friends at the funeral, but almost no family. She never saw their friends since then – as if they had also died in the car crash. Mother was an only child. Father had a gay sister who they moved in with. Six months, later Nicole's little brother, Dexter, hung himself on his fourteenth birthday with the Joker suspenders his father had bought him at Comicon. That was seven years ago. However, the image of him still weighed in her heart, painfully vivid. He did it in the morning, in the garage, wearing his school uniform. Was it a spur-of-the-moment decision? Was it something someone had said to him?

She closed the water and held on to the tap, watching the water trickle down the sterile white tiles. All the unanswered questions and what-ifs drove her mad. Why did they have to go to that freaking Christmas party? Why were there no reflectors on the truck? What if the tired driver had seen the pothole? Stupid questions. Were re-tread tyres so much cheaper than new ones? The only conclusion she had reached repeatedly – if not for the owner who did everything to maximize his profits, her parents would still be alive.

Then that cocky, damaged brute rode into her life with his Triumph and swept her off her feet. Totally unexpected. Not part of her plan. He was so different from the other assholes she'd been dating. Under that macho-don't-care attitude was a hidden gem; sensitive, caring, unselfish and not like his parents. She allowed him into her life, trusted him. He calmed the storm within – numbed her pain like morphine. Greg replaced her nightmares with dreams filled with love, hope, and lust. He was the one. *We healed each other.* In their relationship, there was no space for hatred, revenge, and anger because they'd had enough of it.

Then, when the latter thing happened, her world imploded. The nightmares were back. The storm returned with more intensity and the pain unbearable. If it wasn't for Byron...

But now Greg is back. Can I trust him again?

Fifteen minutes flew by before she stepped out of the shower, refreshed and feeling her age. *A billionaire and can't afford a towel.* She walked to her bedroom, soaked, in search of something to dry herself.

My father's footsteps faded behind me as I ran back to the farm. *Did Byron drag Nicole into this? She worked for him. Not just professional, they worked on each other.* I blocked out the thought, leaping over a rock. My bruised eye was about to pop out of my skull like Mr. Potato Head...my balls too. The pain between my legs reminded me of the albino gorilla, Byron. How sweet payback would be. A meerkat fled into the tall grass as I sidestepped an anthill and ran through a thorny bush. Thorns tear part of my T-shirt and denim, but I felt nothing. The guns were silent. Please, God, not now. I hadn't spoken to Him in a while, so why would He listen. *For Nicole's sake, please.*

Shit! My father had the security card to unlock the small gate in the fence.

I picked up a rock the size of a rugby ball and smashed it into the magnetic lock. It bounced back and landed on my foot. Again, I picked it up and brought it down hard.

Fuck!

Again, and again and again.

"Fuck!" It echoed into the hills. Grandma told me, after burning her hands with a boiling pot, that sometimes the F-Word was acceptable, but never, ever use the Lord's name in vain. He will punish you. Humans disciplined me enough in my life, so I wouldn't want Him to have a go at me. That, and the firm handshake, I'll always remember.

A Baobab tree stood about four metres away from the three-metre-high electric fence with one of its branches extended over the top. I made a leaping jump and grabbed one of the lower branches, climbing until I reached my branch. *Shit!* Looking up, it didn't seem so high but looking down. I stood and prepared to make the leap of faith, unsure if the branch extending over the fence would hold. I took a deep breath. The first few steps were solid, but then the branch wavered. It was now or again – if still alive.

I jumped, screaming Grandma's acceptable curse word. If it weren't for Newton, I would've made it. I landed on the fence, one leg in the secure zone, the other not. Momentum and high voltage catapulted me into the safe area.

A dung beetle frantically rolled a ball of shit away as I regained consciousness. It had to be a she, a man would have left the shit behind.

"What the hell are you doing, Greg?" my father asked, leaning on his knees, panting, sweat dripping from his nose. "You thought I couldn't keep up?" He stuck his hand out. "Let's go."

I pushed away from the cactus, jaw clenched, determined not to show pain, and continued toward the farm. My father followed, panting like a locomotive.

"You still walking in the mornings?" I asked.

"Yes." Heaving. "Why?"

It's not fucking working. "My gun is in my gym bag." I pointed at the cottage and continued toward the main house. I searched for the guards while ascending the steps to the front door. The house was quiet, except for the ticking of the grandfather clock in the lounge.

"Nicole... Grandma," I called in a stage whisper.

I secured the ground floor, tiptoed up the stairs and glanced into the open rooms. Mom's and Grandma's bedrooms were empty. I pressed my ear against the third door. Nothing.

I slowly turned the knob until a soft click. One... two... three.

Nicole uttered a yelp as she flew around, one arm covering her breasts and the other Priscilla.

"Sorry, I was out walking with my dad, and I heard shots. No one was downstairs, so I thought something was wrong," I rambled.

"What happened to you?" She frowned, taking in my appearance.

"I jumped over an electric fence and landed on a cactus." I took in every inch of her beauty. The water from the shower or bath still trickled down her sculpted body. She did not try to grab a cloth or garment. My father's heavy footsteps raced up the stairs and, with my eyes still soaking up every drop, I slammed the door shut behind me. She remained in that awe-inspiring but provocative pose.

"Greg," my father yelled. "The guards said the shots were fired on Piet's farm. Probably shooting foxes again."

"Nicole is also fine, Dad, don't worry."

"Well, that's good, Greg, but have you checked on Grandma and your mother?" His tone dripped with sarcasm.

Nicole suppressed a smile as I rolled my eyes. "But you told me the shots were fired on Piet's farm?"

"I only told you that now!"

I shrugged. "Okay, I'll go check."

"Don't worry, I will!"

"You look terrible." Nicole shook her head.

"I almost killed myself getting to you." It was hard, but I focused on her eyes. All the doubt I had about her melted like ice cream baking in the African sun. Those amber eyes burnt deep into my soul. I felt no more pain, only my pounding heart. Her presence was like a drug, numbing my throbbing foot, aching chest, and smouldering balls. "You're so," I cleared my throat, "beautiful."

A smile played on her full lips as she lowered her arms, exposing herself.

It was the hardest thing I'd ever done remaining by the door. I craved her with everything in me. Why was I such an idiot? I wanted her; I could taste it.

Her playful smile vanished. "Seen enough? This is what you threw away like a used condom. Take your boner and leave."

A woman scorned. The warmth in her eyes turned cold. Wow! I felt more naked than her.

"I see you've thrown away your ring," I said.

She blinked and glanced at her hand. "I always take it off when I shower."

"I also see your Pricilla is now queen of the jungle."

"That's how Byron likes her." Her cheeks reddened. She plucked a T-shirt and shorts from her bag.

"My father told me interesting things about your fiancé, strange that you don't know about him."

"Since when do you believe anything your father says?" She slipped on her denim shorts.

"Maybe that's why you're taking your time with the laptop?"

"Get out," she snapped, fighting to get her T-shirt on. "Now!"

I left the room and went downstairs. Someone was in the kitchen. It was Grandma and Veronica, the old Sotho housekeeper – been with my parents since the time Madiba walked out of prison. The smell of bacon and eggs drove me crazy.

"Morning, ladies." I walked over to the frying pan.

"Master Goodman!" Veronica shuffled toward me with a radiant smile, arms stretched out. "Gogo told me you were here."

"Wait, my—"

She hugged me before I could stop her, forcing the cactus thorns deeper into my chest.

"What in heaven's name happened to you, Geegee," Grandma said, standing teapot-pose with a spatula in hand.

"Still getting into trouble, master?" Veronica gave me a look over. "Eish." She shook her head and gave a click of the tongue.

"I fell into a fu-freaking cactus." I reached for the bacon, but grandma smacked my hand with an oil-soaked spatula.

"Go take a shower first. You smell like a skunk."

"Where were you just now?" I asked, wiping my hand on my torn T-shirt.

"Drew got lost on the way here, so Mom and I went to fetch her in town."

"Drew," I said, eyebrows raised. "Mom's ray of light."

Grandma glared at me. "No."

"What?" I shrugged. "Nicole is taken."

"She hasn't said 'I do' before Him yet." She pointed upward with the spatula.

Veronica stood next to us, frowning, watching us as if at Wimbledon.

"Exactly. Jealousy is sometimes a wonderful thing." I plucked a piece of bacon from the pan and shoved it into my mouth. "Shit." I fanned my mouth with my hand.

The two gogos chuckled.

"Exactly, just be careful. You could get burnt." She slapped me against the shoulder with the spatula. "Go take a shower. The only thing that might get jealous is a female skunk."

Why am I crying? Nicole yanked the laptop from the bag. Last night was too much for her; all the shooting, her beautiful house destroyed, the dead guy next to her bed, Byron, and now Greg. *Things are*

spiralling out of control. And why did I just stand there, naked, taunting him like that? She threw the laptop on the bed, staring at it for a moment.

But he'd remained at the door. *Why didn't he try anything? Does he still love me? I must be certain.* Well, he was... excited to see me. She fell onto the bed next to the laptop and flipped it open. *But what am I going to do about Byron?* A high screeching drew her attention. *What now!* Nicole leapt from the bed and parted the curtains, hiding to one side. Henry Goodman stood next to a woodchipper, showing a gardener how it worked.

He looked up.

Nicole waved and smiled. *Asshole. Your day is coming.*

He stared at her straight-faced for a few seconds and returned to the demonstration.

It's time people pay the price for what they do. It's time the Goodmans realize they can't get away with everything.

I cleaned up and tried to remove the thorns using a mirror and tweezers. After almost biting off my tongue and going cross-eyed, I gave up. I left the cottage two hours later, without a shirt and left shoe, in search of a volunteer. The kitchen had its usual occupants – Grandma and Veronica – but with their eyesight, I might lose a nipple. The lounge only had one, Mom. She jumped from the couch as she saw me. "Geegee, my angel, you came." She cupped my chin and gave me a peck on the left cheek, her usual. "I couldn't believe my ears when Dad told me you're here."

"But your manicure kept you from rushing over to the cottage."

She stepped back and placed a hand on her heart. "What happened to you, Geegee?"

"I fell into–"

"You must put on a shirt, my angel. I need a smoke just by looking at you. Imagine what the other girls will do to you."

"M-o-m!" I shook my head. "I've got thorns in my chest." I held the tweezers out to her.

"You're crazy; I can't hold that with these." She flashed her red nails. "Drew!" She glanced around. "Where's Drew?"

"Yes, Mrs. Goodman." Drew appeared at the front door. "Greg." She said my name with such sultry emotion the tweezers slipped from my fingers.

"Hi, Drew." I picked it up, and as I straightened, looked into her smouldering brown eyes.

"I told you, you need a shirt," my mom muttered and disappeared into the kitchen.

I handed the tweezers to Drew and pointed at the thorns in my chest. She gave a smiling nod and leaned in. I filled my lungs with her scent, the smell of her hair – pleasant but too sweet. It tickled my nose. I could fill my lungs to bursting point with Nicole's scent – delicate, comforting, arousing. The warmth of Drew's breath against my chest awakened little Geegee – like inflating a blow-up doll. *What the hell is going on with me! My testosterone level's in the red. All Nicole's fault!* I broke out in a nervous sweat. Each pluck worsened the situation.

I swallowed. "I think it's enough for now." *Don't look down. Don't look down.* I thought of a gruesome crime scene – baseball would not dampen the spirit.

Then, the law that ruled my life, Murphy, arrived: Nicole walked in. She took one look at Drew and me and clicked her tongue like a Xhosa.

Drew, sensing the sudden tension in my body, stepped away. She stared at Nicole, then me, frowned. "O-kay," she said slowly. "I'm going to unpack."

"I'm sure Greg will join you," Nicole snapped. "There's still one last thorn to be plucked." She looked down.

"I don't know why you're so upset. She was just helping me."

Nicole walked toward the kitchen. "Whatever."

Interesting. I slipped on my T-shirt and strolled with one shoe to the front door. My father spoke with a man, a huge bloody thing – almost seven feet tall sporting a bulging stomach. He was dressed in denim shorts, socks pulled up to his knees, and boots cut from two cows. My father seemed agitated. They stood next to the woodchipper.

"Almost forty rhinos this year," my father said. "We were there before you. Where were you?"

I moved in behind the chipper.

"On the other side of the farm," the man said in an Afrikaans accent.

"You're always on the other side of the bloody farm," my father snapped.

"It's a big farm, Mr. Goodman."

"I pay you good money, Hans, and I'm warning you now, one more, and you're out of here."

Forty times? You had to be fucking unlucky or lucky. I stepped out from my hiding place. "He's talking, Mr. Goodman, screaming like a cricket on a hot summer's night."

My father glanced at me. "What are–"

"The poacher crapped on my shoe while they forced a poker up his arse. Not only do we have cell phone audio of this big ape talking to them, but we've got a confession."

Hans stood motionless. The only presence of life was the whiskey veins in his puffy cheeks and nose darkening to a deep purple.

"I'm Lieutenant Richards from the Task Force." I held out my right hand and stuck my left into the back of my jeans as if reaching for a weapon. "Sorry for the way I look, but the bastard put up a hell of a fight."

Hans cautiously reached for my hand. Bingo. I would have been chipper food if he was innocent. His large, sweaty hand engulfed mine. Luckily for me, my father was at the stage of no-emotion, just before his outburst – so Hans thought my father was aware of all this.

"But, Hans, we've got a problem." I released his grip and wiped my hand on my jeans. "We can't have a judge see this" – I glanced over my shoulder – "fucked-up poacher, he's half-dead, his intestines are hanging out, and he lost an eye in the interrogation." I waved my free hand. "Just horrific." It was like talking to the Paul Kruger statue on Church Square, static and deep in shit. "So, here's the deal, tell us what you know – names, numbers, the contacts at the Musina police department, and you can go home. We'll compare your list and the singing cricket's list, just to make sure you're telling the truth. If not, we'll wait for the translator; he'll probably be here in an hour."

"Translator?" Hans frowned, eyes shifting from me to my father, then back to me.

"We also caught a Zimbabwean who is keen to talk." I smiled. "You've got less than an hour." There must be a Zimbabwean involved in all of this.

I paused for effect, glaring at him with my good eye. "You will be quite the PlayStation in prison with a big hairy white arse like that."

"So, what will it be, Hans?" my father asked. He was white as a sheet, his hands trembling. It took all the Goodman in him not to lunge forward and wring Hans's neck, I knew.

Hans dropped his head and nodded. "I'm sorry, Mr. Goodman. I was–"

"Save it!" my father snapped.

"Is the station commander at Musina in on it?" I asked.

The big man shook his head. "No, it's his second-in-command, Lieutenant Ribeiro."

My father gasped. "What, Simon?"

"That's the name the poacher said as well."

I nodded with pressed lips.

"Mr. Goodman, take Hans to the station commander and let him take his statement. I need to finish here."

"Get in my car," my father barked and pointed to the white Range Rover in the garage.

Hans footslogged away like a cow on the way to the slaughterhouse. I knew he wouldn't run away or try anything on my dad on the way to the station. He was too scared of me and the consequences. I loved frightening big men.

Father turned to me. For the first time in my life, I saw pride and admiration; it stirred something in me – but just a little before it angered me.

"I don't know what to say, Gee."

Gee? A first. "I could have taken his statement, but as you know, I'm not a policeman anymore."

He lowered his head like Hans and mumbled, "I received an anonymous letter. It threatened that if I didn't get you off the case, they'd kill you. You were getting too close." He looked me straight in the eye. "When all this is over, and I'm still alive, I'll get you back in, I promise."

"In other words, I must keep you alive."

He stuck his hand out. "Thank you."

I looked at the gangly hand for a moment before taking it. "I didn't do it for you. I did it for the rhinos. Get going, Mr. Goodman, a man is stinking up your car. I need to stay with the girls. Take three guards with you, two in the back seat and one following you with the Land Cruiser."

He patted me on the shoulder and walked off.

I heard a window close above me; Nicole disappeared behind the curtain.

"Shit! Where's he going?" Byron peered through his binoculars. The two-car motorcade sped through the gate and disappeared behind the tree line below.

Mamba joined him, glancing through his binoculars. "Who?"

"Henry Goodman. He just drove off in his chariot."

"Cobra," Mamba yelled.

"Yes?" The young man struggled to his feet, where he sat amongst the others.

"Yes, who!" Mamba spat.

"Yes, sir, Mamba." He jumped to attention, eyes fixed on the shimmering horizon.

"It doesn't matter what we're doing here – we're still Task Force, and I'm still in charge. We'll handle this as another mission. I want the same discipline. I expect the same discipline." The group of fourteen men stared at him with gaping eyes. "I do not want this. I'm certain none of you want this, but it needs to be done. You will follow my orders to the letter with no empathy. This is for our preservation. You got that!"

"Yes, sir," they said as one.

"That's better." He smiled. "We will go in as soon as our target returns."

He turned and walked to the cliff, calling over his shoulder, "Cobra."

"Yes, sir!"

"Take out the satellite."

Craig grabbed his rifle and ran to the edge of the cliff.

"What's that all about?" Byron whispered as Mamba joined him.

"Motivation. It'll get ugly down there."

The sniper went down on his stomach and did his ritual: turned his Sharks cap front to back, held up his wind meter to determine wind speed, sprinkled dry grass to determine the direction, adjusted his scope and pulled the rifle snugly up against his shoulder and cheek.

"He also checks the mirage to determine wind speed," Mamba whispered.

"Mirage?" Byron whispered.

"The heatwaves or reflection from the tin roof or ground. With an eight-kilometre crosswind, at this range, about one klick, the hold off will be approximately twenty-two centimetres."

"Hold off?"

"We've got left-to-right crosswind, so he needs to aim twenty centimetres to the left of the LNB."

Byron nodded.

"Make me proud, Corporal," Mamba said.

Craig unclipped the safety and curled his finger around the trigger. He took a deep breath, finger curling tighter.

The two men stopped breathing as they peered through their binoculars.

Pop.

A full second passed before the LNB disintegrated far below.

Mamba smiled at the sniper like a proud father.

"Wait a second," Byron said, still peering.

"What?" Mamba raised his binoculars.

"Isn't that the fucking little shit?"

"Where?"

"The front lawn."

Mamba frowned, whispering, "Dammit, Greg." He turned away and kicked at the dust. "Shit!"

"What's wrong?" Lanky Lebo asked, standing up.

"Dammit!" Mamba turned back to the cliff. "What the hell is he doing here? He hates his family." He peered through the binoculars once more. "We need to call it off."

"What!" Byron grabbed Mamba by the arm. "This order came from the top. Everything is set." He pointed at the house. "We killed a busload of his men. Wiped out a village. If we don't do this now, Henry will turn, go into hiding and sing like a fucking canary."

Mamba closed his eyes, shaking his head. "He's one of us. My friend."

"Okay." Byron threw his hands in the air and turned to the men sitting in the tall grass under the trees. "Then, let's go home. Say goodbye to your wife, or girlfriend, your kids, your mommy and daddy." He folded his arms. "Because your life as you know it will be over. Imagine what the thugs you caught will do to you in jail."

"Enough!" Manana barked.

Byron turned to Manana. "Talk to your men. It is what it is." He placed his hands in his pockets and walked away.

Manana balled his fists, glaring at Byron. He took a deep breath before approaching his men. "We've got a big problem."

"Not that big," Craig said from the edge of the cliff.

Manana flipped a thumb over his shoulder. "Meerkat is down there."

The men looked at each other with shocked expressions.

"So, we can all go home, like he said," pointing at Byron standing in the distance, sneering, "or we do what we came here to do. If we don't, we all going to end up in jail. All our excursions over the border, gun-smuggling, assassinations will be headline news for years to come. Our families will suffer the most. I know he's our friend, part of our team."

"Won't Greg join us?" one asked.

Manana shook his head. "I know him." He paused with a pensive frown. "He's such a piece of shit, a loose cannon, but he'll never... turn."

"I'll do him," Sergeant Mike Salts said, scratching his groin.

Manana sighed. "You'll do your own guardian angel. So, those who are in the stand. Those who want to go to jail remain seated."

All slowly rose.

"Good." Byron slapped his hands together and approached.

"Remember," Manana said. "Don't think, just pull the trigger."

"He's mine," Byron smiled. "I'll finish what I'd started."

Mamba draped his arm over Hog's shoulder and steered him away from the group. "While we on the subject, did you order the hit on Greg at Pixies?" he whispered.

Byron smiled. "Now that you're prepared to kill him. Yes."

Manana froze, glaring at a three feet high anthill. "Who gave the order?"

"Order?" Byron frowned. "It was personal." He shrugged. "Or let's just say, a favour for a friend."

The Mamba struck, hitting him in the groin. The Hog's boots raised from the ground before he fell into a heap of pain and dust, groaning. Mamba kicked him in the stomach repeatedly until his men pulled him away.

"What's going on?" Craig yelled.

"I'm fine!" Manana yelled, pushing his men away. "I'm fine," he said, controlled. "Go." He pointed at the trees.

The men retreated.

Manana kneeled next to Byron and whispered, "Do something like that behind my back again, and I'll cut your balls off, fry them and feed them to you. He was part of my team."

8

"Money is sharper than a sword."
Zulu proverb

Goodman Farm
Saturday, 13:02

I struggled with my load toward a tree in the centre of the front lawn. The small wooden table kept slipping from my right hand. Under my left arm, I clutched two camping chairs, and in my hand a bottle of Jack with two glasses. Amazingly, nothing slipped from my left. The only thing slipping, other than the wooden table, was my Bermuda swimming trunks because of my 9mm pistol shoved into the back. I opened my legs wider and wider with every step. By the time I reached the tree, I was walking like a rapper, mooning the house.

I placed the table and chairs facing the river, planted my companion in the centre, my feet on the second chair, and appreciated the view. A fellow needed to create his moments because nobody else would. This was also an experiment – who would join me, Drew or Nicole? Hopefully, the latter.

I lit a cigarette and sipped my whiskey. Jack and Johnny never broke my heart. The flowing river calmed my restless mind; capped the dark hole.

Grandma beat them to it. I smiled at the short shuffling footsteps behind me; it wasn't whom I hoped for, but she was always welcome.

"Old ladies shouldn't sneak up on young men," I said, keeping my eyes on the river.

"What do you expect, flaunting your cute butt like that?" grandma said, ruffling my brush cut. "And how'd you know it was me?"

"I heard a slow, decrepit shuffle. You know, someone who's been through the mill."

"At least I look better than you. For once, I'd like to see both your eyes at once."

"Grab a chair, old lady." I removed my feet from the chair and placed it next to me. "Take the load off." I grinned.

"Give an old lady some of that moonshine. They say it's good for the blood pressure."

"They say so." I poured her two fingers.

She draped her silver weave down her left shoulder and took a sip. "Ah, this will get the old ticker going again."

The salutary river cleared our minds as if we'd placed our fears and concerns into a raft and sent them down the river. We sat for some time, sipping and staring, enjoying each other's company. No need for trivial conversation, no awkward silences – just like Nicole and me.

Grandma broke the silence first. "Your father seemed pleased with you before he left."

I took a sip. "Too late for that."

"It's never too late," Nicole spoke behind us.

A wave of contentment rushed over me and gathered in the pit of my stomach. I wasn't sure if it was the whiskey or Nicole – but something told me it wasn't the whiskey.

Nicole joined us, glass in one hand and chair in the other. "Greg figured out Hans was involved with the rhino poaching syndicate. Asshole."

I jumped up and took the chair from her.

"Not here, maybe later," she said with a smile as I aimed to unfold the chair beside me. "There," she pointed to a spot next to Grandma. "I'm still mad at you, but you do deserve a drink. You know how I feel about animals." She gave me a peck on the cheek.

If I knew it was that easy, I should have joined Greenpeace. I placed the chair at her desired spot and filled her glass – three fingers. Maybe later, she'd said. There's still hope.

"It seems as if all eyes are on me. I can't turn my arse."

"Speaking about your butt, what does that 'B' tattoo on each cheek mean?" Nicole asked, settling in.

"Yes, Geegee, what's that all about?" Grandma asked.

I had forgotten about that.

"It wasn't there when we were dating," Nicole said, staring at the river. "The initials of another girl?"

I detected a hint of jealousy. "Before my incident, the guys and I were celebrating like we do after every successful mission. I was the star of the show, and of course, very drunk. The bar was right next to a tattoo parlour, so they convinced me to get my initials tattooed on my butt. They conspired with the tattoo artist behind my butt to make it 'B' and 'B', instead of 'G' and 'G'."

"Why would they do that? What's so funny about it?" Nicole asked.

"Because now," I hesitated, "when I bend over, it reads 'BoB'."

The two women burst out laughing. Nicole had just taken a sip and sprayed whiskey all over her clothes. I missed this, the laughter.

"Two boys were playing with themselves." I took a sip. "The one said to the other, 'We must be careful – they said you could go blind, doing it too much.' The other one replied, 'Then let's just do it until we wear glasses.'"

Grandma replied through laughter, "If that was true, you would be walking around with a guide dog."

"Hey!"

"Can we join in?" Mom asked behind me. Drew was with her, clutching two chairs.

I flipped a thumb at the spot next to me. "Only if you bring a glass."

Drew filled the space closest to me and presented my request with an eager smile. I poured each one finger and a bit.

"What's the occasion?" Mom asked, holding her glass with two fingers as usual.

"You don't need an occasion to drink, Mother. We're just sitting, enjoying the view and drinking. Relax, let your hair down."

"But my hair is down."

Drew glanced at me and rolled her eyes.

"There is something we're celebrating." Nicole looked at me as if I'd found the answer to life. "He found the asshole who's been responsible for the rhino poaching."

"But you only just got here; your father and the police have been looking for these people for over a year. Who was it?"

"Hans."

"Hans!" She sat up. Without the Botox, there would've been a frown.

"Henry was very pleased with Geegee," Grandma said, patting my leg. "I hope this is the start of the healing process between you two."

Whatever. I was buying my dad's story from this morning, and I didn't know why. Maybe the buzz of the booze?

"You need to forgive those who repent. Otherwise you can't expect to be forgiven." Grandma emptied her glass.

"The Oracle has spoken," I muttered.

"So, will you forgive him?" Grandma asked.

I caught the look she threw at me and realized the direction she was heading in – Nicole needed to forgive me.

"My father apologized to me, and I can see that he feels bad about all the shit that happened between us." I leaned forward and looked at Nicole. "And because I need to be forgiven, I will forgive him," I lied. I would never forgive him for what he did to me. And if he were more involved in the arms deal than he had admitted – then that would confirm my opinion of him.

"That's my boy." Grandma slapped my bare leg. "This calls for a toast." She held up her empty glass. "Get the Bible. The barman is dead."

I poured her another stiff one.

"To forgiveness." She clunked Nicole's and my glass. "So, anyone else in the mood for forgiveness?"

From the corner of my eye, Nicole folded her arms. She wasn't ready yet. *Shit, she's stubborn. Where's her ring? Interesting. What was going on between her and Byron?* Had she already decrypted the file, discovered all his skid marks, and was too embarrassed, or afraid, to tell me?

Grandma also noticed the closed book beside her and turned her attention to my mother. "What about you, Jessica? You ready to ask Henry for forgiveness?"

"What?" she snapped and sat up, spilling the whiskey on her white power suit. "He needs to ask me – all the hell he put me through."

"Recognising your own mistakes is the first step to forgiveness." Grandma elbowed me in the ribs with a wink.

"Refill anyone?" I asked before anyone could grow a set of balls. I wasn't in the mood for any melodrama.

Drew and Nicole accepted.

I settled back. Nicole stared at the bush with a slight frown.

"What's wrong?"

Her glazed expression sparked alive. "Is it safe for us to sit here in the open with everything going on?"

She was right, but I didn't know the entire clan would join me. Besides, I wasn't sure if there would be a hit. I was willing to take the risk, fuck Stewart; I would not hide in a hole like a frightened little pussy. I'm right here... take your best shot.

"With what going on?" Drew asked, sitting up, staring at the river and then Nicole.

"Life's too short to be afraid," Grandma said and raised her glass. We clinked.

"But don't worry," I said after a sip. "I know who's involved. I'll handle him."

"S-shit, here's that bloody prick," Grandma mumbled as the black BMW 530d drove through the gate. "Now, there's a man who I'd struggle to forgive."

"Speak of the devil," I mumbled.

"Who's that?" Nicole asked, shocked at the response beside her.

"Stewart bloody Van Rooyen." Grandma seethed.

"Oh, Stacy's husband." Nicole sipped, watching the car over her glass.

"We don't know if he does, Mother," Mom said. "Stacey would have told us."

"Told us what?" Nicole asked.

"He's a wife-beater," Grandma spat. "I've seen the marks."

"Why then does she stay with the bastard?" I asked. The rage built again. "Why didn't she tell me? I had my suspicions but never found proof. He'd taunt me, but I thought it was just to rile me up. No wife-beater ever boasts about his hobby."

"Because she's embarrassed," Drew said. "She's still in shock, can't believe that something like that is happening to her. It seems so unreal to her. She didn't want you to know because she's proud, and she despises being pitied. And then, there's the fear of leaving him. She knows what he's capable of doing to her and to her family."

I turned in my chair. "When did you speak to her?"

Drew looked at me and smiled. "I've never met her in my life."

Stacey waved with a broad smile on her face and rushed toward the river-watchers. Stewart gave a stiff wave, removed the bag from his car, and disappeared into the house.

"Okay, everyone," I muttered, keeping my lips from moving. "Let's not spoil her day."

We jumped to our feet, smiling.

She threw her arms around me.

"How are you, my little brother?" she whispered in my ear.

"You know me, always landing on my feet," I whispered. "And you?"

"Now, I'm fine." She stepped away, teary-eyed. "Why don't you visit? We live ten minutes apart."

Because I hate your husband's guts. "Been busy chasing bad guys." *Like your husband. Hope he's also on the list so he can be someone's bitch in sing-sing.*

"We can take a walk later and catch up." She winked at me and moved on to the rest of the clan. What was it with my family? Everyone wanted to take me on a walk as if I was a bloody Jack Russell? But I could see she needed a walk; maybe she'd spill her guts, tell me about that husband of hers. I could ask her for permission to kill him. Another reason a walk would do her good was that she'd gained about ten kilograms this year. She seemed tired, the spirit in her big brown eyes extinguished. Her long, black, velvety hair resembled a horse's tail – dull and streaky.

The river-watchers stared in silence as she made her way back to the house to unpack.

"How hot is it today?" Grandma asked.

"Thirty-five, forty," I said. "And she's wearing a jersey."

"There's your proof." Grandma turned to me, her grey-blue eyes flashing. "Fuck the rhino, save your sister," she seethed.

* * *

We disbursed soon after, and I returned to the cottage hoping Nicole might join me later. I wanted to ask her about the list, about Byron, about so many things.

I blamed myself for not doing anything about my sister. However, I could never confirm my suspicions. I was one of those neighbours I interviewed who had his doubts about child abuse next door; was never totally sure until they carried the kid out in a body bag. I couldn't do anything if she wasn't willing to lay charges against him. *There are other ways of dealing with him, with or without her consent.*

I was taking a piss when a knock at the door startled me. *Nicole?* "Just a second." I wiped the lid and floor.

My excitement was short-lived. "Stewart," I said through my teeth. My hands made involuntary fists.

"Where the hell were you?" he said as he pushed past me. "Where's the laptop?"

"Don't tell me you're still playing this game?" It took all my self-control not to leap forward and squeeze every drop of pus from his vile body. "Your team almost killed us last night!" I screamed. "You've got the laptop."

Steward frowned. "What the fuck are you talking about? What team?" He was in so deep that his only defence was denial.

"Oh, please," I snorted. "Losing Thero wasn't part of the plan, was it?"

He stared at me as if I had completely lost my mind. "What do you mean I lost Thero? Did he resign?"

"Stewart," I shook my head. "Nicole already decrypted the file, and your name is on the list. I've got you." I bullshitted with a smile. "You were in bed with Bolton, so you can stop this charade."

"What fucking charade?" He stormed toward me, his face as red as a fire engine. This time, however, I was ready for him. A quick jab to the throat and gut had the desired effect. He stopped in his tracks, mouth gaping, gasping for air.

"That's for my sister. And this is the one I still owed you." I dribbled and kicked him between the legs – Beckham would've been proud. He landed on his side, clutching his privates. "And this one is for trying to kill Nicole last night." I pulled his head up by his Tin-Tin tuft and wrapped my legs around his neck, locking my feet. "I once had Manana like this," I seethed.

Stewart opened his mouth like a little bird waiting for a worm, his tongue and face turning into the colour of my bruised eye. No more self-control or thinking about consequences. "You killed my cat, you tried to kill me" – I tightened – "and kill Nicole."

His arms fell limp to the floor. I gave him some rope, wanting to hear him beg. "How much did Byron pay you?"

He sounded like a car not finding gear but then said hoarsely, "I... fucking promise you, I... did not do it. I don't have the laptop. I... did... not order... my men. The... order did not come from me. I swear on my life."

"Then why did you order me to get the laptop from Byron? Why do you want it?"

He remained silent.

"Why!" I tightened the grip.

"Because... because I want your father to pay."

"What! I thought you were on his side?"

"That... bastard doesn't give me or Stacey a cent of his fucking money. We live like fucking paupers, while he lives like a politician. I wanted to bring him down – the mighty Henry Goodman."

Fuck! I was appalled; we had something in common. I released my hold on him and jumped to my feet. Stewart rolled on his back, gasping and coughing for air.

"Thero didn't resign; I killed him last night."

"How... many were... there?"

"Two destroyed Nicole's house, but later the Task Force van drove in to clean up the mess. I don't know how many men were in there."

He shook his head. "It must be Modise."

"It could be. We'll know soon enough."

Stewart struggled to his feet. I'd never seen so much hate in a man's eyes as I did when he glared at me.

"You're not off the hook yet." I pointed. "If you ever raise your hands to my sister again, I will kill you."

He stumbled out the door without a word, one hand clasping his throat and the other his dinglings.

Between him and my father, I was still undecided whose side to take. I had to admit my father was taking the lead, slightly. It was like choosing between North Korea and Afghanistan as a holiday destination.

* * *

16:06

"The ego has landed." Byron turned to the group relaxing under the Marula tree. His face distorted with pain as he touched his stomach.

Mamba rose to his feet. "Get the patsies into the awaiting chariot. It's time to clean house."

They dragged the four Zimbabwean men into the bus, handcuffed and blindfolded.

Byron looked at his cell phone before pointing it at the skies. He lowered his arm, coughing, holding his ribcage. "I think you broke one of my ribs," he mumbled.

"I told you there's no reception," Mamba said. "This is the fourth fucking time today."

"I was hoping for a miracle."

"Miracles only happen to good guys. What do you want to tell her?"

"That I love her." Byron stared at the Mini Cooper parked in front of the farm. "And ask why she didn't call me last night."

"We both have somebody down there. As you said, it is what it is. You should have kept her out of this when there was still a chance."

Byron turned to Mamba. "Remember, it's my call if she lives or dies. Tell your men to leave her alone. If any of them touch her–"

"They know."

He turned his attention back to the Mini and whispered, "Hope we're still a team, Nicky."

* * *

16:10

I contemplated my next move while devouring bacon and scrambled eggs at the kitchen table. Yes, I took a shower.

"You want some coffee," Grandma asked as she wrestled with the dough on the table. She prepared one of her favourites – vetkoek and mince.

"Don't worry, I'll make it myself, Grandma. I can see you've got your hands full. Besides, you always make it too strong."

"Sissy," she mumbled and wiped her hands on her apron.

"Your coffee looks like chocolate sauce."

She picked up a bottle of cooking oil and emptied it into a pot on the stove. "When I was your age–"

"Here we go," I mumbled. "They didn't discover the coffee bean yet, or the wheel."

"Men were men. They ate red meat three times a day, drank coffee that resembled chocolate sauce, ate fat the size of a Polony roll, and they shaved nothing but their beards."

"And their life expectancy was a ripe thirty-five."

"Grandpa lived until he was sixty."

"Wow, a whopping sixty." What did she know about my father's dealings?

"What?" She frowned, hand on hip.

"Nothing." I shrugged and pushed my plate away.

She dropped her shoulders and sighed. "Don't even think of playing your *nothing* game with me. What is it?"

I folded my arms and straightened both legs. "What do you think of your son's shady dealings? He's placed everyone in harm's way."

Grandma gave a wave of the hand before rolling out the dough. She kept quiet for seven or eight rolls, then said, "I've known some bad people in my life, Greg, and your father is not one of them. I don't know how he got involved with this, but I'm dead sure he didn't mean for us to get dragged into it. He will get us out of this – you'll see." She looked up from her creation, and her eyes softened. "I know you hate him for what he did to you in the past, but he was young and fierce. And stupid."

"I don't hate him for the past, Grandma," I said with an innocent expression. "I hate him for who he is now."

She attacked the paper-thin dough and mumbled, "You must forgive your father and move on."

"He's not my father." I shifted in my chair. "So, I don't have to."

"He is your father." Grandma slammed the rolling pin down and glared at me. "I think the dough is ready."

The skin under her chin jiggled as she shook her head. "Don't you think the reason you're not getting along is the fact that you're so alike? You're both so bloody stubborn." Her cheeks flushed.

"Take it easy, Grandma, don't pop a vein or break a hip."

She glared at me for a moment and then smiled with a slow shake of the head. "Greg, what am I going to do with you?"

I stood up and approached her with open arms. "Give me a hug, you old fart."

She wrapped me in those tender arms and whispered, "I forgave your father, just like I'd forgiven you so many times. That's what the Man upstairs wants us to do."

"What man upstairs?" I glanced at the ceiling. "Don't tell me you're back on the market; it's only what – fifteen years since Grandpa died."

She tightened her embrace. I missed her consoling arms, our chats around the kitchen table. We'd talk for hours about shit before she cunningly ventured into my soul, giving me advice or nudging me in the righteous direction. She was my barometer between right and wrong. However, as she admitted, I'm a stubborn prick who did things my way.

"Not in the kitchen, you guys," Nicole said as she and Stacey entered the room.

Grandma wiped her tears as she broke free. *Why's she crying?*

Did I bring back memories of Grandpa, or was she upset about her son – more than she wanted to admit? Or was it me?

"Koeksister, anyone?" Grandma held out a plate towering with the syrup-soaked woven dough.

Stacey grabbed one with eager fingers.

"No thanks." Nicole glanced at me.

"Did anyone see Stewart?" Stacey asked with bulging cheeks. "He said he wanted to talk to you, little brother, and he never came back."

Grandma and Nicole glanced at me, shocked.

I shrugged and plucked another piece of bacon from the plate. "We talked, and he left."

"Maybe he's still at the back somewhere." Stacey aimed for the back door.

"No!" Nicole and Grandma said as one.

Stacey stared at them, confused.

"I saw him in front by the guardhouse a few minutes ago," Grandma said.

"Okay." Stacey exited the way she came in.

Grandma walked to the door and made sure the coast was clear. "What did you do to him?" she said, holding her head. "I didn't mean for you to hurt him. Did you kill him? Must I call Bongani?"

"We can't call Bongani; there must be no witnesses." Nicole grabbed a koeksister from the plate and stuffed it into her mouth.

"Don't worry," I said. "They'll never find him."

Grandma stroked her busty chest, wheezing. "It's all my fault. I'll take the fall." She pulled out a chair and fell into it. "I don't have long to live."

Nicole stared at me with her big green eyes. She seemed sad.

"They'll never believe that you broke his neck and legs, Grandma."

She raised her hands, eyes piercing. "These hands fought many a war."

"The bastard deserved it." Nicole seethed and plucked another koeksister from the plate. She showed an emotion I only saw once before when I allowed Byron to beat the shit out of me – heartlessness. *How well do I know her?*

"You two worry me." I stood up. "Stewart's fine. The only things that got hurt were his ego and balls."

A koeksister flew past me as I ran for the living room. "At least I know you've got my back," I yelled over my shoulder.

Nicole followed close behind and leapt onto my back, wrapping her arms around my neck. "Now I've got your back, you bastard."

We fell onto the couch, and I flipped over. Nicole sat on top of me, pinning my arms under her knees. "Now I've got you," she said through clenched teeth.

"It's heartening to know you'd be an accessory to murder for me."

She looked deep into my eyes and smiled.

We remained in that position, not saying a word, delving deeper and deeper into each other's soul. She inched closer. My heart revved up. The space between us was supercharged. My body tingled all over... more at certain places. I swallowed. *This is it! Breathe Greg!* I filled my lungs with her minty-fresh breath and closed my eyes, preparing for those sweet lips.

"Daddy!" I heard Stacey's outside. "Oh, I missed you so much."

Nicole dismounted and ran up the stairs.

What the hell? "Shit." I needed another cold shower. Or something. I gave a long-drawn sigh and sat up, rubbing my aching shoulder. The stairs seemed so inviting, but I reined myself in. I had to wait a minute before heading for the front door. *Are blue balls a real thing? I'll google it later.*

Stacey and my father stood in a tight embrace as I stepped outside.

"I tried to visit once or twice," dad said, stroking her hair. "But you were never home."

"I've been so busy."

She lied as if a sign hung around her neck. Her eyes told the truth. She stepped back, folding her arms.

"But you resigned." He frowned. His eyes were soft, filled with love – something I'd never experienced. His angel, his only child, was home.

"That's just it, Daddy. I'm a little housewifey now. I must go to the shops, pay bills." She always turned into a little girl around my father. She was home; she didn't want you to see her bruises.

He pulled her closer and draped his arm around her. "It's so good to have you here." They walked past me into the house. I felt like Patrick Swayze in Ghost. How could my father be so relaxed? Was his life really in danger? He had the most to lose with Bolton talking. Was it he who organized the hit? I glanced at the two guards roaming the grounds. *Why did the extra guards only arrive today?* A man with his money could have a hundred of them within an hour if he wanted the protection. Was he fabricating the hit on his life to emphasize his false innocence?

I glanced around, searching for Stewart. *Where the hell are you?* Maybe a lion ate him. *No, that's ridiculous; Christmas only comes once a year.*

"Better late than never, but are they needed?" I whispered as the Goodman security van approached the gate.

9

"There is no hillside without a grave."
Zulu proverb

16:20

"Why don't we just shoot the guards and drive through; they can't call for help," Byron highlighted his lack of tactical skill as the bus approached the gate.

"Because Greg is in the open." Mamba applied the handbrake. "Craig can take him out before we strike."

Byron snorted. "I can't believe you are so afraid of him."

"I'm not afraid of him," he snapped. "Know your enemy's weaknesses but be aware of their strengths."

"That's very nice, but why is he still standing."

"Because Cobra is waiting for my order."

"Okay," Byron drawled. "What are you waiting for?"

Mamba kept his gaze on the man he'd known for years. He loved him as a brother. A little brother.

"Think of your wife and kids. You want them to visit you in jail for the rest of your life? Don't you want the best for them? Schools, toys, holidays–"

"Stop patronizing me. I know what I have to do." He shook his head and pressed the button on the transmitter dangling under his neck.

"You have a go." He glanced at the ridge where Craig waited for the order.

"The guard is approaching," a passenger said. "Do I take him out?"

"Not until Meerkat is down." Mamba pulled down his Orlando Pirates cap.

"What's he waiting for?" Byron muttered as Bongani knocked on the window. "Ask him!"

"Not now. I'll distract him."

* * *

"Affirmative." Cobra trained the crosshair on Greg's temple. "Sorry, Greg." His finger tightened around the trigger. He took one last breath, exhaled, and squeezed.

His finger froze as warm steel pressed against his temple.

"You forgot one of the first rules I taught you, always be aware of your surroundings. You concentrated so much on your target that an elephant could've stepped on you. I saw the reflection of your scope – very sloppy."

"Lieutenant Van Rooyen," Craig whispered, shocked.

"Who's the target?" Van Rooyen nudged Craig with his 9mm.

"Everyone."

"Even me?" he snapped.

"Everyone on the farm, so, yes, sir."

"I take it my entire team is on the bus?"

"Most of them, Lieutenant."

"Give me your transmitter."

Craig removed his earpiece with a trembling hand and passed it to Van Rooyen. He shoved it into his ear. "This is Lieutenant Van Rooyen. Whom do I have the pleasure of speaking to?"

No response.

"You better talk to me. The rifle is not pointing at Greg anymore... if you know what I mean."

"So, how are we going to play this, Lieutenant?"

He heard the familiar tone in his ear. "My goodness." Van Rooyen chuckled. "I'm surprised to hear your voice."

"I'm surprised to hear yours."

"Let's deal then," Van Rooyen said, kneeling next to Craig.

"I'm listening."

"I want in." Van Rooyen wrenched the rifle from Craig's hands. "In my position, I can open a lot more doors." He tucked his 9mm into the back of his pants and mounted the sniper. Craig groaned as Van Rooyen made himself comfortable. "I can make any operation seem legitimate."

He aimed the rifle at the bus. "Who's the white man next to you?"

"Byron Wolf, our rainmaker."

"Well, you've got thirty seconds to convince him before all hell breaks loose. I can see the guard at your window getting agitated, and little Greg is getting suspicious. And, oops, the other three guards are also approaching."

Van Rooyen listened as the voice in his ear frantically explained the situation to Byron. Twenty-five seconds later, Byron gave a nodding smile.

"I see he's in agreement."

Seconds later, Byron gave him the thumbs up.

"Good, now tell Corporal Davis here that I'm part of the team." Van Rooyen pushed the earpiece into Craig's ear.

"I copy that, sir." He gave a few nods. "Yes, sir."

"What?" Van Rooyen asked.

"They want to witness your commitment, Lieutenant. You must take out Meerkat."

Van Rooyen grinned. "That'll be my pleasure." He dismounted Craig and took up a position next to him. "And I was so not looking forward to this holiday. Turns out to be my best Christmas present ever."

*   *   *

What's wrong, Bongani? He knocked for the second time on the driver's window. I strolled toward the gate about a hundred metres away. *Who's the guy with the cowboy hat?* Both the driver and passenger wore hats; both kept their chins down.

But then the passenger glanced at the ridge, smiled, and gave a thumb-up.

Byron. Fuck! He had given someone the go-ahead to take me out, a sniper. *Craig. He must be on the ridge. Shit! He never misses.* They wanted me out of the way before blowing Bongani's brains out.

Fucking clever, Greg. They couldn't have caught me at a better time; dressed in swimming trunks, T-shirt, barefoot and 9mm in the cottage.

The house was three hundred metres away. *I'll never make it.* The bullet would hit me before I heard the pop, but I'd see the puff of smoke before the bullet hit its target. I'd have a second to react. As I turned to the ridge, I realized that all snipers used smokeless gun powder. I looked up at the heavens. *No, I dare not ask. Just a please?* "Please," I whispered.

"Bongani, run!" I shouted while keeping my eyes on the ridge. "Run! Call for help! Run!"

My body tensed – a wound-up spring; my heart swam in adrenalin. The tall yellow grass on the ridge rustled alive as a gust of wind swept in from the east. *Thank you.* Craig needed to adjust his aim; the slightest breeze at that distance could deviate the trajectory of the round two or three feet. I made an about-turn and ran for the treeline. *The shooter must be on the ridge, in a straight line above the farmhouse – that's where I would be.*

All hell broke loose to my right, screams, gunfire, more screams, more gunfire. I sidestepped to my left, into the wind, and could almost feel the graze of the bullet as it whisked past. The round slammed into the ground ten metres in front of me. Only then did I hear the faint pop.

Please, God, let it be Craig up there. I dared again because the arrogant sniper only loaded two rounds into his rifle – one for the head and one for the heart, to make sure. I zigzagged my way to the treeline, but unpredictable. Predictable equalled a bullet in the back.

The shooting to the right of me continued; the other three guards had joined the fight. I kept my eyes on the approaching treeline. A few angst swerves, and I would be out of the son-of-a-bitch's firing line.

I thought of Nicole as she appeared before me in her room. *The last thought, if my luck ran out, must be of her.*

* * *

Damnit!" Lieutenant Van Rooyen struggled to keep the crosshair on Greg.

"Aim at the opening in the treeline he's aiming for," Craig advised.

"Shit." Van Rooyen handed Craig the rifle. "You do it."

"Bloody hell, Lieutenant." Cobra positioned himself. He never thought he'd have the crosshair trained on Meerkat. He liked Greg – always in the mood for a party. But he also knew not to fuck with him on an off day. Greg was stubborn, unpredictable, and ruthless.

But he had no choice – life was good for him and his girlfriend; he'd bought a house in Fourways, a new Golf GTi, and gave the contractors the go-ahead to start work on his man-cave. No way this could fall apart.

Hitting a swerving target at this distance was impossible. A true meerkat. Craig aimed at the opening as he had recommended to Van

Rooyen, marking the spot – high and into the wind. He took a deep breath and squeezed the trigger. The rifle jolted.

His target made a rolling dive and disappeared into the woods.

"I think you got him," Van Rooyen whispered, peering. "Lucky son-of-a-gun."

"Luck had nothing to do with it, sir," Craig said, taking a deep breath.

Diving the last few strides prolonged my life a little longer – like playing Russian roulette with one bullet instead of two. The round slammed into a tree a few feet in front of me. They would want to make sure I'm out of the way before attacking the rest of my family. I hoped it gave my family time to call for help or to escape. I took a glimpse at the bus before continuing farther into the bush. Three guards lay beside it. Why didn't they run, get the hell out of there? They were outgunned – *Suicide*. Did they do it for my father? Who would willingly die for him? *Idiots*.

"I thought you said the guards would scatter like flies." Byron dusted glass from his hair and shoulders.

"Anyone hurt?" Mamba called from the front of the bus.

"Two dead. Smith and Plaaitjie. Three wounded, but not too serious." Sergeant Dube released Smith's wrist. The operative sat head slumped, glazed eyes pinned on his crotch.

"Headshot."

"Dammit." Mamba slammed the windscreen with his fist, leaving a crack. "This is going all wrong. How am I going to explain this?" He shook his head. "Okay, there's no time to waste. The element of surprise is over, and we might have Greg to deal with still. Open the gate from the guardhouse."

* * *

It took Nicole a good minute to realize the magnitude of the situation. She watched from her window as if viewing an episode of CSI. She held her breath as Greg swerved his way toward the trees.

Please, God, let him make it.

"No!" she cried, covering her mouth. *Did Greg dive, or was he hit?*

One by one, the guards fell until none were left. The gunfire ceased. She darted from her room and down the stairs where Henry, Jessica, and Stacey stood frozen, staring out the window.

"Call the police," Nicole said. "I-I think they'd shot Greg." Only when she heard her own words spoken did she realize how much she loved him. The sudden emptiness within made her dizzy – a black hole in the pit of her stomach devouring her being. The room spun. She stumbled to the nearest couch and fell onto it. She took deep breaths, fighting back a wave of nauseating heat.

"Stop it!" Henry snapped. "Not my Greg. He won't go down that easily." He glared at Nicole with lightning-brooding grey eyes, fists clenched. A towering defiant figure.

"My husband is right," Jessica echoed. "I know my son." She emphasized each word. "He is a survivor." Her fiery gaze settled on Henry. "Like my husband."

"Daddy, what are we going to do?" Stacey ran into Henry's arms.

"The lines are dead." Grandma entered the lounge clutching a twelve-gauge shotgun. "Where's Stewart and Greg?"

Veronica followed close behind, gripping a carving knife, hand trembling.

"I saw Greg outside." Nicole nudged aside the curtain. "I don't know where Steward is." She glanced at Henry.

They're right. Greg is as tough as a honey badger, a thick-skinned bastard, unyielding when he sets his mind on something. "We can leave through the back door." With renewed hope, Nicole leapt from the couch and ran toward the kitchen. "We need to find Greg before we go." She regretted so many things now.

"Nicole."

She stopped in her tracks at Henry's tone.

"What?" She turned, annoyed. In a different time, it would've been the perfect picture: A wealthy family – father, mother, daughter, and grandmother – but today it was an obstacle to freedom. They wouldn't last five minutes out there with those trained assassins behind them, even with Greg.

"It'll be dark soon. They'll track us down like pigs and kill us one by one. They have night vision," Henry echoed her thoughts.

Drew stormed down the stairs clutching her suitcase. "We need to get going. The gate is opening. Let's take one of the 4x4s and get the hell out of here." She ran for the front door.

"It's too late. The cars are all parked in front!" Henry grabbed her by the arm. "It'll be suicide."

"We will die if we stay." She pulled free and headed for the kitchen. "Who's with me?" she asked, almost begging. "Come on, Nicole, we can make it – call for help."

Nicole shook her head. "I can't leave." She glanced at the front door. *I can't leave without Greg.*

"She's right," Grandma said. "They don't know Nicole and Drew are here. They want the Goodmans. They won't waste time looking for them." She turned to Veronica. "You must go with them, my dear."

The old help shook her head, tears welling up. "Haikona, I won't leave you here. I'm not a coward."

"Gogo is right, Veronica." Henry placed his hands on her bony shoulders. "You're the only one who knows the farm. You can get them to safety. Please."

"Why is this happening?" She wiped her tears with the point of her headscarf.

"Go now, please," Henry whispered and hugged her.

"I'm not going." Nicole raised her chin.

"I'll go with you." Stacey looked at her father with begging eyes.

Henry frowned, taken aback. "I'm sorry, Stacey, but then they will look for you. Drew, Nicole and Veronica will have no chance of escape if you do."

Stacey gasped. "So, you want them to kill me? All this is your fault!"

"I'll take her place," Nicole snapped, peering through the window. "If it comes to that, I'll pretend to be your daughter. You need to leave now. They're halfway up the driveway already."

"Go get help, my baby," Jessica cried and hugged her daughter. "Go!" She pushed Stacey through the door. Drew and Veronica followed, glancing over their shoulders with tear-filled eyes.

"Mr. Goodman." Nicole grabbed his arm. "Henry!"

He blinked back to reality and glanced at Nicole.

"We need weapons and a place to hide. Somewhere we can defend ourselves."

"That's the spirit." Grandma cocked the shotgun. "Now I know why I like you so much. Those bastards think they can walk in here. Fuck them."

"Jessica," Henry whispered. "You with me?"

His wife wiped her mascara-stained cheeks and approached him. "They'll kill us all." She wrapped her arms around him. "This is all my fault."

"We need to go." Henry jumped into action, grabbed Jessica's arm and ran down the corridor leading to his study. Nicole and Grandma followed.

"Park it," Mamba ordered, standing behind the driver's seat.

The Goodman security bus came to a halt halfway up the driveway.

He glanced at his watch – 15:12 – then at the unrelenting sun.

"We're behind schedule." He wiped his brow and nape with a handkerchief. "Kit up!"

Twelve of the sixteen occupants checked their automatic assault rifles and exited one by one.

"The three wounded stay with the bus. Make sure nobody leaves." Mamba placed a hand on Sergeant Dube's chest, stopping him before he exited. "Take three" – he glancing at the treeline to his left – "no, four men and search for Meerkat. The rest of us will take the house."

"You want him dead or alive?" Dube asked, fastening his bulletproof vest.

"I don't think you'll have a choice, Sergeant."

"What about the Zimbabweans?" Byron asked.

"Leave them on the bus. We will deal with them later."

"I think it was a waste of time bringing them along," Byron muttered. "Your plan's not going as expected."

"Nothing has changed," Mamba snapped. "We can still make this work."

He glared down at Sergeant Dube. "What are you waiting for?"

"Mike, Martins, Lebaka, Lebo, you're with me," Dube called out and ran toward the grove Greg had dived into.

"The rest of you, follow me." Mamba exited the bus. "Watch your sixes."

* * *

I burst into the cottage and retrieved my 9mm in the bathroom. *Byron Wolf! Unfucking believable! Well, the wedding is off.* I wanted to be with Nicole, protect her, but I had to split them up, divide and conquer. I could handle three or four at a time, but these men were as good as me. Even one-on-one could be a problem.

I slipped into my running shoes, and on my way out, emptied the last bit of Jack. *I'll stop after this if I'm still alive. Promise.* I froze at the memory boiling from the pit – I was on my stomach, someone on my back forced my head upward. The blade reflected a streetlight. I wanted to scream. *Breathe. Hold still.* I touched my scar as I remembered the knife slicing flesh, blood spatter on asphalt. *This is for...* I keeled over and vomited in the doorway. How could I forget such fear? *Fuck!* I took deep breaths.

"Not now," I whispered, then vomited the last chunks of Grandma's food. Wiping my mouth, I straightened – took another deep breath. "This is for what?" I whispered.

I approached around the left of the house, hoping they'd also approach from that side. How did Byron convince members of my team to go rogue? *After everything, we went through.* I climbed into a tree and made myself comfortable on a branch about three metres off the ground. No amount of money would turn me. Through the branches and leaves, I counted eight men.

If I had been sure about the hit – of my father's innocence – I would have brought along Manana. We could've handled them. Just like we dealt with those drug dealers in Hillbrow – the operation where everything that could go wrong did. From then on, we coined the phrase: This operation was about to go Hillbrow.

My team had received a tip-off about a drug manufacturing plant and had to go in hard. In the raid, the factory caught fire. I was in an office in the centre of the building, trapped. My comms system was faulty. I could only receive. I heard Modise and Van Rooyen call off the search for me; they thought there was no way I could still be alive – assholes. I kept to the floor, hiding from the smoke. It filled the room like a fast-descending elevator.

I took my last breath and held it until my lungs were about to implode. Then, as I filled my lungs with the toxic air, I heard him call my name. He sounded more terrified than me because he couldn't find me. I screamed his name with the suffocating smoke bellowing out my mouth. It only took him ten excruciating seconds to break through a wall. He tossed me over his shoulder as if I were one of his little girls and covered us in a wet blanket he brought. I protested, yelling at him that I could get out myself, but he kept going, running through the flames as if nothing – as if it was the source that gave him his strength. That was the smallest I'd ever felt, but also the most loved.

In the back of my mind, I hoped he'd be here at the last minute, just like that day, and this time I would not protest.

"Where are you, Stewart?" I whispered, hoping he'd joined my father in the house. We hated each other's guts, but now we had to act like we were family. I hoped that blood would run thicker than water - -=this time.

Five men broke away from the group. I checked my 9mm, fifteen rounds – that was it. *Make it count, Greg.* I cocked it and waited. A colony of termites gnawed at my stomach. I took a deep breath, trying to steady my hand and calm my nerves.

This wasn't like any other operation. If I messed this up, my whole dysfunctional family and the only woman I'd ever loved would be dead. As I waited, a big, black, hairy spider sauntered over my hand. Every one of its eight legs triggered an explosion of goose pimples. I shook it off and almost lost my footing. Usually, I'd have leapt out of the tree and run like Forrest Gump. I heard the impact when it landed on the ground. *Fuck, I hate the bush. Especially this December heat.* I wiped my face with the front of my wet T-shirt. Another shudder rippled through my body. I could still feel the ghostly cold body on my hand.

The first of five men appeared through the trees. Dube, you son of a bitch.

We'd always had each other's back. I'd saved his life twice. I had dinner with him, his wife and two daughters a week ago. The image of him sitting on the couch with his two girls dressed in their pink pyjamas and bunny slippers popped into my head. He was so proud; his big chest seemed double the size, and when he spoke to them, always softly, they stared at him with such love and admiration.

I remembered how Patience, his wife, stared at me, almost pitying me. The perfect family, I wanted that. And here I was, aiming my weapon at him, about to destroy that picture. *This isn't right.* I felt like the villain, the one who would break into your house and kill you while sleeping next to your loving wife. It was easy for Byron to convince my team to turn against my father. I was about to destroy ten or twelve perfect pictures because of one screwed-up family – mine.

I couldn't pull the trigger; he had to make that decision. *Maybe when he sees me, he'd reconsider.*

Dube approached, every step calculated, as trained. I raised my weapon and aimed. The other four would have spread out, appeared to the left and right of him, in a V-shape – like ducks in flight.

He scanned the area from right to left before his eyes crept up my tree. Dube froze as our eyes met.

A heartbeat passed; it felt like minutes. "You gonna shoot me?"

"That depends on you."

"Why did you come here? You could've just stayed away, become part of our team."

I shrugged. "It's my family, and you know me. Can't stay away from a good fight."

"You hate your family."

He was playing for time. "It's still my family."

"You know you're not going to win."

"Maybe, but at least I'll go with a clear conscience."

"I'm doing this for my family."

His teammates were getting close, their boots crushing twigs and leaves – Dube heard it too.

"That's why you're still breathing," I said. "You sure about this? We can make a deal."

Our time ran out; two of the four appeared to the left and right of Dube. I didn't fire; I wanted them to decide. The other two made their way around – as trained.

If I took my eyes off Dube, he'd make his move. So, I did; I glanced at Lebaka to his left. All three raised their weapon as one and fired. *Decision made.*

I jumped down the back of the tree; the recoil of their weapons would make it almost impossible for them to hit me. On my way down, I fired three shots, shattering three families' lives. Two went down at once, headshots. Dube went down slower; I hit him in the throat. He kept his eyes on me, blood squirting through his fingers. The father of two gargled, coughed blood, and fell backward.

The remaining two opened fire to either side of me, splitting my tree in half. I jumped and rolled into the nearby bushes and made a run for the cottage.

* * *

"Help me move this against the door" Henry grabbed hold of the mahogany desk. Nicole hesitated a moment before grabbing the other side. It screeched toward the door.

"They're in the room down the hall!" someone shouted.

"Come on." Henry groaned with clenched teeth. The desk inched closer.

"Push, dammit," Grandma said, aiming the shotgun at the door.

Heavy footsteps thundered closer. A loud thump gave them the surge of adrenalin they needed. The desk gained momentum.

"Shoot the lock," someone yelled on the other side of the door.

"Oh, no, you don't." Grandma aimed and fired. The buckshot blew a hole the size of a rugby ball in the centre of the door.

"My fokken arm!" Someone yelled in Afrikaans.

"Okay" – Henry heaved the table – "get away from the door."

A sinister silence followed as the four occupants stared at the closed entry.

* * *

I darted to my left as bullets ripped into a tree to my right. The rounds followed me as I dived over an anthill, but it offered no protection. The two-foot-high clay heap exploded behind me. I turned and fired two shots into the bushes. It slowed my pursuers, giving me the split-second I needed to reach the cottage. I slammed the door shut, pushed a couch against it, and hid behind the nook where my father and I'd sat this morning. *My father.* For the first time in my life, I depended on him, on his stubbornness, his will, his short fuse, his cunningness. *I hope he can keep them at bay until I'm done here.* Henry Goodman was many things, but he was no coward. He was the only reason I even considered running away from the house.

A shadow moved past the window next to the door, then another...and another? I aimed but hesitated; something was wrong.

The doorknob rattled.

"Greg, it's me, Stacey. Please open!"

I jumped up, tucked the weapon into the back of my jeans, pushed the couch to the side and unlocked the door. Drew, Stacey, and Veronica scurried inside, glancing over their shoulders.

"I thought you were in the house." I scanned outside.

"We thought we could make a run for it, but the gate was locked, and we didn't have a card." Stacey wrapped her arms around me. "I'm so glad we found you."

"Wait in the bathroom," I ordered.

The three women scurried away and closed the bathroom door behind them. I turned to close the front door but stared down the barrel of a gun.

"Hello, Greg." Corporal Lebo smirked.

I stood my ground, smiling. "What brings you here?"

"An annoying tick that just won't die."

Sergeant Mike Salts appeared in the doorway. What a contrast. Not the obvious, but Lebo and Mike were as different as – I wouldn't say salt and pepper, but they were as diverse as a tissue before and after you blow your nose.

Lebo was the before tissue, neat as a pin, his clothes ironed with starch, his shaven black dome always glistening, and he smelt...flourishing. Mike was the after tissue, sloppy, stuck in the Seventies with long, wild, bushy sideburns connected to an unruly moustache. He smelled like a worn-out bicycle seat and always scratched some rash somewhere private. The only problem, they were good at what they did.

"You forgot to wipe your arse, Lebo," I said and glanced over his shoulder at Salts.

"Fuck you, hobbit," Mike muttered, scratching his chest.

"What are you waiting for?" I slowly reached for my weapon in the back of my jeans. "Difficult when you know the man you're about to kill."

"I don't know. How did it feel to kill Dube, Lebaka and Martins." Lebo prodded me with the rifle.

"I gave them a choice."

"Unfortunately, I can't give you that choice."

"Fortunately, I can still give you that choice."

The two of them chuckled, but only for a second, then Lebo snapped, "Drop your weapon." He stepped back, pointing his rifle at my chest, his trigger finger taut. "If I don't hear it hit the floor in three, you're dead."

I slowly turned around and clasped the 9mm between my thumb and index finger.

"Careful."

I eased the weapon out and dropped it to the floor."

"Nice moves out there, but this bullet you won't be able to dodge." Lebo curled his finger tighter. "Any last words."

"At least nobody turned me." My miserable life flashed before my eyes and paused on Nicole.

"Wait," Mike barked from the doorway. "Shooting him is too easy. Too quick." He strolled in, scratching his behind. "Martins was my best friend. This piece of shit needs to suffer."

Mike glanced at the bathroom door. "Is that where you're hiding the three sluts?" He smiled, his stained teeth underlining his foul moustache. "I'll bet you one of them's his sister."

"You, in the bathroom," he yelled. "Come out, or I'm gonna shoot your little brother."

"I'm the eldest."

"You know what he means," Lebo muttered.

"I'm gonna count to three," Mike yelled. "One...two—"

A trembling voice on the other side of the door interrupted the count. "Okay."

"Lebo, please," I begged in a whisper. "This isn't right. Let them go. You want my father and me."

Lebo showed no emotion, keeping his eyes and rifle on me.

I looked over my shoulder at the door opening.

"Everyone. That's the order," Lebo said in a chilling whisper.

I glanced at my feet.

"Don't even think about it." He kicked my weapon across the floor.

Drew, Stacey, and Veronica crept out of the bathroom like frightened kittens, holding hands, glancing around the room.

"Afternoon, ladies." Mike scratched his groin. "Our orders were to make it sloppy. Make it look like a farm murder." He turned to me, beaming. "I can think of a couple of things to do."

I leapt toward him, but it felt as if the roof came down on my head. My legs gave way, and I fell on my stomach, fighting to stay conscious.

"Don't do this," I groaned, rolling on my back, holding my head.

Lebo stood over me as I forced my eyes open. He was ready to crush my skull with the butt of his rifle. My shoulders and back warmed as blood seeped from my head.

"Don't kill him yet," Mike smirked. "I want him to see this."

A sharp pain shot through my body as I tilted my head to the right. Stacey trembled as if she stood in a blizzard.

Drew stood with her fists and lips clenched, eyes filled with rage. Veronica had a blank look, no anger or fear as if she had switched off.

"Get on your knees," Mike ordered.

They stood, unresponsive.

"Now!" He fired a shot into the wooden floor beside Drew.

Stacey screamed and fell to the floor, weeping.

"Not you, Gogo," Lebo said as Veronica aimed for the floor. "Go stand in the corner."

"Yes, go," Mike barked.

Veronica looked at Lebo with pleading eyes and said something to him in Sotho.

"Go," he snapped.

She kept her eyes on the two girls as she shuffled away.

"What are you waiting for?" Mike seethed as Drew stood in defiance.

The blood squished beneath my head as I turned back to Lebo. He still stood over me, feet planted by my shoulders. He'd flipped his rifle around, aiming it at my head.

"My father is a rich man, Lebo," I whispered. "I'll give you two million if you shoot Mike and help me free my family."

For the first few seconds, I thought I had him, but then he frowned and burst out laughing.

"It's too late for that. Besides, I can't wait to see your family go down. You think you can fix everything with money. Your family raped our land." He grinned, eyes filled with hatred. "And now it's time for payback."

My eyes stung as tears of anger welled up. My body felt numb and cold. I grabbed at his legs, but again he expected my rage. A bomb exploded within my head as his rifle slammed into my face. Each blow was blinding agony, a searing white flash, inescapable. Until, thank God, an invisible force yanked me away from the light and tossed me into a painless black pit.

* * *

Nicole froze as Grandma walked closer to the gaping hole, smoke still flowing from the shotgun barrel.

"Mom," Henry whispered. "Get away from the–"

Wood fragments and books exploded through the room as bullets riddled the door. Nicole and Jessica scrambled into the corner, away from the firing line. Henry ran to his mother's aid as she fell on her back, clutching the shotgun, chin trembling and eyes searching.

Henry fired six shots over the desk, silencing the carnage.

"Mom!" He lifted her head onto his knee. "I'm sorry." He wiped a strand of silvery hair from her face.

She smiled as her eyes settled on him. "Don't cry for me, Henry," she whispered, her breathing shallow. "I had a wonderful life." She raised a trembling hand and grabbed hold of her son's arm. "Promise me before I go."

"Anything, what?" He whispered.

"Accept Greg as your son." She closed her fading eyes, squeezing out a tear. "Stop being such a dick with him."

He took a deep breath as he fought back the tears. "He is my son, Mom. I had a paternity test done."

She frowned. "You stupid idiot, it was never about that. Greg is your son. God gave him for you to look after. It wasn't his fault."

Henry nodded.

Her eyes broke away from him and settled on the corner of the room. "He's here," she smiled.

Henry frowned, staring at the corner. "Who?"

"I told you He was real." Her hand released its grip and fell to the floor. "Beautiful," she whispered, exhaling her last breath. Her eyes flickered shut.

"I know, Mother," he whispered and kissed her on the cheek. "I know."

He fell back into a seated position, head buried in his hands. Another volley ripped through the door, peeling plaster from the wall.

"Please get away from the door, honey, please, we need you – I need you," Jessica cried.

His trembling hand took hold of the shotgun, and he pulled it from his mother's hands. "I'm coming," he whispered, and the leopard crawled toward them.

Jessica wrapped her arms around him. "I'm sorry." She sobbed.

"No, I'm sorry."

The day of the Goodman reckoning, and I'm caught in the middle. Nicole stared at the shotgun. She'd to come to the farm to find out if Greg loved her. She had fallen in love with him all over again. *But will he forgive me for everything?* She had forgiven him.

Nicole glanced at Henry – *got to accept the entire package. But, how can I? Can I live without Greg? No. Simple – forgive. Let God judge them. As He will judge me.*

Nicole grabbed the shotgun from Henry's hands. "Are there more bullets for this thing?"

He shook his head. "In the kitchen."

"What!" Nicole shouted as a gunshot dwarfed his response.

"In the kitchen!"

"And for your gun?"

He nodded and pointed to the riddled bookshelf opposite the door. "In the safe."

"What's the combination?"

"No." He sighed. "I'll get it."

"You need a moment." She forced sympathy into her tone. "What's the combination?"

"I had my time," he said and stroked his wife's arms. "Greg will never forgive me if something should happen to you." He stood up. "If something should happen to me, it's an electronic safe. The code is nineteen, forty-one, zero, two."

"Mom's birthday," Jessica whispered, staring at the lifeless body.

A beeping sound interrupted the moment; Nicole was already at the safe, punching in the code. She glanced at the door with every key she pressed.

"Nicole, dammit." Henry ran toward her.

Bullets tore through the door as he slammed into her, knocking her off her feet.

"I told you, Greg will kill me if you die before me," he whispered, laying on top of her.

"Thank you, Mr. Goodman." She groaned.

"I think in the position we found ourselves in, you can call me Henry."

"I didn't know you had a sense of humour." She rolled on her stomach as he shifted off her.

"Facing death brings out the worst in people."

The attack continued as they crawled back amongst the falling debris, shredded paper, and wood fragments.

"Damn it," Henry said under his breath, sitting up with his back against the wall. Jessica and Nicole followed.

Henry removed his pistol's magazine. "All out." He looked at the safe.

"Henry Goodman," a man called from the other side. "We only want you and the evidence. Come out, and we'll spare the others."

Nicole stared at the Goodmans; Henry and Jessica glanced at each other as they recognized the voice.

Shit.

Henry frowned, studying Nicole for a moment.

"I almost married him," she said and rested her head against the wall.

"I think it's time to break off the engagement." Jessica took Nicole's hand.

"So, what'll it be, Henry," Byron called.

"It's over between us, Byron," Nicole shouted. "I found out you blocked all e-mails and messages from Greg on all my devices. You even paid the guard. And you did it before you even asked me out. Greg tried to contact me two weeks after... after he– "

"Ran away like the chicken shit he is." Byron sneered.

"Five months I tried to figure out why the hell he left me! You knew what I went through before. How much that hurt me! How it influenced my...decisions?"

"Why didn't you just call him?" Henry said.

"That's not how it works," Nicole snapped.

"Okay, Nicky," Byron said. "I apologize. However, you and I go back much further than that. I know you must keep up the pretences because you're locked up in there with them. Your secrets are safe with me. I'll play along because I love you. We'll discuss things later."

Nicole shook her head and whispered, "He's crazy."

"We are getting side-tracked here!" Another man hollered.

"What if we give you all the evidence and you go away," Henry asked.

"You're a businessman, Henry. You know that's not how it works. Somebody needs to pay," Byron said.

"What guarantees do I have that you will let the others go?"

"Henry, no," Jessica whispered, grabbing him by the arm. "You know he's lying."

"There are no guarantees in life, Henry, but what other alternative is there? If you don't come out, we will blow the door and kill everyone inside."

"Okay, I'll come out with the evidence, but I need to get into the safe first."

"Henry, no," Jessica repeated, still holding on.

"It's okay." He tapped her hand. "They're not getting me that easily."

"Okay, we've got a deal," Byron called.

"It'll be fine, you'll see." Henry embraced his wife and kissed her on the lips. "Do you know how to handle this?" He handed Nicole his pistol.

She nodded. "I went out with Greg, remember."

"Good – be ready." Henry wrenched himself away from Jessica and stood up. He took a deep breath and walked toward the safe.

Nicole also stood up and removed the magazine. Waiting. Her heart pounded in her throat.

Henry turned his back on the door as he reached the safe. Again, he took a deep breath and punched in the keys. He closed his eyes for a moment, and then with one swift motion, pulled the safe open and grabbed the box of 9mm rounds.

The door behind him exploded, catapulting the desk and debris across the room. The explosion flung Henry against the bookshelf. He held on to the safe door and tossed Nicole the box.

Jessica screamed. She ran to her husband, catching him as he fell to the floor.

Nicole tore the box apart and started loading the magazine with shaking hands. She managed two rounds before she heard the approaching footsteps. *Where are you, Greg!* She inserted the magazine, cocked the pistol, and aimed. *I'm about to kill someone.* The weapon weighed a ton, becoming heavier and heavier as the footsteps approached. What if the first person is Byron? Her gaze was drawn to Grandma, her apron now drenched in blood. Nicole's hand steadied, she aimed high. She breathed, just how Greg had taught her. Jessica screamed.

It was like a reflex as the first man appeared. Without thought, she fired. Blood sprayed the wall as the bullet hit him in the head. The man collapsed without a sound, hitting the floor face down. She returned her aim to the door and fired as the next man made his appearance. The bullet struck him in the ribs, knocking him against the wall. He turned toward Nicole, shocked, left hand clutching his right side. Blood spurted from his mouth as he coughed. He wiped his mouth with the back of his hand and stared at the blood. His legs buckled, and he slid down the wall.

"I'm sorry," Nicole whispered as he kept his eyes on her.

The third man dived and rolled into the study and fired at Nicole. She went down, screaming, and covered her head as bullets slammed into the wall behind her.

"Stop firing," a thundering voice commanded.

The automatic rifle fire ceased.

"Get her weapon," the same voice commanded.

Her attacker rushed over and grabbed the weapon from her hands.

Byron walked in, glaring at the two men, then at Nicole. "What the fuck, Nicky," he snapped. "Were you serious?" He threw his hands in the air. "Really?"

"Take your bitch and get the hell out of here before I shoot her myself," Manana seethed.

Byron pulled her up by the arm. "Can't believe Chicken Little turned you. What is it with you and that guy?" He licked her cheek and whispered, "You will regret this."

Nicole locked eyes with Jessica. "Please tell Greg I love him."

10

"Rain beats a leopard's skin, but it doesn't wash out the spots."
Zulu proverb

I woke up in the cottage, lying in blood, tasting it in my mouth. It took me a moment to recollect. Then came the screams. I turned my head and what I saw...My mind instructed my body to move, but it couldn't. With every scream, life returned, fuelled by rage. My extremities stirred alive with excruciating intensity.

Lebo stood over my sister's battered body, laughing. He raised his boot and brought it down on her stomach. She let out a bloodcurdling scream and rolled into the fetal position. Her bloodshot eyes had focused on me but closed in pain as Lebo gave her another kick.

"Please," she begged, reaching out to him.

"You had enough, bitch?"

Drew's pleading cries muffled behind the closed bedroom door.

Then I felt it, the cold steel slipping in under my hand. I gathered strength and raised my head. Veronica crouched by my feet, shivering, tears streaming down her face. She closed my hand over the weapon. My fingers curled around the grip, tighter and tighter. A surge of power ran up my arm and through my body. She pulled me by the arm, helping me to sit. My head weighed a ton, throbbing as if someone beat it with a hammer. I spat blood as Veronica helped me to my feet.

Lebo straddled my sister, hands wrapped around her neck, teeth clenched. She clawed at his face, mouth gaping, searching for air.

I raised my hand and aimed at his head. Stacey looked at me. I'd never forgotten her expression as long as I breathed.

"Lebo." I waited for him to raise his head. He stopped, panting, and looked up at me. The madness in his eyes vanished. He opened his mouth to say something.

"Close your eyes, Stacey." I pulled the trigger.

She didn't. She watched as the side of Lebo's head exploded. Perhaps it was something she needed to see. He fell back on top of her, his legs twitching.

I reached for his arm to throw him off, but Veronica intervened.

"I will help her, Ntate," she whispered. "Help nonnie." She pointed to the closed door.

I moved slowly, painfully, my arms hanging limp. It was as if the real me stood in a corner and instructed my body what to do, like a zombie, detached. I preferred it that way, distancing myself from what had happened.

The pleading cries behind the door had stopped. I didn't know when. "I take it you're finished," Mike yelled from within the bedroom. "I'm almost done here."

I turned the doorknob and pushed open the door. My soul returned and filled me with anguish. A gut-wrenching scene. Drew lay spread out on the bed, cut open from her chest to her stomach. Blood covered the walls and bed – smeared by a sadistic hand. Mike stood at the end of the bed, naked, clutching a knife and covered in blood, admiring his handiwork. He turned to me, smiling, thinking I was Lebo. The smile dropped from his face.

I aimed.

He raised his arms in reflex, covering his face, thinking I would shoot high. He was wrong – that would be too quick.

I fired. The first two rounds shattered his kneecaps. He fell with half his body on the bed, clutching the blood-drenched duvet, afraid his knees might touch the floor. I took careful aim at his dangling private parts and squeezed off another round. Mike fell to the floor, his knees not his primary concern anymore. He looked at me, his eyes owl-wide before he started howling, crawling away from me.

I fired another two shots, one for each arm.

"Stop, please," he screamed and turned on his back. He tried to raise his arms, but it was no use; they dangled at his sides. I picked up his knife and knelt beside him.

"I heard Drew scream those same words," I said in a calm tone and buried the blade in his stomach.

I held him down and silenced his screams by placing my knee on his throat. Again, these hands weren't mine, as if someone else commanded my body. It was a sharp knife; cut through him as if a lump of fudge. Was this the righteous path? *Maybe... I don't know.*

I draped a sheet over Drew and picked up Mike's rifle and a bulletproof vest from the floor. Veronica sat holding Stacey when I stepped out of the room.

"Don't go in there," I ordered and closed the door. There was no time for comfort. *I'll leave it to Veronica.* Nicole and my parents were my next priority. I placed my hands on my sister's shaking shoulders. "Stay here. I'll be back."

Stacey looked at me with drained eyes; she wanted to say something but decided against it – too tired to offer any resistance. I was glad because I was equally tired. Before leaving the house, I reloaded my pistol and removed Lebo's magazine from his rifle. My movements were sluggish; every step ignited excruciating pain.

* * *

Craig Davis sat, legs crossed, tossing stones over the edge of the cliff. Van Rooyen lay on his stomach, peering through the scope, searching for any movement below. Craig paused after a throw. "I can't believe you're so relaxed."

"What do you mean?"

"I mean, your wife. She's probably dead by now."

Van Rooyen glanced at Craig with a pensive frown before returning to the scope. "Married her for the money," he murmured. "Which never came. At least I'll get some insurance money now."

Craig shook his head, tossed another stone. "You're one heartless son-of-a-bitch."

Van Rooyen glared at him. "One heartless son-of-a-bitch, Lieutenant."

"I'm sorry, Lieutenant."

"There's something wrong," he said, peering. "It's taking too long. Here..." He handed Craig the sniper rifle. "I'm going down there." He stood up and dusted himself off. "If anyone but our team sticks his head out, you know what to do."

Craig grinned and took Van Rooyen's position. "Affirmative, Lieutenant."

* * *

I walked around the right of the house, aware of the sniper on the hill. The trees would shield me, and I wanted to enter via the kitchen door. The image of Drew flashed through my mind once more. I leaned against a tree with one hand, closing my eyes, taking deep breaths. There was no time for it, I knew, but I was going to pass out or vomit. I'd seen some horrible things in my life; however, those victims never spoke to me, never looked me in the eyes. It was just another case, another body bag. That's how I handled it. I never thought about their life before it was taken from them. Survival instinct, I guess; otherwise, I would've been in an asylum by now. *Is this the tipping point for me? Have I seen too much?*

Pull yourself together, Greg!

The tears flowed. I wrapped my arms around a thorn tree as my legs gave way. *Shit! Not now!* My body refused to carry on. I let go of my anchor and fell to the ground, focusing on the shades of orange beyond the branches. A gentle breeze rustled the leaves and eased my aching body. The enthusiastic chatter of the birds signalled their settling for the coming night, oblivious to the circumstances below them.

"Okay," I whispered and took a few deep settling breaths before sitting up. *Nicole and my family need me. No time for a breakdown, or a panic attack or whatever happened a moment ago.* I struggled to my feet and took another deep breath. My heart thumped like a diesel engine in my chest, my body clammy with sweat.

The always-bustling kitchen lay quiet. Grandma's vetkoek sat in a dish on the table. The aroma angered me even more. Voices carried through the house. I peeked into the lounge. No one. Cries came from my father's study. Bullets riddled the corridor walls, and the section of the study in view was destroyed.

At first, I only noticed two bodies of my team amongst the debris, but then I saw Grandma's green slippers and legs protruding from the mangled desk. I froze and leaned against the wall with clenched fists. *Keep it together.* I wanted to scream, break down the wall, but I kept the rage inside; it would help me continue. The familiar smell of sulphur filled the house.

I kept to the wall as I approached the study, rifle ready. My hands shook, and my sight blurred. *I'm too late.* The thought repeated over and over in my head. I grew faint and nauseous. Blood still trickled down my back and legs, soaking my running shoes. It made a squishy sound as I walked. I stopped halfway down the corridor and removed them. *Just a little while longer.*

Pausing by the door, I listened.

"We need to get him to a hospital, please," I heard my mother plead. "I'll pay you double what Byron is paying you."

Then whatever I had left in me died as the man replied.

"It's too late for that, Mrs. Goodman," Manana said in his soft, calm tone. "I can shoot you in the face, or you can turn around. I promise you won't feel a thing."

How could I have been so stupid? I don't know if it was anger or losing Grandma or losing my best friend or losing my faith in humanity, but I cried once more. If they could turn Manana...

I stepped out of my pool of blood and into Grandma's with my bare feet. Her blood was warm.

Manana and another of my team stood over my parents; Mom held my father in her arms, glaring up at them, her designer suit drenched by his blood. My father was still breathing, but every breath laboured. His pale complexion stressed his gaunt features even more. My heart pounded in my throat. *Where's Nicole?*

"I'll pay you triple, "Mom said, stroking my father's hair, unaware of my presence.

"Okay," he smiled. "The face it will be."

"How do you want it?" I peered through the scope of the automatic rifle.

My mother gasped.

Musi swung around, weapon in hand. I shot him in the face. A pink substance splattered the books behind him.

His body landed beside my shocked mother.

Manana turned around but still had his weapon aimed at my mother's head.

We stared at each other in silence, not knowing what to say. I couldn't believe I had the crosshair trained on my best friend. Energy charged the room; any movement or noise could set off a chain of events that would be irreversible.

"You look like poop, Greg," Manana said with a raised brow.

"You can drop the fucking act, Manana. Murder is much worse than swearing."

"It's not murder when you do it for your country."

"What are you talking about? This is just to save your ass." I did not move an inch, not even flinch. How long could I hold this stance?

"Byron thinks so, and I'm making some money on the side, but what he doesn't know is that the order came from the top."

"From Modise?" I lowered the rifle.

He grinned. "Much higher than that, my friend. Your father is," he stared at the fading man, "was a very resourceful man, Greg. He sold weapons to rebel forces all over Africa, causing instability and genocide."

"Why not arrest him, take him to trial and throw him in jail?"

"Therein lies the problem. Your father couldn't accomplish his achievements without help. He was like cancer, infecting and infiltrating the government on so many levels."

"He was framed," I snapped. "Bolton was the kingpin."

Manana lowered his weapon. "Why do you think Bolton left Goodman enterprises? He couldn't live with himself anymore. He wanted out. He was the one who wrote the letter to the president. In the beginning, he included your father but later saw that he'd never receive immunity with your father on board."

"Then why kill him?"

"We didn't kill him." He looked at my mother. "Tell him, Jessica. Who killed Bolton?"

She glanced at my blood-soaked feet. "He's talking nonsense, Geegee. Look at what they did." She pointed to Grandma.

"She paid Thero and Eddie to retrieve the laptop that night."

I scratched the back of my head and almost fainted as I re-opened my wound. "I saw the van. You were there."

"We were following Thero. We knew he was working for somebody else."

"Mom?"

She kept silent, stroking my father's head, dazed.

"Mom!" I barked.

She snapped out of her trance, blinking. "That laptop held all our family's sins. My meeting with Byron. Your father's dealings with the rebels...everything. I had to destroy it." She looked at me. "After everything we did for Byron, he wanted to destroy us. They were nothing before us. Nothing."

I lowered the rifle. It almost slipped from my fingers. "What about his wife and kid?" My legs wobbled. I was hot and struggled to hold down whatever was left in my stomach.

"That bitch knew everything. She convinced Byron to throw us to the wolves. She hated our guts," she seethed, and then her wild expression faded. "The boy...I couldn't let the boy grow up without his parents. He would've been an orphan."

"What? I can't believe what I'm f-fucking hearing," I whispered. "Thero almost k-killed Nicole and me." I had my problem under control, but this situation set me back. I was in grade five, in my father's study, which I was.

"I told him to get the laptop, nothing else. If I had known you were there, I would never have told him to go. I swear that, Greg. And I didn't tell them how to kill the Boltons. I only told them to get rid of the problem."

"How did you know Nicole had the laptop?" I asked.

"Thero put two and two together when he overheard you talking to Nicole at your flat," Mom said, eyes shifting all over the room, refusing to look at me.

"I'm sorry it had to come to this, Greg," Manana whispered. "But I had my orders. The government didn't want a trial. With your family's money, it would've lasted for years and State secrets exposed. Unlike you, I'm proud of my country, and orders are orders. Sometimes you need to know when to shut up and obey."

"Where d-does Van Rooyen f-fit in?" I was angry, angry at my parents, angry at my best friend, angry at the world. I wanted to scream and run into the bushveld, run until I could go no farther, and then keep going some more. Hopefully, Nicole would wait somewhere at the end. I'd fall into her open arms and cry, cry until I had no more tears. And then, I would sleep. Sleep until I had no more nightmares.

"We kept Van Rooyen on the side-line," Manana interrupted my reverie. "We did not know where he stood."

"You killed him too?" I said, hopeful.

Manana gave a regretful frown, shaking his head. "He was with the sniper on the hill. The Goodman's aren't popular at the moment."

"They had beaten Stacey to within an inch of her l-life. They r-raped and gutted, Drew.," I glanced at my mother.

She gasped, placing her hand over her mouth. "No, no, no..." she whispered, shaking her head.

"Yes, Mother." I gained control of my emotions, and for a moment, reveling in her pain. "This happened because of your greed, your actions. You played with fire. It was okay to allow these things to happen to other families, just not yours."

Manana snapped his weapon toward me as my legs gave way. I ended on my side but had the crosshair on him. We hesitated.

"What now?" I groaned, struggling to keep conscious.

Manana smiled. "We could stay like this until you pass out."

"Is Nicole safe?"

He gave a nod. "She left with Byron. I'm sorry, Greg, but they involved her. She played you like a banjo."

I looked at my mother. "Is that true?"

She met my gaze, stroking my father's hair. "The way they spoke to each other, yes. I'm sorry."

I lowered my weapon. "I'm so fucking tired. Let's be honest. My fucked-up family deserve what's coming to them."

"Geegee?" my mother gasped.

Manana's image blurred as the tears returned. "I can't do this anymore." *Without Nicole, my life is meaningless.*

"You've got us. Let my son live," Mom begged. "He doesn't deserve this. He is the only good man in this whole messed-up family. And that must mean something."

"Quiet!" Manana snapped. "A lot of good people die in this world. There are no rules. And that scares the shit out of me. It's because of all the good people that I'd seen dying that I'm doing this.

I cry every time I look at my girls. The fate that awaits them if I'm not around. After this mission, I'll have enough to take" – he slammed his chest with a closed fist – "my good people away from here. Those are the only ones I have the power to keep safe. I gave up on the rest." He expelled the anger with a sigh.

"And that's why I can't do it, Meerkat. I love you, umfowethu." He walked over to me and kneeled by my side. "I have the power to give this good man a reason to live – a reason to kill a bad guy. I only found out this afternoon that Byron was responsible. He was the one that attacked you. I lied to you because I didn't want to upset you." He snorted. "How ironic." Manana pointed over his shoulder with his thumb. "I don't know why she lied to you, but the truth is Byron dragged Nicole away from here against her will. She loves you, pal. I planned on killing him after all this shit, but I think you'll do a better job." He rose to his feet. "You weren't here today. After I complete my contract, I will take you to the hospital. You will find Nicole, kill that mother-trucker, and make some babies. Keep walking Greg, like Johnny, your best pal, suggests. Because every step will take you farther away from today."

He shrugged. "And keep doing what you're doing, Meerkat, because you're fucking good at it. Face it, your useless doing anything else. The good people of this country need a badass like you."

"Thanks for helping my boy, Manana, but that's what mothers are for." Mom sat up, holding Musi's automatic rifle. "I have the power to save a Goodman. And you know me."

Manana's shoulders slumped. "Rookie mistake, turning my back on the enemy." He looked at the rifle in my hand and then at me.

I shook my head and whispered, tears streaming down my face. "I can't."

He nodded with a sigh. "Love you, brother. Take care of my girls." The barrel of his rifle swung like a pendulum toward my mother.

The volley from Musi's rifle lasted a couple of seconds. A devastating couple of seconds. Manana was no more, sprawled on his back, blood boiling from his mouth. A horrific sight – watching a friend die.

My mother lowered the weapon. "We need to get to the hospital." She felt my father's pulse. "It's still strong."

I struggled to my feet. "The devil looks after his children." My head spun, and I stumbled back. The wall halted my fall.

"Greg." My mother grabbed me by the arm. The manicured nails, still perfect, cut into my flesh. "I need help with your father, and besides, even if you do go after Nicole, you can't do it in your state."

"I know," I whispered. That was more painful than the hole in my head. The only thing preventing me from going insane was Byron's love for Nicole. *He won't harm her. Or will he? There's such a fine line between love and hate. I know; I was at the crime scenes.*

"Grab his feet," my mother ordered, snatching me back to reality. I don't know how she did it, maybe desperation, love, but she picked my father off the floor – me carrying his feet – and we shuffled toward the front door. I was a robot, following orders. Too tired to resist.

"Put him on the couch," I said as we reached the lounge. "I need to take care of something before we leave."

I struggled up the stairs to my father's room and removed his hunting rifle from his gun safe. He kept the key in a leather Bible pouch next to his bed. I remembered my grandmother commented on it once. "The only time Henry opens his Bible is to go hunting." And then he would say, "Criminals never steal Bibles."

The rifle wasn't the only thing in the safe.

* * *

All dressed up and no one to shoot. Craig searched the property. The sun touched the horizon, illuminating the top of the trees with a bright yellow halo. He closed his eyes for a moment, dowsing the burn. *Go down already.* The unforgiving sun had taken its toll. He licked his chapped lips and swallowed, trying to moisten his parched mouth and throat.

"Okay," Craig sighed and continued his search. He started with the gate, then moved the crosshair over to the bus. However, the tinted windows on the side only reflected the exterior. "Rest in peace, brothers," he muttered, searching for any movement through the windscreen. *They must be dead.* The crosshair moved to the trees on the western side of the house, searching every branch and shadow. *Where's everyone?* The rifle tilted down to the front of the house, past the front door, and around the eastern side. *More fucking trees.* Again, he explored the branches and leaves. The crosshair moved to a small window on the second floor. He kept the scope on the closed window for a moment. *Nothing.*

Then he moved back to the bus. "Hello, I thought we had killed you all," he whispered as a guard ran from the gate toward the bus.

His finger curled around the trigger but relaxed as the guard disappeared behind the bus. "Don't worry, I'll get you when you climb out, Rasta."

* * *

Bongani waited by the door, catching his breath and calming his nerves. He took three deep breaths before entering, aiming the pistol. A mixture of dried blood, sweat, and heat filled the bus. He wanted to cover his mouth but needed both hands to steady his weapon. A man sat by the door, head resting against the window, chest drenched in blood. He looked dead or close to it. Another man, also sitting upright in the seat behind the dead one, showed more signs of life, but each breath required all his strength.

Bongani sneaked closer, reaching for the pistol in the man's hand.

The man opened his eyes, pointed the pistol, and with a growl, pulled the trigger. The round whisked passed Bongani's head and shattered the window on the other side of the bus.

Bongani fell back in the seat behind him as he returned fire. His attacker arched his back before his body went limp. The weapon slipped from his hand and dropped to the floor between his feet.

"Shit." Bongani wiped the dreadlocks from his eyes and the sweat from his brow and continued down the aisle.

A third passenger sat with his head slumped forward. He nudged the body and noticed the small entry wound by the man's temple.

Another shallow breather lay in the next row of seats. His blood covered the seat and pooled on the floor below. He removed the man's weapon and threw it on an open seat.

There were four bodies lying face down in the aisle, hands and feet tied. He had noticed them earlier but thought they were dead. One raised his head, staring at him with wide eyes. "I'm here to help you," Bongani said, lowering his weapon.

The remaining three also raised their heads, eyes wild.

The eldest of the four whispered, "Please let us go. We must bury our wives and children."

* * *

"Thanks for opening the window." Craig grinned as the bus window blew apart. He searched the opening, but the setting sun behind the trees cast a shadow over the vehicle. It was difficult to identify any occupants.

"Come out, come out, whoever is alive," he sang.

The bus rocked as people prepared to exit.

The crosshair moved from the front of the bus to the back, unsure in which direction his target would escape.

"There you go," he whispered as a group of men ran from the bus toward the gate, one of them, Rasta.

"You first." He aimed slightly in front of the running target.

* * *

Among the contents of the gun safe were a bottle of Johnny Walker Blue and a packet of Stuyvesant Blue. I cracked open the cap and swallowed a respectable amount. It numbed the holes where my front teeth once glistened. For the first time in my life, I drank to numb the physical pain. And it worked; I could carry on.

The image of Byron dragging Nicole away mulled in my head. *She loves you, pal.* "I know, brother."

I opened the small bathroom window and searched the hill with my father's Mauser M03 hunting rifle. "There you are, shithead," I whispered.

Craig scanned the area and was on his way back to my location. I closed the window and waited thirty seconds before reopening. He was concentrating on something to his right and preparing to fire. He parted his legs and snuggled up to his rifle.

Whoever he aimed at was a friend of mine. I had to take him out first. As I framed his temple, my conscience gnawed at me; he was only following orders, and I liked the guy; he was a Sharks supporter. Lucky for him, he was not a Blue Bull fan. I moved the crosshair to his tightening finger. No, that would kill him; being a sniper was his life. I had to decide. *Sorry, Craig.* It was time for a career change, or if he truly loved his job, he could teach himself with his left hand.

My ears almost popped as I pulled the trigger in the confined space. The recoil of the powerful weapon elevated every ache and injury in my body. I almost peed my pants.

Craig's weapon and hand exploded in a red vapour.

I filled one of my father's backpacks with the contents of the gun safe and made my way down to where my mother attended my father's wounds. I'd never seen her perform like that with him – concerned, compassionate, and loving – the only good thing to come out of this mess. Still, I couldn't digest what she did.

What frightened me the most about her was in her mind, she did what was necessary; to protect the Goodman name, her name, her status, her way of life. Once an orphan, growing up in utter poverty, she did what she had to do. Nothing would take that away from her, nothing, not even a mother and her defenceless child. Especially not them. It would've been like a Gladiator surrendering to a puppy.

Over the years, I watched her transform from a caring mother and housewife to a pretentious socialite. She added layer upon layer of falseness as her stature in society grew. A woman once content with tap water now only drank Evian natural spring. She also switched from brandy and Coke to Gin and Dubonnet. From Defy to Gaggenau – not that she ever used the latter appliance. However, the domestic workers were ecstatic. "It's to die for," she would always say with a limp wrist, nails dripping with red. Never did I imagine she will actually kill for it.

The queen and I stumbled our way to the Land Cruiser and placed my father in the back seat. He groaned, which was a good thing. Dusk had fallen, the birds had settled, and the stars switched on one by one.

"Where is Stacey?" my mother asked, with tears in her eyes.

"In the cottage, I'll go get her."

"No, I will," she whispered but did not move, only stared at the cottage.

"It's okay," I said and left her in the car.

The cottage door was open. *I told them to lock it!* Again, for the umpteenth time that day, an overwhelming uneasiness hit me. I approached the door from the side and peeked in.

In a second, I took everything in. Veronica lying on the floor next to the couch. Van Rooyen and Stacey on the sofa, struggling. He had his hands around her neck, face distorted with rage.

"Leave her alone!" *When will this fucking day end!* I was like a clock, ticking over, going through the motion, one tick at a time.

He released his hold and grabbed at his pistol, tucked into the back of his pants. Stacey pushed his arm as he fired. A split second later I landed on top of him, fighting for the weapon. *Am I hit?* Another round went off into the ceiling and another. I didn't care anymore. The gun slid out of play as we landed on the floor. The events of the day physically and mentally depleted my strength. Van Rooyen detected it.

"Why don't you just die," he seethed, flipped me onto my back and wrapping his hands around my neck.

My mouth opened, not sure why, because I wasn't even trying to fill my lungs. I had nothing more to give. This was it. I looked into the eyes of a madman. Saliva dripped from his distorted mouth. My head wound had reopened; wet warmth oozed under my body. His image faded, unfocused, like an untrained projectionist searching for clarity.

"Let him go," Stacey said from far away. I blinked. Her image sharpened; she was on her knees two metres away, aiming his pistol.

He looked at her and only registered after a beat.

"Let him go," she repeated.

Van Rooyen raised his hands and stood up, moving away.

I filled my lungs. "Don't, Stacey." I coughed, clutching my neck.

She looked at me, eyes filled with rage.

"You're shot," she said.

I looked down and saw the fresh blood seeping from a wound in my side.

"Don't," I said again. "Your hands are clean." I struggled upright.

"He's right, Stacey. I'm unarmed." He winked at me. "You need to take me in."

Tears streamed down her ashen cheeks. "You never loved me." Her hands trembled as she gathered her strength. "You allowed what happened here today."

"No," he said, shaking his head. "I loved you."

I stumbled to her side and reached for the weapon.

She looked at me, frightened. "No, you can't take him in. He'll get away...he'll come back and kill me."

"Give it to me, please," I whispered. "Once you pull the trigger, everything will change." I placed my hand on her trembling fingers. "I know what I'm talking about."

She nodded, crying.

"You're doing the right thing, Greg." Van Rooyen smirked. "I'm glad you remember our chat in the van. You're a cop."

I took the pistol from her hands and aimed it at Van Rooyen. "What I meant was, Stewart, *her* hands are clean. No gun residue. And you were right. We all have a tipping point."

His shocked expression as he looked down at the hole in his chest was priceless. This one would not keep me up at night.

"See you in hell, Meer–"

A bullet through the right eye silenced him. "I hate being called that," I whispered.

My brother-in-law dropped to the floor like a marionette, its strings cut – the devil had released the control bar. Stacey was right; he would get off with everything that had happened here today. He would turn State witness and tell the story the government wanted to hear.

I rushed to Veronica and searched for a pulse. *Nothing.* He broke her neck. My mom rushed in, gasping, wielding a revolver. Her shocked eyes skipped from Veronica to Stewart, to me, and settled on Stacey. Mother and daughter ran into each other's arms, crying.

"It's over." I collapsed onto the couch. I was so exhausted.

"Greg!" They screamed in unison, rushing over.

"Stacey, listen to me," I whispered.

"What," she said and lifted my blood-soaked T-shirt. She looked at my mother.

"Put pressure on the wound," my mother ordered and ran for the bathroom.

"Listen to..." I groaned as she placed her hand on the seeping wound.

"What?" She leaned forward.

"In my gym bag is the number for Inspector Coetzee. Phone him when we're in town. Tell him everything. Promise me." I fought to stay awake.

"I promise."

"Also, give him the notebook in Nicole's room. Get it before you leave."

"Okay, Greg," she said, nodding wide-eyed.

"And don't tell Mom."

My mother stormed from the bathroom with towels. "Let's get him to the car."

Those were the last words I heard before everything went dark.

11

"Directions are sought from those who have travelled the path
before."
Zulu proverb

I had no idea of time as I drifted in and out of consciousness. The
physical pain had subsided, but the nightmares prevailed. I lay in the
hospital, but where I didn't know.

The first time I woke, briefly, I looked at the ceiling and then at
my mother sitting next to my bed. The next, I woke and saw my
mother and sister arguing. Another time I woke and noticed my
mother with a washcloth and bucket – I was naked. She smiled at me.
I tried to protest, but I couldn't move or speak. I dreamt of Nicole,
and Manana, and Grandma; I dreamt a lot about Grandma. All good
dreams. However, the nightmares would always return.

Then one morning, I woke. I didn't open my eyes because my
mother spoke to a man. They stood by the door.

"I'm trying my best, Mrs. Goodman. Just give it some time."

"We don't have time," my mother snapped.

"We've got him on dialysis..."

"He can't be on dialysis the rest of his life, Doctor."

My eyes flew open, and I searched for the dialysis machine. Not that I knew what to look for, but the only thing I noticed was a heart monitor and drip.

"Remember, we not only need a donor, but the person must also be a match as well. Otherwise, the body will just reject the kidney."

Fuck, I lost my kidneys. I reached for my back, searching for any wounds or scars.

"Geegee!" Mom ran to my side. "You're awake! My Geegee! How do you feel, my darling?"

"I don't know. How long can I survive without kidneys?" I grew faint thinking about it.

She managed a brief frown with all the Botox and shook her head. She was back on form as if nothing had ever happened. "No, my darling, we were talking about your father. The explosion ruptured both his kidneys."

"Can't he buy a couple?"

My mother glanced over her shoulder and leaned forward, whispering, "All eyes are on us – the media, the police. We need to lie low for a while. Our sources in the police told me that the prosecutor is building a case against us. I don't know how long we've got." She sat up with tight lips. "Somebody handed them everything. All the evidence. They want you. An Inspector Coetzee was here twice trying to talk to you." She placed her hand on my arm. "We need to leave this fucking country as soon as possible."

"Heard anything from Nicole?" I stared at the ceiling. I cared nothing for what my mother just told me.

She hesitated, inspecting her manicured nails.

"What?"

"Byron and Nicole skipped the country. The police told Stacey that they crossed the border into Mozambique. And I'm afraid with everything that had happened here, they're not high on their most wanted list."

"They are." I scowled.

She touched my arm, eyes filled with sorrow. "Manana lied to you. Nicole went with Byron willingly."

I shook my head. "I don't believe a word you say anymore, Mom."

Her hand retracted as if I had a sudden attack of leprosy. "You rather believe a man that tried to kill us?"

Don't worry. I'll find out soon enough. "Whatever," I muttered. *I miss her, everything about her.* If I confirmed what my mom said was right, I could make an end of the bad memories. No need to keep going then. "How long since..."

"That day?" My mother stared at the row of bouquets on the four hospital dinner trays parked against the wall.

"Two weeks."

I dropped my head back onto the pillow. *Two weeks!* I took a deep breath. "How's Stacey doing?"

"She'll be fine," Mom said with a wave of the hand. "I've got her at the best psychiatrist in the country – mine."

As always, everything is fucking fine. "I hope he does a better job with her," I mumbled and lifted my head from the pillow. "Did you send the flowers?"

"No." She smiled. "Since the day the news mentioned you as a survivor, all these flowers started arriving." She stood up and read some cards.

"Hope you get well soon, Greg. Call me...Bianca."

"I'm not mad at you anymore, G. I'm still here for you, Nikki."

"I can make your pain go away. Always yours, Sam. Sam?" Mom raised an eyebrow.

"Samantha," I mumbled.

"I don't mind, my darling, it's the in-thing these days. As long as you are the husband in the relationship." She looked me over. "But with your size, it will be difficult."

"What are you talking about?" I said, annoyed. "I fucked up guys twice my size."

"So, you'll look into it," she said, eyes wide with anticipation.

"What the fuck, mom! Look into what, a butthole? I'm not gay." I pointed at my groin. "There will only be one penis in my relationships." I threw my hands in the air. "Because it's the in-thing. What if living in a caravan park is the next in-thing?"

She clutched her heart, horrified. "Okay, don't work yourself up like this. I get your point. But..."

"But what?"

She touched my arm. "A trailer park will never ever be the in-thing."

"I've got a headache. Please leave."

She continued with the cards. "Get well soon, Greg. I'm always here for you, SS."

"And those dead roses over there?"

"They arrived yesterday." My mom picked up the card and glanced at me before reading it. "These flowers represent my heart. Why did you not call? You deserve that bullet hole and cracked skull. CALL ME!" Mom forced another frown. "I'll send her my shrink's number."

"I get the idea," I said before she could read another blueprint of my past. A past I would not revisit. "Let's get back to Dad, not that I want to, but because I promised someone. Stacey should be a match?"

She started playing with her nails. The ticking noise drove me mad.

"I need to tell you something," she said, tick, tick, tick.

"What now?" I scowled. "You're about to detonate a nuclear bomb over Jo'burg."

"Dad had you tested when you were in the hospital. We tested Stacey last week–"

"Aids," I interrupted. "I know all these flowers are not a good sign, but–"

"Geegee, please," my mother snapped. "This is serious."

"So is murder." I wouldn't, couldn't, forgive her for what she did to little Sammy.

She bowed her head in shame as she ticked away. At least she was showing a little remorse. "What?"

"I ran some more tests out of pure desperation to see if you or Stacey was a match."

"So, I take it Stacey is too attached to her kidney."

Her lips tightened. "Remember the lawyer?"

"My father," I said dryly. "The one who forgot to register your antenuptial contract."

"Well." She sighed, shaking her head ever so slightly. "Stacey was not a match."

I frowned at the ceiling for a long time. "Is she the lawyer's daughter?"

She stared at her nails.

"What about me?" *Slut.*

Then she broke into a smile. "You're a match."

I closed my eyes and took a deep breath. *Fuck!*

"I told you, you were his son." She leaned forward and rested her hand on my arm.

I shuddered. It felt like the spider that had crawled over my hand.

"You should have allowed the paternity test. It could've saved you a lot of trouble and alcohol."

That explains dad's sudden change of heart. I recalled his words, "...because it doesn't matter anymore, if you're my biological son or not. You are my son. I want to make things right between us."

Asshole.

I felt terrible for Stacey. She never doubted the fact that she was a true Royal. As for me, all these years, I believed I wasn't a Goodman, and now that I was, I despised it. I hoped I was only fifty percent, Goodman. The other fifty percent, I believed, came from a man my mother had met in a far-off place or planet, a mysterious man, a hero, a good man. *Congratulations Gee; you are one hundred percent Goodman. Fuck!* I thought I was half good; now, I'm all bad.

Reality struck me like a bucket of arctic water in the groin. I fought against the paternity test for this reason. "How is Stacey taking the good news?"

She forced a smile, like a mannequin trying one. "I know you're still weak, and your father doesn't want to hear anything about it, but–"

"I'll do it," I said and switched on the television suspended from the ceiling. Images of the farm flashed on the news with the heading: Pandora's farm.

"Oh," she said, shocked. "Thank you, Geegee; you don't know how–"

"Today or tomorrow," I said. "I want to get out of here as soon as possible."

"The doctor said that you should be up and running within a week or two." She removed a tissue from her purse and dabbed her eyes. *She's back, all right.*

"How do you like your new teeth?" she asked.

I ran my tongue over my front teeth, remembering I'd lost them. "I hope I don't look like Bugs Bunny."

"No, no, my boy. I had the best dentist flown in."

"Let me guess, yours."

"Of course. I couldn't let a true Goodman look like a poor white."

I rolled my eyes and noticed Coetzee standing in the doorway. He wore the same clothes the last time we met – a short-sleeved, red checked shirt with grey flannel pants. The only thing different was the Mickey Mouse tie.

"I'm glad to see you back in the land of the unscrupulous," he said and glanced at my mother.

"My son is too weak to be interrogated," she snapped like a lapdog over her shoulder.

"I'm here for a chat, one cop to another." He walked in and stood behind my mother.

She shifted her shoulders.

"I don't know if you heard, but I'm between jobs at the moment."

"That could change." He blinked at me from behind his thick-lens glasses, then glanced at my mother.

"Give us a moment, Mother."

Her eyes narrowed. "Remember, we Goodmans stick together."

She stood up and shifted past Coetzee as if he had an incurable disease.

He closed the door behind her.

"How you feeling?" He took a seat and placed an envelope on my bedside table.

"Stop the bullshit." I stared at the television. "You here to arrest me?" I noticed his crooked smile from the corner of my eye.

"No, I'm here to crap on you for dropping the evidence in my lap."

"You need the exercise."

"I needed to retire. This mess will postpone it for at least two years."

"Retire." I snorted. "I'm sure Bingo will do without you for a little while longer. You know this shit came from the top. Good luck going against the president."

He grinned and leaned back into the chair, pushing out his bulging stomach, "So, I take it you haven't heard?"

"Heard what?"

"The president had been, what did they call it, oh yes, recalled. I gave the evidence to the Public Protector. It was like throwing a bomb into a long drop. They suspended Modise and several ministers. The public will not know the real reason for everyone's sudden departure. They said that it would tarnish the country's image, make it look like a banana republic, and scare away investors."

"What was the reason they fed the public?"

"The country's current economic state, cut back of the government's wage bill, blah, blah, blah."

"I take it you're not here to wish me a speedy recovery."

The chair creaked as he sat forward, his face hardened. "They want what happened at the farm to be a clash between two rival syndicates or gangs. That everyone involved was dead or caught, and that it did not go higher than that. They want a witness who can substantiate it."

"So, I must lie."

"Not lie. Just not tell the whole truth. Like Trump, alternative facts."

"Might I remind you that one of the rival gangs–"

"I also told them you would never testify against your parents."

"And then what did they say?"

"They will offer you immunity and Modise's job if you do."

"And if I still don't?"

"Then they will prosecute you and your sister and offer the deal to" – he removed a little notebook from his shirt pocket and paged through it, licking his fingers with every page – "a Mr. Byron Wolf."

He already knew the name; it was for effect. I kept my eyes on the suspended television. The weather was on. I focused on the country to the northeast of South Africa. Coetzee's gaze burned holes into my temple.

"I don't want Modise's job," I mumbled.

"Okay," he slapped the armrests and prepared to start his ascent. "I gave you a lifeline, and you–"

"I want Van Rooyen's job." I left Mozambique and looked at him. "I want to be in the field."

He hovered with a frown and then smiled, descending back into the chair. "I'm glad to hear it, Lieutenant Goodman."

I returned to the television, crumpling the sheets with my hands.

"There's a catch, of course," Coetzee said.

"Of course."

"Because you accepted the deal, you need to silence the man who did not. He has so many secrets of the government that we cannot afford to bring him in."

Is he talking about my father?

I felt trapped, like a meerkat living in a foxhole, and the fox had just returned home.

"We don't want to involve anyone else, just you."

"Who is it?" I said calmly, but inside, my words echoed.

He smiled, pushing out his belly. I almost closed my eyes, afraid that a button might come loose. "Mr. Wolf, of course, haven't you been listening? I threw that one in as your Christmas bonus. Take that as your first assignment."

Suppressing the excitement was difficult. He gave me a licence to shoot a polecat.

"Just him?" I asked.

"Yes," he frowned. "Anyone else you want to shoot?"

"No." I shrugged. "Just asking."

"What can you remember of that night?"

"What night?" I asked.

"The night someone gave you a permanent smile."

"Not much. They found Rohypnol in my blood after the attack, so someone spiked my drink. That's why he could do what he did. Fucking coward."

"It sounds as if you know who did it." His grey bushy eyebrows inched together like two fireworms preparing for a headbutt.

"Well, Manana told me it was Wolf," I said. "But I'll confirm that before killing him."

The fireworm headbutt almost happened. "Why?"

"Probably to stop me from investigating the arms-dealing shit." I tried to change the channel on the television. "I'll ask him."

"It never works," Coetzee shook his head. "Pay two-thousand rand a day."

I threw the remote on the bedside table. "What's that?" Pointing at the envelope.

"If it was Byron, he wasn't working alone. I checked the CCTV footage of that night and found the woman responsible." He handed me the envelope. "She did it while you punched some guy in the background. You sat together at the bar, but I couldn't see if you had arrived together. What was the fight about?"

The asshole called me a Smurf. "I can't remember," I muttered and pulled a photograph from the envelope.

"The image is too grainy to run through our database. Can you remember who she is? Were you on a date with her?"

What the fuck! Dominique! I slowly shook my head and said as calmly as possible, "No." I placed the photograph back into the envelope and handed it to him. "She bumped into me on the dancefloor, but I can't remember her name."

"Don't worry." Coetzee rose to his feet. "Take it easy. It'll come back to you. We will find her."

I nodded.

He placed his business card on the bedside table and turned for the door. "I'll tell Task the good news. One of their best is back." Coetzee winked. "Phone me when you get out of here. We've got a lot to talk about."

"Will do," I said before he disappeared around the corner.

The black wall of that night filled up like a YouTube video collection. I crashed into the mosaic and landed face down in a desolate part of Pixies parking lot, concealed by a black SUV, with a gorilla grinding me into the asphalt. A hand clutched my forehead, forcing my head back. I knew how to escape, but my body refused to cooperate.

"Hold still," the man mocked in a whisper and licked my right ear. "You see this Buck hunting knife." He wielded it inches from my nose, a parking lot light reflected in the steel blade. "One of the sharpest knives in the world. Let me show you."

The knife dipped from sight. *Wait, wait, wait!* From somewhere, I gathered the strength to flip over and elbowed him in the face. I wriggled free as he fell on his side. The parking lot – filled with cars – started spinning around me as I jumped to my feet. I fell against the SUV and grabbed hold of the side-view mirror.

"Just fucking die." The coward's big hand covered my face as he yanked me to his chest. The sudden pain hit me like a bucket of boiling water as the razor-sharp blade cut into the flesh under my left ear. My body went numb, surrendering to the inevitable, but my mind played catch-up – after one drink, the room started spinning, and Dominique said she'd take me home. The last thing I remembered was stumbling out of Pixies into the crisp winter night, guided by Dominique. Then poof, darkness.

The blade reached my right ear. My attacker did it with such ease and pace, for a split second, I thought he was fooling with me, trying to scare me. But the pain and what had to be blood cascading down my chest told me otherwise. My time had come...my mind had caught up with my body. *I'm fucked.*

I landed in a pool of blood as the coward released his grip and stepped back. "New fucking shoes," he whispered.

I twisted my head to the side, not to drown in the expanding pool of blood.

Then I heard approaching sirens. It was white noise in Jo'burg, but maybe, just maybe, somebody saw him dragging me away.

"What the fuck?" the man whispered.

Please, God, let it be for me. Please. I will not be one of those victims I found at so many crime scenes; that receives a shake of the head, a report and a body bag before they move on to the next.

The sirens grew louder.

The man moved into view and bent down. He was masked, dressed in black, and wearing gloves; impossible to identify.

"Why?" I whispered under my breath. Blood oozed into my mouth.

"This is for the sins of your family and breaking my girlfriend's heart." He cleared his throat and spat in my face.

I shivered. *Not long now.* I closed my eyes. The ground gave way, like quicksand, sucking me into the abyss. Maybe to hell.

A car started and drove off quietly, like a funeral hearse.

I forced my left eye open – the SUV was gone. The surge of blood into my head deafened. I couldn't hear the sirens anymore. Surrounded by tyres, I didn't know how far I was away from Pixies entrance.

Stay awake! Or, as I'd instructed on so many occasions, "Stay with me." And the poor sod left, anyway. Now I knew why; so easy to drift off. So peaceful. *Just wait.*

I forced my chin to my chest, and with a hand that weighed a ton, I cupped my throat. *They'll never find me here. I will not be a victim. I will not die for my fucking father's sins.* And I didn't see the light. That scared me. *How do you eat an elephant? One bite at a time.* Manana told me the African proverb.

With grinding teeth and tears of anger, I raised my head from the blood. I took my first bite. Still clasping my throat, I shuffled with one arm to the nearest car – another bite – and grabbed hold of the tire. I waited, gasping for air, blood seeping through my fingers. *I will not die for my father's sins!* "One," I seethed, preparing to stand. "Two." Pressing down on the tire. "Three!" I took a huge fucking bite as I rose to my feet.

Pixies entrance was about a hundred meters away. People still entered, deafened by the pumping music. It reverberated in my chest – boom, boom, boom.

One bite at a time. One step at a time. I kept my eyes on my bloodstained Nikes – left...right...left...right. *Don't faint.* Black balls floated around my feet. I bumped into a car. Turned and shuffled around it. The balls grew bigger. My Nikes weighed a ton. Left...right.

I stopped as the balls turned from black to red and blue – bouncing amongst the cars – from windshields and panels.

"There he is!" somebody shouted.

I leaned back, afraid to raise my head. My legs gave way as the paramedics and cops ran toward me. Thanks, Manana – I had devoured the elephant.

"We've got you, buddy."

That was my last memory of that night. The mosaic completed.

Clive Christian's blue bottle of perfume smashed into the mosaic. I'd never forget the fragrance or name, *Chasing the Dragon*. Mom was nearby. I opened my eyes.

"What were you thinking about?" she asked, concerned.

I shook my head. "Nothing. Let them know my remote doesn't work."

She rose from the chair. "Did you tell the inspector anything?"

"And don't come back. I want to be alone."

She looked like a puppy that had pissed on the carpet. The Goodman curse had caught up with her.

How did my intense dislike for my father, eating an elephant, and my height save my life? My dislike gave me the strength to get up, and Manana's eating-an-elephant proverb gave me the strength to carry on. Because of my short height, when Byron slashed my throat, he sliced too high and upward, missing my windpipe and one carotid artery – the main artery supplying blood to my brain. He severed the artery where he started his procedure but only sliced skin where the blade left my throat under my right ear.

They carted me to the operating room the following day with my mom faffing around me like a hummingbird. She wanted to make sure I went through with it. The doctor was not pleased; I was still too weak, but my mom's constant threats swayed his mind. Although I also wanted it done, her brushing aside of my condition for the Goodman name angered me.

I wanted to get this over with, leave this place, never to return, never see my parents again. *Never is a long time, I know, but what they did is unforgivable.* I thought of little Sammy, his mother, Grandma, Veronica, Stacey, Drew, and... Beatrice. Their greed had caused all of this, everything in the name of Goodman.

They parked my gurney in the corridor, just short of the cold, intimidating, steel doors. I waited, the knot in my stomach tightening. The moment dawned on me – a blanket woven out of threads of fear. And then, a spark of excitement at the same place the knot had tightened. *Maybe I won't wake up.*

My father's gurney, with all his equipment, parked beside me. He was pale, hollow-cheeked, and bony. He looked at me with rheumy, sunken eyes as if sucked in by his starving body.

"Give us a minute, Jessica." My father chased away the hummingbird.

She kissed him on the forehead. "I'll be back in a minute."

He waited until the rapid clicking of her high heels faded. "I don't want you to do this," he said hoarsely and unconvincingly.

"Take it as a Father's Day gift."

He managed a weak smile and lied, "I knew deep down that you were my son."

"It's a shame you hadn't realized that sooner. You could've had a thirteen-year-old grandchild running around. You made me feel like a failure all my life, like a stray dog. You treated me worse than the people who worked for you. You never had to say anything. You just had to look at me. And now Stacey will get that same look."

"Why are you doing this then?" he asked after a laborious breath.

"I made Grandma a promise, and..."

"And what?"

"Every breath and every step and every piss you take from now on, you will owe to me. I thought of reminding you, every day, for the rest of your life, of that fact. But you know what, I'm a better man than you. I will not do unto you as you did to me." I glared at him. "After this, I want nothing to do with you."

He just stared at me with lifeless eyes.

"Another thing, Inspector Coetzee visited me. He wants me to testify against you and mother. I agreed because he offered me my job back. I'm telling you this, not to help you, but to save me from testifying against my parents. I don't want Stacey to go through something like that. So, as soon as you're up to it, get on your plane and fly to your fucking island. The promise you made me the other day that you'll get my job back came true. Thanks, Dad." I needed a hanky to wipe the dripping sarcasm from my mouth.

"I'm sorry, Greg," Father whispered. "For everything."

"Whatever."

"Coetzee visited me too." He shut his eyes, groaning, face distorting with pain.

"And you made a deal," I said under my breath.

He shook his head. "I've handed myself over. Will plead guilty. I'm not going anywhere."

"Why?"

"I have to fix things between us, even with Nicole. You've got an amazing girl there. Don't make the same mistake twice."

A whirlpool of emotions overwhelmed me – rage, frustration, fear, and panic.

He grabbed my arm; the life had returned to his weary body, his tired eyes. "I can wait. Go!" he said with urgency. "Before Byron realizes she will never love him back. I was with her those last moments." He smiled, squeezing my arm. "That love will get you through your darkest days."

I frowned, taken aback by his tears.

"You deserve it, please," he said through gritted teeth before falling back. He started shivering, teeth chattering – I almost expected him to exhale a cloud of vapour.

"Dad?" I searched the corridor. "Doctor! He needs a doctor!"

Dr. Pepple, my father's surgeon, a timid Nigerian woman, burst through the double doors. "We need to do this now!"

"Dear God, Henry!" my mom cried, trotting toward us on her high heels. "Help him, Dr. Pepper!"

A series of unstoppable events followed that moment, one of which, if I had stopped, would have resulted in a man's death. A man willing to die for me to experience that love. A love I was sure he had never experienced but longed for his entire life. However, his love for power and money made it impossible to find that love; he had to let go of half before starting his search – a crazy ball-busting journey.

12

"You cannot fight an evil disease with sweet medicine."
Zulu proverb

Six days later
Northern Kwa-Zulu Natal
Friday, 14:21

This could be heaven. I stood next to the road, taking a piss, looking down at Kosi Bay. *Where is Nicole in all this?* I thought of Grandma and smiled. *She's where she wants to be.* I told no one what had happened to me that day in the cottage after Lebo had sent me off to La-La land – she had been with me: I'd felt her comforting arms around me, smelt her scent – vanilla, she always smelled of vanilla. She spoke to me in a tender voice, begging me to wake up, asking me to save my father, that he wasn't ready. That was the reason I gave up my kidney.

The fact I discovered he was my biological father didn't change a thing. It still didn't change the past. However, after the mosaic – reliving that night – I'd decided the past would not shape my future.

Who I am. Playing the victim, blaming my father, for everything gave him power. And it was tiring. *I will not be the victim any longer.* I could only be free if I let go of the hatred. I would forgive, but not forget. I needed to remember; keep my guard up; otherwise, they'd hurt me again. There were more assholes in the world than daisy pickers.

I wanted Nicole to be up here with me. I pictured myself standing behind her, arms wrapped around her warm body, burying my head in her silk-soft hair. I filled my lungs with moist air, imagining her scent. Without Nicole, this was not heaven. It was just another lonely beach. I carefully zipped up and returned to my government-sponsored white Land Rover Defender.

At first, I'd been appreciative, but as the bumpy Swiss-cheese road took its toll on my kidney scar, I wished I were in politics, where a Range Rover was a standard entitlement. This was the ninth piss stop I'd made, as the aggressive Nigerian doctor ordered me to gulp down as much water as my butchered body could handle. In the beginning, I thought, screw you, but that would be like cutting off one's arms to spoil one's penis.

Hope you appreciate that kidney, Daddy-O. I eased back into the Defender and made myself comfortable on the excessively stuffed pillow, which I had bought at an Indian shop five pisses back – and wouldn't you know it, he sold it to me at the best price.

Not far now. My emotions flip-flopped from anger to fear, settling on fear. *What if Byron has hurt Nicole? Killed her? Can't think of that now.* I was thirteen kilometres from the Mozambique border post and another ten kilometres from my destination – Punta D'our, only accessible by 4x4. It sounded like twenty minutes, but it could take hours.

My parents took me to Punta for a holiday when I was still an innocent sixteen-year-old boy. I had my first sexual experience and my last holiday with my parents. Her name was Beatrice, her parents called her Betty, and I called her Barbie. She was sixteen, blonde, and as sweet as fudge. Barbie was on holiday with her boyfriend's parents.

His name was Claude; I called him Clot. A successful rugby player from Springs - a big oaf. He was twenty and had finally graduated from grade twelve that December – or so I hoped for his parents' sake; the results were still pending.

Betty eyed me one hot summer's evening skinny-dipping in the resort's pool. I was alone and high on a beer that I'd bought from a local. She arrived, angry with her oaf, and caught me as I climbed out. I leisurely strolled past her and slipped into my swimming trunks. Surprised by my shameless reaction, she chatted me up, then we talked, then laughed. As dawn broke, we ran to the beach and watched the sun come up. It was so beautiful, even at sixteen.

That was the last time I saw the sunrise as a child. We had another rendezvous, same place, ran to the beach again, but this time before dawn. Had awkward, clumsy sex, but at sixteen, it was terrific. We picked at the bright stars as we lay with our naked butts in the sand and spilt our unfulfilled dreams. And then it happened: Claude arrived, drunk, blind with rage, and clutching a cricket bat. Beatrice tried to stop him, but he tossed her aside like a spoiled baby, an unwanted toy.

He was double my size but slow as a half-dead sloth. I attacked with the ferociousness of a meerkat protecting his young, plucking at him from all sides. I threw sand in his inflamed eyes and got hold of the bat.

Beatrice pulled me off him as he lay unconscious in the sand. The police said it was self-defence, thanks to my size, the witness, my father's money, and his name on the bat. Our holiday was over, and so was Claude's rugby career. I left him brain damaged. That was the first life I destroyed.

I never saw Beatrice after that day.

Two years later, I was eighteen; Stacey, angry at my parents, told me Beatrice had fallen pregnant after our rendezvous on the beach. My father had persuaded her parents she must get an abortion. He'd offered them one million rand to kill a child. *My child.* The Goodman black magic can make anything disappear.

That night when I learned the truth, I confronted him, stuttering. It was a battle I could not win. His words left me as defenceless as Claude had been. I remembered him screaming, "I'm already raising one bastard. I will not raise another. That child was not a Goodman, you are not a Goodman, and I will prove it."

That's when he'd fetched the syringe to draw my blood, and I had fled to Granma's house.

I phoned Beatrice many times after that but could not get a word out – not because of my disability, but shame. What could I say to someone whose life I'd destroyed?

One hour fifteen minutes later, I drove into Punta D'our. I stopped by the only petrol station, filled up, emptied my stretched bladder, and bought a pie. The sandy road was a bustle of fat South Africans, skinny Mozambicans, and oversized 4x4s preparing to leave. The holiday season was coming to a sudden end.

I asked for directions to Mount D'our. It wasn't a Mount, more a dune covered in forest. According to the intelligence report, Wolf's property stood on top of the mount.

As I drove past the pristine beach. A pang of guilt enveloped me, like two hands cupping my heart, squeezing the life from it. I took a deep breath and tried to clear my mind.

The log cabin, with a green roof, was elevated above the dense forest by wooden stilts. Easy to find. I turned right onto a narrow sandy road, which snaked its way up through the dense forest toward his lair. The impregnable canopy blocked out all sunlight as if trying to protect a dark secret.

I wondered where Nicole is. Please, God. I prayed Byron didn't keep her locked up. I pictured her roaming the streets, visiting the beach, and strolling through the market, picking beads for a new necklace. She loved doing that – creating jewellery. My mother would self-destruct if any of those creations should ever touch her, like Superman with kryptonite or Dracula with holy water. How could somebody with such creative innocence be dragged into such evil?

After parking the torture chamber halfway up the Mount, I walked the rest of the way. The air was humid. I reached the top, clothes drenched in sweat and my backpack weighing a small hippo. The road made a sharp bend to the left, and in the distance rose the wooden stilts of Byron's hideaway. I left the road and struggled my way through the forest.

One of my nightmares came true. Everywhere I looked were spider webs, as if they held the forest together. Big eight-legged creatures with red bellies lingered in the centre as if crucified, waiting patiently for their next quivering strand. I froze four strides into the woods, pondering my decision. Was it so crucial for Byron not to know I'm on my way?

"Shit." I sighed. "Time to face your fears, Gregory," I said and gave the next step.

Goosebumps flooded my skin as I tiptoed and danced my way through the forest like a ballerina performing The Nutcracker. I'd never seen it, but I would have nailed a scene where the ballerina glanced around petrified as she heard the most horrid sounds emanating from the forest.

My backpack was my shield, nudging the spiders with their sticky creations out of my way. The most important aspect of it all was that the spider must still be visible once I'd passed. Halfway through my expedition, I had forgotten why I was there; the only thing on my mind was not to walk into a creepy arachnid. I slowed my breathing as my face numbed. I hyperventilated.

As I waited for the feeling to return, a spider came into focus inches from my face. It descended on its strand, legs grabbing at my nose. I slapped at the strand and shrieked as the spider landed on my arm. After swiping at the spider with a shuddering vigour, I heard the body fall amid the carpet of rotting leaves. I'm sure my tombstone would read one day:

Here lies a Goodman, an arachnophobic, stuttering alcoholic.

An hour later, I stood next to one of the three-metre-tall stilts, looking up at the floorboards. There was no way I could enter from below. The front door was the only way in.

No sign of life twitched or shifted or breathed as I moved up the stairs, keeping as low as possible. I halted my crawl three stairs from the top, listening. The only sounds came from the forest and, in the distance, the crashing white noise of the ocean. A streak of sweat followed me up the stairs. I was so thirsty, my swollen tongue stuck to the roof of my mouth.

The double wooden doors were wide open, too inviting, but I had no alternative. I reached into my backpack and removed my pistol.

One...two...three.

I leapt from my position and did a flying roll into the cabin. It was an open-plan design: kitchen to the left, lounge area in the centre – four wicker chairs and a coffee table. The bedroom was in the far-right corner. A door in the centre of the back wall led to the bathroom. *No hostiles or occupants.*

But then, on the double bed covered by a sheet, a body. I approached, weapon in hand, aiming. The person was still alive; its head moved under the sheet. I reached out, took hold and snapped it from the bed.

"Nicole!" I called out. Chained to the bed, drugged, and face covered in bruises, my worst nightmare came true. Her eyelids flickered as she struggled to open them. I threw the weapon on the bed and clutched her head in my hands.

"Nicole, I'm sorry. I'm so sorry." I should've chased after her three weeks ago. I could've made it. Or let my father die. I could've spared her six days of torture. *Three fucking weeks! What did he do to her all this time!*

She opened her eyes. "What took you so long?" she whispered. She managed a faint smile. "I thought you were dead."

"I'm right here." I kissed her on the forehead. "I'll never leave you again."

She stared at me with glazed eyes and raised a heavy hand, but the clinging chain prevented her from touching my face. Teeth grinding, I grabbed at the chain and pulled. I knew the futility of my action, but the rage within compelled me to.

Nicole's eyes widen with fear as a weapon cocked behind me.

"I waited for you," Byron said. "My contact at the border phoned me over three hours ago."

I stared into Nicole's tear-filled eyes.

"I love you," she whispered.

"You took your time admitting it," I said with a wink. She was still in there.

"Get up," Byron barked, drilling me with the barrel.

I kept my eyes on Nicole, unmoving. "What did you see in this albino?"

"Absolutely nothing."

"We had a fun time these last couple of weeks. Tell him, Nicole."

She closed her eyes, lip trembling. The rage within me built up like a volcano before erupting.

"Were you ever planning on marrying him?" I asked in a calm tone.

"The moment I saw you again, I knew he wasn't the man for me."

I felt the barrel tremble against my head.

"Remember the night I allowed him to beat me up. It was the greatest sex I ever had."

She smiled and played along. "Me too."

"Bastard!" He raised the weapon above my head, preparing to crush my skull.

I swung around and punched him twice in the chest and once under the chin. He stumbled back and fell over one of the wicker chairs – no time to search for my weapon. I dived on top of him before he could return fire. We rolled around on the floor, fighting for control of the gun. He was a big man, his arms the size of my legs. I needed both hands to keep the weapon away. He tossed me over like a rag doll and rolled on top of me.

I didn't enjoy being on the bottom. The weapon inched toward me.

"I'm going to have sex with Nicole next to your dead body," he sneered and spat in my face. I used every ounce of my strength to keep the barrel from turning my way, but he was too strong.

If you can't beat him, join him.

I relaxed and moved my head out of the way. The barrel slammed into the wooden floor beside me. I sunk my teeth into his thumb.

Byron roared in pain. My new pair of front teeth sliced through his flesh and came to a grinding halt against bone. His blood filled my mouth.

I slammed the weapon out of play as he tried to switch hands – time for payback.

"Grandma's waiting for you," he said through clenched teeth, clutching his thumb.

I spat his blood into his face. "Tastes like pork."

"Time to shut that fucking mouth of yours." He straddled me.

"I can't believe you're still under the impression you whipped my ass that time."

"This time, I won't stop."

I flew into a sitting position and slapped both his ears with cupped hands. He fell back, groaning, grabbing at his ears. He left himself wide open for my next volley – two jabs to the throat. Gasping like a fish on dry land, he came upright. His eyes nearly popped out of his head. He was still on top of me, pinning me to the floor. I did another sit-up, grabbed him behind the head with one hand and forced my thumb into his right eye socket – not stopping until my thumb disappeared into his skull. He squealed like the pig he was and leapt from my lap.

"Where are you going?" I seethed.

He crawled away, searching for the weapon, leaving a streak of blood. I sprinted past him and kicked the gun away.

"Shooting you will be too merciful." I dribbled and kicked him in the face. His head whipped back. Big arms collapsed under him. I raised my boot and brought it down on the back of his neck. Byron's legs straightened as if poked by a cattle prod.

I knelt next to him and whispered in his ear, "This is what I do. I'm good at this. Where's the key?"

He reached into his pants pocket with a shaking hand. While staying facedown, he tossed the key onto the bed.

I rushed to Nicole's side. She was sitting up, staring blankly at Byron. I removed the chain and wrapped her in the sheet.

"I'm here. It's okay," I whispered, wiping a tangled lock from her bruised cheek. *So beautiful, so fragile.* The hell she went through was my fault. The Goodman curse did it again; my mother sacrificed another innocent life to preserve her status.

A window shattered behind me; Byron had leapt to what he assumed would be safety. I rushed to the gaping hole and saw him disappear into the forest below. I jumped, crushing a fern on the way down. His escape sounded like a charging elephant. I followed his heavy footsteps, running at full speed and in a straight line.

Nothing would stop me from killing him, no phobia, no injury, no conscience – a madman with only one goal. The gap between us closed swiftly. Every clumsy step, he glanced over his shoulder with his functioning eye, arms waving like a person drowning. I craved his fear.

Every stride brought me closer until I could taste his vile odour and smell his heavy breathing. His sweat burned my nose; the sight of his cumbersome body enraged me. The thought of him with Nicole propelled me forward.

I dived onto his back and wrapped my arms around his thick neck. He kept going, bursting through thorny branches and tenacious spider meshes. My arms tightened. His heavy breathing became a gurgling gasp. Wolf's stride slowed to a stumbling walk, slower and slower until he stopped. It was the last step he would ever take. I clenched my teeth as I used every grain of strength, tighter and tighter – allowing him no breath. His arms fell to his sides, and his knees buckled.

A spider scurried to safety down my back as I waited for Byron to fall. Then, too soon, he went down on his knees and fell forward onto the rotting foliage.

I released my grip. The Wolf filled his lungs with a desperate gasp and rolled onto his back. Covered in dirt, mouldy leaves, and mud, he clung to his gaping eye socket and mouth. A spider ran over Byron's face and into his mouth, unaware that it would be its final resting place.

It didn't take me long to find what I was looking for. I stumbled back to Byron's side. "You didn't break Nicole or me. I know what you did. We will live happily ever after. You won't. Look at me."

He granted my wish and emptied his lungs with a roar.

I brought the boulder down onto his head, screaming, "We will be happy!"

His body twitched and went still. Even the forest fell silent, shocked by what it saw. It was over. He couldn't hurt Nicole anymore.

"Sorry, Grandma," I gasped, stepping back, knowing she wouldn't approve.

I left his corpse behind to rot, to be devoured by the forest – the only pure act of his life.

Nicole lay asleep by the time I got back to the house. While I waited by her side for the drugs to wear off, I made the call to Coetzee. It was time to end the Goodman curse. I told him about Byron, about the secret runway on my parent's farm, and about the island. My father would not flee, but mother was quite resourceful.

I told him I had their passports, which I'd removed from the gun safe in my father's room. And, most important of all, I told him who ordered the murder of the Bolton family. I was the witness to my mother's confession.

He agreed I could take two weeks off. Well, he didn't have a choice in the matter.

Nicole woke a few hours later, frightened and confused, searching the room for Byron. I climbed into the bed beside her and wrapped my arms around her, whispering, "He will never hurt you again."

She nestled into my arms, crying.

"I'll never leave you again."

Her arms opened around me. "Promise."

"On my life." So much for silencing my nightmares. Well, we'll chase away each other's nightmares.

I wanted to hold her like this forever, protect her.

As if reading my mind, she said, "Hold me tighter."

Her healing breath brushed against my chest, warming my lifeless heart. I felt alive. Whole.

She raised her head and looked at me. I smiled, and she smiled. No words were needed; she loved me, and I loved her.

"I need to take you to the hospital." I reached out and stroked her cheek with the back of my hand. Her skin was soft and pure, my hand coarse and bloody. I pulled back, afraid of spoiling her purity.

"I don't need a hospital. I need you...I need you to take me away from here." She grabbed my hand and placed it back on her cheek. Her smouldering eyes welled up, fresh tears following the path of the old.

I fetched the Land Rover, helped her into it, and returned to the cabin, gathering whatever belonged to her. *Nothing of her must remain, nothing.* On my way out, my eye caught the engagement ring on the floor beneath the bed. I stood frozen, unsure.

"Shit," I whispered and fetched it. Women are strange like that. It must be her choice to get rid of it. I tucked it into my pocket and ran back to the Land Rover.

We left Punta, regretful that such a perfect place bore such painful memories. One day we might return. The future was unpredictable and intoxicating – filled with Nicole.

I had ulterior motives with the place I picked, Richards Bay. Not the best destination; a town built on industry, but still nice. Nicole didn't care where we went. It was away from Punta and with me. However, she got that dubious expression as we drove into the town.

She peered over the dashboard with narrowed eyes, a slight frown, and flared nose. The flared nose rarely went with the look, but it was at that moment the aluminum mine had vented after-gas. It smelled like those silent-but-vile heated farts. I had to roll down the window to prove to her it wasn't me. We'd caught Richards Bay with its pants down.

I booked us in at a secluded self-catering chalet on the beach. The holiday season was over, so I had no trouble finding us the perfect place. Afterwards, we drove to the local shopping mall. Nicole waited in the car – brushing shoulders with shoppers frightened her. After scribbling down her sizes, I bought her clothes at Mr. Price, as my Goodman-stripped budget did not allow for non-Chinese and double stitching. I had to convince the flirty male cashier that I was not a crossdresser by showing him my weapon.

That first couple of days were difficult. Nicole would stare, sometimes for hours, at the angry waves with tears in her eyes. She would shudder when I touched her without warning. I hated Byron even more. And my mother. At nights, she would disappear into the bathroom, showering for what felt like hours. I prayed the warm water would be a magical potion to wash away all her nightmares.

When we went to bed, she'd lie in my arms with the light on, her body would shake, and she'd cry again. I cried too. Afterwards, we'd speak about trivial things, avoiding the elephants in the room. She pretended to fall asleep, me too. We would "wake up" in the morning and go for a walk. With each new sunrise, I wished today was the day Nicole would awaken whole, but the crying and the tearful gaze at the waves continued. It was easy not to drink to block out my nightmares. I needed to be there for her, one hundred percent. So, in caring for her, I healed myself.

The morning of the thirteenth day started like all the others. The suffocating night lifted; the sunrise every day these last two weeks was a relief. I made us coffee and carried it to the bed. Nicole lay with her back toward me, dressed in white pyjamas, watching the red ball gain intensity as it climbed its way into the cloudless sky, maybe to dry her tears. Soon she'd turn over.

"Just how you like it," I said as I approached with the steaming cup. Nicole glanced over her shoulder and forced a smile. The eyes never lie.

Please, God, help me get her through this, I don't know what to do.

I didn't know if I stumbled or if He nudged me, but I spilt half the cup on her back. She leapt out of bed and stood on the other side.

"Shit, I'm sorry," I called out."

"No," she snapped. "Stay back."

I remained on my side of the bed. "I'm sorry."

"Men can only hurt," she yelled. I'd never seen her that angry; her face mirrored the flaming-red sunrise behind her.

"It was an accident," I pleaded. "Sorry."

"Stop-saying-sorry," she screamed. With each word, she straightened her arms, fists clenched. "Sorry-can't-fix-me."

"Well, I'm..." I swallowed and shrugged with wide eyes. "What do you want me to say?"

"You left me again!" She picked up a stone-carved elephant statue from the bedside table and threw it at me. I didn't duck or flinch for the fast-approaching ornament. It hit me on the right cheekbone and landed on my left foot. I remained static, not even raising my hand to touch the expanding bump.

Nicole raised her hands to her mouth.

"Do you feel better now?" I said, dripping with sarcasm. It wasn't the best reply, but I wanted her to take it all the way. I didn't know where we were going, but it was better than where we were at the moment.

She lowered her hands as her eyes narrowed. "I watched you sidestep a bullet. You could've ducked. You're just trying to make me feel sorry for you, like the other night with..." She pressed her lips, unable to utter his name. "Fight with me! Stop treating me like a molested little girl."

"I don't want to fight with you," I said with another shrug.

"Why not!"

"Because I love you."

"Bullshit," she shrieked at the top of her lungs. "You left me with that monster for three fucking weeks!"

I felt the rage build within, not targeted against Nicole, but at the situation we found ourselves in. "I w-was in t-the hospital. I told you this."

"Your entire life, you hated your father, and then you chose him above me! I could only play along for so long, waiting for you. The last six days would've made all the difference!"

I took a deep breath. "Why d-did you take so long with the d-data? You knew him. Why were you still planning on marrying him the d-day they attacked?"

"I wasn't going to marry him," she answered more calmly but still flaming red. "I had broken off the engagement a day after seeing you again. I wanted to make you jealous. I wanted you to want me so badly. And for the data, I saw your mother's name in the report; I wanted to spare you the shock. You were going through a tough time. Now I wish I hadn't protected her."

I didn't know what to say. I'd messed up. *Will she ever forgive me?* I avoided her piercing eyes, staring at the coffee-stained sheets.

"Say something," she screamed and walked around the bed toward me. She took an aggressive stance in front of me.

Her breath heaved against my face. My right eye swelled shut.

"I-I'm..."

"I-I'm what?" she mocked.

Her rage radiated from within her trembling body, like the sun behind her, already a blinding yellow. Nicole was angry at the world for allowing something like that to happen to her. She wanted to denigrate a man, as he denigrated her. It would take time before she'd trust a man again. Trust me again. She knew I would never harm a hair on her head, that she could vent all her rage on me. Perhaps she was testing me; seeing if I would lose it like I had lost it with Byron.

"Cat got your tongue?" She continued her barrage, panting. "Oh, I forgot, your cat is dead. Skinned like the pussy you are."

Seeing her like this ripped my heart apart. I fought with everything in me not to cry for her. Glaring at her through a narrowed eye, I pretended to be angry.

"Say something, you little shit. You're the size of a dwarf. And you're a baby killer."

I flinched – she'd touched something – but I remained calm. With Nicole, it was easy. I'd told her about Beatrice a couple of days ago.

"It doesn't matter what you say to me," I whispered. "I will never leave you or hurt you. So, if you need to say these things to get over what you're going through, it's fine. Just remember, I love you, and I want to spend the rest of my life with you."

I let it sink in, waiting for another volley of anger. The sun flared behind her, shining through her tangled golden locks. She looked like an angel.

The anger in her eyes vanished. Tears welled up and ran down her flushed cheeks. I closed my eyes as she grabbed me by the collar; I was expecting another attack, but she jerked me toward her and kissed me hard on the mouth. Her tongue forced my lips apart, and her hands clawed into my back. I wrapped my arms around her and pulled her tight against me. I would not take it further unless she wanted to.

She threw me on the bed and ripped off her white pyjamas. A button came loose and hit me on my swollen cheek.

"I should have spilt coffee on you that first day," I said, staring at her approaching breasts.

"Shut up." She pushed me onto my back. I stared at the ceiling, my heart surging in my throat.

It was unreal, a dream. I pushed myself away, admiring her beauty as the sun illuminated her body. Her skin shimmered as if covered in gold dust. Our eyes locked. No woman had ever looked at me the way she did. I saw what my father saw – that love. Her eyes were a tranquil mountain pond, a magic pond which washed away all evil within me, all my troubled thoughts, all my rage, all my self-pity. We kept the bond, lost in each other's eyes as we made love.

She flipped me onto my back and straddled me. Her nails clawed at my chest as she increased her rhythm, her breasts bouncing playfully. I grabbed at them, caressed them, suckled them. I wanted this moment of euphoria to last forever. The power-play continued as I tried to flip her onto her back again, but she resisted, clasping her thighs, clawing my chest.

Nicole increased her rhythm, unstoppable, her movement almost uncoordinated. I clenched my teeth and took a deep breath, trying to prolong the inevitable. She threw her head back, like an athlete crossing the finish line. Her hips shuddered. I groaned as every muscle in my body contracted, my fingers digging into her hips. She fell on top of my trembling body, gasping for air. Our hearts beat as one, our breathing coordinated.

Together, we were whole.

It was also the first time I'd made love.

"Marry me," Nicole whispered in my ear.

"Thought you'd never ask."

13

"There is no medicine to cure hatred."
Zulu proverb

Richards Bay
Two days later
09:30

Nicole and Greg sat in the Defender in front of the modest house with a white picket fence, new jungle gym and kept garden. Christmas trimmings still decorated the white front door and brass bell. The perfect picture – Nicole remembered Greg telling her the day before. She hoped it wasn't covering a cracked wall, for Greg's sake.

He'd been here yesterday but couldn't ring the bell. She rescheduled for today. The woman was dubious over the phone, but she agreed to see him after telling her Greg's story.

"You want me to go with you?" Nicole placed her hand on his shaking leg.

He clutched her fingers in his sweaty palm and gave a stiff smile. "No," he whispered. "I need to do this alone." He leant over and gave Nicole a tongue-twisting kiss.

Her stomach fluttered as she looked into his lively blue eyes. "You'll be okay, don't worry."

He took a deep breath and opened the door. A white Maltese poodle came running around the house, tail wagging.

"That's a good sign, Meerkat." She pinched his butt. *Couldn't resist.*

He glared at her over his shoulder with narrowed eyes; he hated that name. "I'll let that one slip, but next time I'm gonna pull you over my knee and spank you pink and blue."

"Promises, promises."

He sat with the door open, feet on the pavement.

"You took out an entire Ops team. I'm sure you can handle a twenty-seven-year-old woman."

He snorted. "Of the two, it's the women I'm afraid of." He climbed out and walked to the front gate. "Love you," he said over his shoulder and pushed open the gate. The dog jumped up against him, tail wagging and yelping.

Bitches love him.

Greg sauntered to the door, wiping hands on his jeans, and took hold of the string. He rang the bell and waited with head slumped.

The door opened, and a beautiful blonde woman appeared. An awkward handshake followed. She smiled and stepped into the house. Greg glanced over his shoulder before disappearing inside too.

Nicole's heart lodged in her throat, her hands grew sweaty. She started reading a novel and at page seventy-two, not remembering a word. The door finally opened. They hugged each other. Greg walked toward Nicole, beaming from ear to ear.

She swallowed a lump and wiped the fast-forming tears from her eyes.

He closed the gate behind him and walked toward the car without looking back.

"So?" She asked as he slammed the door shut.

He smiled. "This picture ain't hiding nothing."

"So, she's okay?"

"We were kids. We can't be blamed for our parents' mistakes. She's happy. She's got a family now – four-year-old twins."

He looked at her with those searching blue eyes. "Are you okay?"

"It'll take time, but time is on our side." She took his hand. "What about you?"

"When is our appointment at the head doctor?"

"Tomorrow at three."

"Then we better get moving."

I can never be truly free if I don't let go of the hatred. Greg's words struck her like a brick in the face. Her hatred for the Goodmans had consumed her life – almost destroyed her future. Henry Goodman's hunger for profit destroyed her family. He'd fitted all his trucks with re-treaded tyres, and most were not roadworthy, including the one that had killed her parents. He also forced his drivers to do double shifts.

All of it changed after the accident. False statements, reports, and bribes secured a not guilty verdict. His company dodged a bullet – but not Nicole's judgement. Working as an IT specialist for the National Intelligence Agency, she'd approached Byron and fed him the illegal arms dealing plan – how the Goodmans and Wolf could profit. That was it. She planned to gather evidence until she had enough for the NPA to prosecute – enough to destroy the mighty Goodmans.

Nicole was shocked at how it all escalated. The greed of those in power caught her off guard, as well as Henry and Jessica Goodman's resourcefulness. In a matter of months, even the President was on his payroll. As Henry went for the politicians, Byron went for law enforcement, including Greg's team. Nicole had lit a fire she couldn't control.

Byron boasted what he had done to Greg after the night he'd destroyed Greg's bike. He'd involved Dominique, Nicole's best friend, to spike Greg's drink. That was when she broke off the engagement. Nicole couldn't go to the police because he had most of them in his pocket, and he had evidence implicating her. *But Byron is dead now, and we are not.*

As Nicole drove them through the neighbourhood, she knew they'd never see the place again, just as she knew they'd never see Punta again. The past was behind them, the future ahead, unpredictable and, as she looked at him, intoxicating.

She fell in love with him back then. It was unplanned. That he was a Goodman quenched her appetite for revenge. She couldn't love a person entirely if she despised his family. *There's no space for hatred in our relationship.*

Byron took advantage of the situation when Greg had left. She never loved Byron, but she despised him the moment she'd realized he'd kept Greg away.

"At least this is done," Greg whispered.

"Not yet," Nicole said as they approached a four-way stop. "Pull to the side of the road."

He frowned but obeyed.

"I can't have this with me a second longer." She removed Byron's engagement ring from her handbag and exited the Land Rover. A woman, begging with her infant child, stood next to the stop sign.

"Here, take it." The diamond glistened in the sun as Nicole offered it to her.

The woman reached out with an open palm, dubious.

"Buy food or a house with it." Nicole dropped the ring in her hand.

Her eyes flickered alive as she stared at the shiny rock.

"Worth a lot of money." Nicole closed her hand around it.

"Ngiyabonga mamma," she whispered with tears welling up.

As Nicole walked back to the Land Rover, the woman shouted once more, "Ngiyabonga."

"Now we can go." She shut the door.

Greg looked at her as if wanting to say something but decided against it. Instead, he cranked the engine into gear and drove off.

"What?" she finally said.

"I don't know how she'll sell that thing. Probably gonna end up in jail."

"She'll find a way." Nicole placed her hand on his leg. "Never underestimate a desperate woman."

He nodded. "That's true."

* * *

Houghton, Johannesburg
   Two weeks later
   Friday, 9:22

Nicole was better because she wanted to visit my mother. I was dead set against it. We were more alike than I thought. Dr. Lippitz, our shrink, told her to face her fears; it would help heal her wounds. But I didn't think he meant this. My mother wasn't in jail yet. She was out on bail, awaiting trial. The wheels of justice were as slow as a one-legged turtle, even slower for the rich.

"You sure about this?" I engaged the handbrake.

She nudged her head down, staring through the windshield at the ivy-covered, double-storey mansion with blooming flowerpots suspended in front of every window.

"No." She squeezed my leg and gave me a peck on the cheek.

I took a deep breath before opening my door. She, however, waited for me to walk around the car and open hers – a first. She needed more time.

"What do you want to say to her?" I took Nicole's hand.

She arched her mouth and shrugged. "I don't know. Why did she tell you I left willingly with Byron? Why did she not tell the police

Byron kidnapped me? She was the only one who saw what had happened, besides the bad guys. What did I ever do to her to deserve it?"

I slipped my arm around her slender hips as we made our way up the stairs. "I'm glad I moved out of here when I had the chance."

She nodded, keeping her eyes fixed on the front doors.

"No, I mean when I moved out, the ivy-covered only half the house." I pretended to shudder. "Imagine all the spiders."

She glanced at me, smiling. "I thought Mozambique cured you?"

"I think it made it worse." I turned to her as we reached the top. "I wake up in a cold sweat every night."

Her smile faded. "I know." Nicole knew what I meant. She had her demons, and I had mine, and they weren't spiders. We were both diagnosed with post-traumatic stress disorder. I didn't tell Coetzee, though.

The door opened, and Tito stepped out. "Master Greg." He gave me a stern nod but only glared at Nicole. I've never seen him so frigid. My mother probably told him another bullshit story about how the world was turning against her.

My father appeared in the doorway. "It's okay, Tito."

Tito gave him a nod and shuffled away.

I couldn't resist. "How's my kidney doing?" I smiled. "Up to standard. Is it good enough?"

"Yeah, yeah." He smiled and gave my hand a limp shake. Not the handshake I grew up with.

My father looked ten years older since the last time I saw him; gaunter, ashen, and hair as white as Santa.

"Morning, Mr. Goodman," Nicole said.

"You can call me dad." He held out his arms. "Heard you got married in front of a judge."

"Too soon," she mumbled.

My father nodded and stepped aside, waving us in. "I would've been there."

"Why?" I followed Nicole inside.

"Because I want to be a part of your life." He closed the door and turned to me. "A man can change. Grow up." He shrugged. "For some, like me, it takes longer."

He gave me a heartfelt look with those sunken grey eyes.

I didn't know what to say.

"Look at you,"–he pointed at me with an open palm – "all grown up." My father stepped toward me. "It might be too soon, but it can never be too late. Please," he begged.

He had never spoken to me in that tone or looked at me in that way. He had a point; I couldn't expect Nicole to forgive me – which she already had – and me not forgive my father.

His gaze shifted to my left. With the way he cast his eyes up at the chandelier and sighed, I knew my mother had arrived.

Nicole and I turned around as one.

"Mother." I almost choked on the word.

"Geegee! Darling!" She approached me with open arms.

I stood static as she gave me a peck on the cheek. She turned to Nicole with the same fake smile but had the wisdom not to invade her space.

Nicole looked like a pressure cooker about to explode, cheeks flaming red and fists clenched to her sides. Her rage was palpable.

"Let me look at the ring." Mother leaned forward.

Nicole opened her right hand. I was about to tell her that the ring was on her left when she struck my mother with such force, the bun on top of her head came loose.

I frowned at Nicole, shocked, and then glanced over my shoulder at my father. He stood at the door, expressionless as if he'd missed the entire thing.

My mother's eyes still fluttered like a butterfly when I turned back to her. It seemed as if she tried to wake up from a nightmare.

"That's for telling lies about me," Nicole said in such a calm tone it scared me.

My mother regained her composure. She swallowed, almost choking as she said, "I'm sorry."

"Let's go." Nicole marched toward the door.

My mother stood, head bowed. It seemed as if she had only realized now what she'd done. As if Nicole knocked some sense into her. A queen stripped of her crown.

"Mr. Goodman." Nicole gave my father a nod as she walked out of the house.

"Nicole." My father mimicked, expressionless.

I halted in the doorway. "I uh...I have a game on Saturday."

"A game?" he frowned.

"I've started playing again, club rugby. It's just a friendly."

His grey eyes flickered alive. "I would love that." But his elation faded. "Isn't it too soon after your operation? I mean, I'm still" – he touched his back – "tender."

I shrugged. "The doctor said I could play. We can grab a beer and steak afterwards."

"Wouldn't miss it for the world. I've got a lot of catching up to do." He held out his hand.

"Pick you up at eight." I shook his hand. The grip I grew up with was back.

I left the house feeling better after choosing the more righteous path. Nicole waited for me in the car, rubbing her right hand.

"What took you so long," she snapped as I slammed the door shut. "Hope you didn't apologize."

"You're crazy. She got off lightly." I turned the key in the ignition. "I invited him to the game on Saturday."

Her gaze bore into me for a moment. "You know he's not innocent in all this. He's a shrewd businessman who destroyed innocent lives."

"I know." I looked at her. "No one is really innocent."

She blushed.

I slipped the Mini into gear. "How's your hand?"

She inspected her swollen fingers. "Hurts like hell."

The cast-iron gates at the end of the drive parted as we approached.

"I don't think Dr. Lippitz had this mind." I smiled. "But do you feel better?"

She mulled it over in her head. "Yes." She nodded. "Much."

14

"Love is a painkiller."
Zulu proverb

Hillbrow, Jo'burg
Six months later
Thursday, 21:56

A quiet night for hell. One square kilometre cramped with seventy-five thousand people. On the surface, all seemed normal – minibus taxis streaking the roads, homeless sleeping under bin bags, prostitutes trying their hardest to harden someone, forgotten street kids sniffing glue trying to forget, and prowling hoodies. Every couple of steps, the music changed like a scanning car radio, as did the scent of food mixed with the occasional piss whiff. Within a hundred metres, I travelled Africa. I loved everything about this, feeling alive, scared, and excited at the same time.

As the only whitey out this late on the streets of Hillbrow, I didn't attract too many dubious stares. It meant only one thing; they saw me as a junkie in search of my next fix – whatever it took, usually by selling my AIDS-infected body to a willing weirdo. In everyone's street smart opinion, they thought I belonged to a drug lord. Well, I looked the part; I hadn't shaved for a week.

My destination was close, I could tell; the drunk I'd stepped over was Corporal Mataruse, and the trolley-pushing bum across the street was Sergeant Blomhuis. Seven of my team watched every move I made.

"Okay, ladies, I'm a minute away. Stay sharp." I snaked my way through four glue-sniffing street children.

"Lieutenant Goodman," Sergeant Bingham said in my ear.

"Yes, Bings."

"What will your pregnant wife say if she finds out you're moonlighting in Hillbrow?"

I smiled as the image of Nicole popped into my head. "She knows." I kept the answer short; the less they knew about my private life, the better. She wasn't home but working late to stop the spread of a virus that had breached a financial institution's firewall. If she'd been home, she wouldn't sleep until my Triumph's headlight beamed through the bedroom window and then would pretend to sleep.

I need to trade in my Triumph for a daddy car – something with four seats and a cup holder. *Daddy – me?* The thought made me more petrified than what I was about to do next. The kid would grow up without grandparents. It would be better to tell him they were dead than tell him they were in prison. *Hope it's a boy.* My mom was still out on bail, pending her trial for murder, and my father had made a deal, receiving fifteen years for – I can't even remember. I was glad there was no trial, as I would have hated testifying against him. *He should be out in eight.* I'd miss him – never thought that possible – but he tried to be the father he never was before he went in. He came and watched every game I played. We had a few lunches, a few heated discussions about our country, about the future of our children. You know, just talk...like, father and son. He even bought me a new Triumph – using the excuse that my previous bike disappeared on Company property.

Because of his criminal record, he had to resign as CEO. He wasn't upset about it. I believed he changed, using my life as proof. As our relationship healed, so did my speech impediment. My sister was not doing well. She had a breakdown and was placed on antidepressants that could knock out a Sperm whale. She was never that strong, always crawling into a corner when life threw her a curveball. *Is it because she's not a real Goodman?*

"Hey, sugar." A hooker tugged at my T-shirt and tried to keep up in her high heels. "Want some fun?"

I showed her my ring finger and increased my pace.

She laughed. "Most of my clients are."

"This one's for real."

"Fuck off then." She disappeared in the misplaced crowd behind me.

Three steps on, I heard her voice again, "Hey, sugar, want some fun?" That hurt my feelings.

"Hey, Lieutenant," Bings chuckled in my ear. "I'm gonna tell your wife."

"I will tell your mother you're screwing a one-legged hooker in Newtown."

"She'll be glad to know. It's one leg more than the previous one I had."

"Enough fucking around," Captain Sithole vibrated in my ear. "Showtime, everyone."

I stopped in front of The Virgin Cafe; only the "V" and "C" were still flickering in pink neon.

"Infrared shows two hostiles with the kids in the room next to the bar," Coetzee said. "If we go in now, we'll have a hostage situation. You think you can create a diversion and get everyone in the bar area?"

"I'm sure I can think of something."

"We can then go in via the window and secure the kids before neutralizing the traffickers."

"Okay, let's do this. I miss my wife."

"Remember, they must not get the idea that you're a cop, otherwise–"

"Otherwise, they will join the kids," I interrupted Sithole. "Don't worry, I've been doing this for a while, old man."

"Well, go do your thing then, snot-nose. Stick you for a beer afterwards."

"Make it a coffee at my house, and it's a deal."

"Six months married and already pussy-whipped."

"You know it, snitch."

I walked up the grime-covered stairs, pushed open the smutty black doors and strolled down the dark corridor with flaking walls. On the left, barely visible, a snake and on the right a Nigerian flag. I stopped at a bright green door. The monotonous rhythm of rap music hammered my ears. A trickle of light lit up the tips of my boots. I took a deep breath, trying to settle my pounding heart. Since that day, my phobias included darkness. *Pathetic.*

I pushed open the door.

A large room hanging so thick with weed it burned my eyes and nose. Five men stood around a pool table, and six sat by the bar with their backs toward me. I stopped by the end of the corridor and removed a packet of cigarettes. By the time I'd flicked my Zippo, I had everyone's attention.

Placing my hand on my hip, I blew out a cloud of smoke and yelled, "Who's been screwing my girl without paying. She said it was an ugly fuck with a small penis, and from the looks of all of you, it could be anyone."

As the eleven approached and the two entered the bar area from the adjacent room, I thought of my tombstone again:

Here lies Gregory Goodman, an arachnophobic, stuttering alcoholic (recovering), husband, father, and brother who tried to be a good man.

It was fine for now. However, I knew the inscription would shorten the more I found myself. Hopefully, one day it would read:

Here lies Gregory, a good man.

Nobody is perfect; who the heck wants to be? I accepted my imperfections, the path that had let me to this day. There were no coincidences in life. Every flaw and every decision were part of the bigger plan. *If I'm lucky, and my life is part of the bigger plan, I might see my kid grow up a good man, grow old with Nicole, and then, one day, I will see Grandma again; taste some of her vetkoek.* Because if I had the power to change my past, I would be dead. I would have wanted to be taller and have a loving father.

* * *

Northcliff
  Thursday, 22:01

At five months pregnant, Nicole barely showed. *The boy has his father's genes.* The last six months went by like a dream. Unimaginable. Finally, she was whole. They were one. Inseparable. Nicole lay awake at night and watched Greg sleep – so peaceful. Byron still haunted her at night, but before he could lay his filthy hands on her, Greg would appear and slaughter the demon. In her dreams, Greg was a giant in life – her anchor, her lighthouse, her everything. She'd never felt so safe. Content.

Greg still had the occasional nightmare, but Nicole was there for him – every step of their precious union. She would do whatever it took to secure their happily-ever-after. Only one demon remained.

Nicole had left her phone at home. The chance of Greg tracking her location would be too risky.

She parked the Mini around the corner of the apartment block – just in case. Still busy this time of night, it was reasonably safe. She could've parked in the building's basement but opted against it; too creepy – at least ten horror movies came to mind. Nicole checked the street for weirdos, placed Greg's Lions cap on her head, and grabbed her handbag.

A winter breeze cut through Dexter and her as Nicole climbed out. She zipped up Greg's camo jacket and pulled the hoodie over her cap. Nicole thought of naming their boy Gregory junior, but Greg had refused. He'd said calling a kid after his father was stupid, uncreative, and confusing for everyone. Greg added that their son must have his own identity – no boy grew in the shadow of his father. *Although it wouldn't be a big shadow,* she'd told him. He'd flipped her the bird. She'd suggested the name Dexter after her late brother, and he'd accepted. Nicole had told him about her past but left the Goodman part out of it. For her husband and child, she had to let go. *Husband and child! I'm a wife and mother!* The future was so exciting.

A tall blond guy held open the glass door as she walked up the stairs. She kept her head low, hiding behind her cap's visor. "Thanks," Nicole mumbled.

"Almost didn't see you there." He pointed at her camo jacket.

She walked past the elevator and headed for the stairs – only four flights. Her stomach churned as she reached the third floor. *Hunger or nerves?* Nicole had devoured twelve Vienna sausages on her way over. *What am I going to say?*

404...405...406

Nicole stopped at door 407, heaving like a five-month pregnant woman who'd just run up four flights of stairs. *Take it easy. Greg'll kill me if he finds out.* A minute later, after catching her breath, she knocked.

No answer. Also, no CCTV in the corridor.

She knocked again.

"Yes?"

"It's me, Nicole."

"What!" Dominique yanked open the door. She took a step back, shocked. She had tied her curly red hair up – it looked like a spewing volcano. She fidgeted with the belt of her pink gown.

"Sorry." Nicole slipped the hoody off and removed Greg's cap. "It's cold out."

Dominique shook her head, shrugging with open hands. "How did you...Wow, what a surprise."

"Been almost a year."

Dominique nodded, looking up and down the corridor.

"It's only me. Can I come in?"

"Of course." She stepped aside.

"When did you move here?" Nicole knew she was renting because the title deed wasn't in her name.

"Almost a year." She pointed at the Chesterfield couch. "Take a seat."

They had bought it on special – buy two and receive a fifty percent discount on the second. Dominique only paid twelve thousand five hundred rand.

Nicole took a seat on the left and placed her handbag between her legs. Dominique remained standing, unsure, awkward.

Light colours made the small apartment look bigger. It had a white, open-plan kitchen with granite tops. *No boyfriend. No picture frames. Minimalistic. Grab your suitcase and run décor.*

"Glass of wine?"

"I'm pregnant."

"Wow." Dominique took a seat next to Nicole, taking her hand. "Congratulations."

"Five months. It's Greg's."

Dominique let go of Nicole's clammy hand, wiping her fingers on her robe. "Greg's?"

"You know, the guy whose drink you spiked. Greg told me they have footage of a woman called Dominique that threw something in his drink."

She paled and stood, turning her back on Nicole, staring at the city lights through the window. "Byron told me he wanted to rough him up. That you asked him to do it. I didn't know what else to do to get you out of the hole you found yourself in." She turned, eyes filled with tears. "The stuff you said that you wanted to do to Greg..."

"People say stupid things when they hurt, but you knew how I felt about him. You knew I wouldn't do anything to hurt him."

Dominique covered her face, sobbing. "The next day, when I found out what Byron did, I got scared. I ran. I didn't know he wanted to kill Greg." She fell on her knees before Nicole. "I swear I didn't know. He told me he wanted to–"

"Rough him up. I know!" She rose. "Well, Byron is dead now. Greg killed him. That's what couples do for each other."

"I'll hand myself over to the police," she cried.

"And tell them you were my best friend<" Nicole seethed. "That I blamed the Goodmans for my parents' death because of a broken-down truck? They'll think I'm crazy. Greg will then think I had something to do with his attack because I allowed Byron to rough him up once before..."

Dominique looked up, confused, tears streaming.

Nicole bent over. "Nothing will come between Greg and me. Our love. Nothing. This child"–she pointed at her stomach–"will grow up with both parents." She straightened. "If I can find you, they will find you. Tell me, why did you try to call Greg?"

Her tear-filled eyes shifted, searching for an answer. "Just...just to tell him I'm sorry. That...that Byron forced me to do it. That I didn't know."

Nicole shook her head. "You wanted him all for yourself. You wanted to tell him I told you to spike his drink. It's so easy to fall in love with him, isn't it?"

"No," she sobbed.

One advantage of being married to a cop was the amount of stuff they neglect to hand in after a raid. Nicole reached into her handbag and withdrew a Glock 17 with a silencer – serial number filed off.

"Nicole?" Her eyes widened with shock. She reached for the weapon.

The gun recoiled. Louder than expected.

Dominique looked at the hole in her shaking hand and then at the increasing bloodstain on her chest. She looked at Nicole, lips parting.

"Nothing will destroy our love. Our family. Nothing. I won't allow it. I'm a Goodman now."

Dominique fell onto her back, staring at the ceiling.

Should I feel something? Should I ask forgiveness? She gasped, touching her stomach; it was the first time she felt the baby move. *A sign.* As the life drained from Dominique's eyes, so the precious life grew within Nicole. Dexter kicked again.

"Yes, my baby, I hear you," she whispered, stroking her belly. "We'll be home soon."

Nicole placed the Glock back into her bag and knelt next to Dominique. She had been a wonderful friend. She untied her blood-drenched bathrobe, ripped the white underwear from her body and splayed her legs apart. *Strange, this kind of thing would have freaked me out. But now that I'm fighting for my family and the preservation of Greg's love, it dulls the senses. No sympathy. It is what it is – Manana's words.*

As she placed Greg's cap on her head and slipped into his camo jacket, she thought about Jessica Goodman, her mother-in-law. Nicole now understood why Jessica did what she did. The survival instinct of a mother to preserve her family was primal. Brutal. *I'm a Goodman now, and Goodmans stick together. Unlike me, Dexter will have a father, mother, grandfather, and grandmother.*

The evidence against Greg's parents was only bits and bytes, stored on some computer. Greg thought they were part of a bigger plan – everything happened for a reason.

If that were so, Dominique would still be alive. *But she's dead, and we're not. I did it for Greg, my husband, a good man. I know what's good for him. That's what couples do for each other, isn't it?* The meaning of life for her, after finding her soulmate and falling pregnant, was to preserve their love, happiness, and family, at whatever cost. The rest of the time, she'd be good.

ABOUT THE AUTHOR

Johan Thompson is a writer by night and manager of a law firm by day. He lives with his wife, two boys, and two dogs in Johannesburg, South Africa.

After studying creative writing, screenwriting, and watching every science fiction film created, he decided to draw on his interest and imagination to create his first Science Fiction novel.

The Goodman Curse is his fourth book.

ALSO BY JOHAN THOMPSON

The Clone

The Monster Within

www.ingramcontent.com/pod-product-compliance
Lightning Source LLC
Chambersburg PA
CBHW060151180626
46813CB00007B/2697